HEXED

MICHELLE KRYS

CORGI BOOKS

HEXED

A CORGI BOOK 978 0 552 57165 4

First published in Great Britain by Corgi Books,
an imprint of Random House Children's Publishers UK
A Random House Group Company

This edition published 2014

1 3 5 7 9 10 8 6 4 2

The Random House Group Limited supports the Forest Stewardship
Council® (FSC®), the leading international forest-certification organisation.
Our books carrying the FSC label are printed on FSC®-certified paper.
FSC is the only forest-certification scheme supported by the leading
environmental organisations, including Greenpeace. Our paper procurement
policy can be found at www.randomhouse.co.uk/environment.

MIX
Paper from
responsible sources
FSC® C016897

Corgi Books are published by Random House Children's Publishers UK,
61-63 Uxbridge Road, London, W5 5SA

www.randomhousechildrens.co.uk
www.totallyrandombooks.co.uk
www.randomhouse.co.uk

Addresses for companies within The Random House Group Limited can be
found at: www.randomhouse.co.uk/offices.htm

THE RANDOM HOUSE GROUP Limited Reg. No. 954009

A CIP catalogue record for this book is available from the British Library.

Printed and bound in the CPI Group (UK) Ltd, Croydon, CR0 4YY

For Brandy – my ultimate cheerleader

1

Exactly twelve minutes into cheerleading practice, and I already wish I were dead.

Sweat collects along my hairline. Blood fills my head, and a hammering pulse pounds in my neck. I can't be the first to fall, but my arms quiver under the weight of my body until, finally, they buckle and I collapse onto the cold blue mat of the school's gymnasium.

"What the hell was that, Indie? My grandma could do a better handstand." Bianca Cavanaugh, Fairfield High's resident slave-driver cheer captain (and my best friend), marches up to me with her hands on her hips.

Julia tosses her peroxide-blond head back and laughs. So

of course the rest of the squad erupts into giggles. Even Thea, the little Chinese girl Bianca treats like crap because she can barely speak English and only keeps on the team because she weighs ten pounds and makes a great flier. Bunch of traitors.

Gritting my teeth, I push myself up onto my elbows. Most people would assume that the coach not being able to make it to practice would mean we'd get to slack off for an hour and a half. Nope. When Coach Jenkins is absent (read: every second practice, due to her various commitments to French manicures and online dating), Bianca uses her power to practice medieval torture methods on the squad. Which, okay, I'll admit it, didn't bother me too much until she turned on me too—coincidentally around the same time I started dating Devon.

"Well?" Bianca says. "What do you have to say for yourself?" She shifts her weight to her other foot.

I almost spit out my standard apology. Almost. "I guess I just fail to see the point of a two-minute handstand, unless your plan is to bore the opposition to death." Titters from the squad bolster my confidence. "And if Granny is so much better than me, why not ask her to join the squad?"

Bianca takes one step closer and stares down her ski-slope nose at me, eyes narrowed to slits. A casual observer might call it a death stare, but after nine years of friendship I know better; it's an "embarrass me in front of the squad again and you'll come to regret the day you were born" stare. Big difference. Still, I decide to back off.

"Sorry," I say. "I'll try not to suck so much next time."

Bianca cocks her head.

I sigh. "And your grandma's actually aging really well. I bet she'd look hot in spankies."

Bianca rolls her eyes, then twirls on her heels to face the rest of the squad. "The point of a two-minute handstand *isn't* to bore the opposition to death or even to flash them our awesome asses. It's to improve our balance and stability." She claps her hands so hard a few girls startle. "Now get on your feet, losers. Three minutes this time." And with a pointed look at me she adds, "That includes you, Blackwood."

Exactly fourteen minutes into practice and I decide I'd rather Bianca were dead. I get through the rest of practice by imagining thirty-two ways I'd like to kill her.

When the clock strikes five and the basketball team charges into the gym to boot us out, the break in tension is practically palpable. The squad stops just short of celebrating, in light of the fact that Bianca hates complainers, and limps off toward the locker room for scalding-hot showers. It's only September. It's going to be a *long* year.

"Hey, bitches, I need help taking these mats back," Bianca says. By "help" she means do it for her.

Pretending not to hear her, I hightail it to the locker room, strip out of my practice T-shirt and shorts, and escape into the first shower stall available.

I turn the tap to the hottest temperature possible and let

the burning spray massage the tense muscles in my neck, watching the water circle the drain. I'm in love with this shower. I'd like to make out with this shower. If I could move into this shower, with its gloriously strong water pressure and hell-hot spray, I would. But Mom will kill me if I'm late for work again.

I turn off the tap and reach for the towel hanging on the hook on the other side of the curtain.

Bianca whips the curtain open. "'Bout time."

"Mind?" I scramble to cover myself with the towel.

"Relax. No one cares what your tits look like. Right, girls?"

"Right," twenty girls confirm in unison. Crazy how it can appear as if they're going about their own business—toweling off, getting dressed, fighting for a spot in front of the mirror to apply their makeup and blow-dry their hair—but really be watching every move Bianca makes.

Bianca perches on the bench outside my stall and starts passing a brush through her thick blond hair. "So listen, sorry if I was a little hard on you today."

I snort. "A little?"

"Okay, so a lot." She leans toward me and lowers her voice. "But I kind of have to make an example out of you, you know? I can't have the other girls thinking I'm going easy on you or they'll never respect me when Jenkins is away. I thought you'd understand."

I don't care if it sort of makes sense and we'd probably

suck a lot of ass if it weren't for Bianca going extra hard on us in place of our absentee coach—I consider her paddle brush as Way #33 to kill her.

"So," she continues, "did you hear everyone's going to In-N-Out Burger?"

"Yeah, I heard something about that." I tighten the towel around my chest and move past her, wet feet slapping against the gritty tiles. I can guess where this is going.

She follows me. "Devon's coming too."

Ding, ding, ding!

Bianca leans against the locker next to mine and pretends to check her hair for split ends while I pretend to be really interested in the contents of my bag, because I just don't know what to do when she gets like this. I thought she'd be over Devon by now. We've been best friends since the first grade, and he's just some guy. Some sickeningly hot, captain-of-the-football-team guy.

But if I'm being honest, there was friction between us before Devon ever came along. Things got a little weird around the time Bianca became morbidly obsessed with popularity and dragged me along on her mission to become high school royalty.

Supposedly it's normal; Mom says friends can drift apart as they get older, as their interests change and their person-alities develop.

This is bullshit, of course. Bianca's the person who pushed

Stacey Miller in the first grade after she told me my hair was ugly, and then offered me half of her banana sandwich. She was there for me when Grandma died when I was eight and I thought the world was ending. She's the girl who dressed up in fur hats and muffs with me when we were eleven and traipsed around the mall pretending to be my Russian sister. Who gave me the giant collage of pictures of us for my fifteenth birthday last year, a collage that was (and still is) so awesome it had me both spitting Coke out of my nose and tearing up. We'll always be best friends. This is just a little rough patch. And since she shuts down any attempt to talk about it and won't admit there's even a problem, I'm left with Door #3, which is to ride it out until she gets whatever *this* is out of her system.

Still. Doesn't mean I have to like it.

"What about Sebastian?" I ask. "He going too?" Sebastian is a friend of Bianca's older brother who she's had a mambo crush on since forever. He's got an acne problem (as far as I can tell from the pictures), but he's older and plays lacrosse, so I guess that makes him awesome. He's her date for homecoming.

She dismisses my comment with a wave. "Like he wants to hang out with a bunch of high schoolers."

Someone should tell Bianca she's in high school.

"Anyway, it's too bad you're working," she says.

"Yeah, too bad." I yank my denim miniskirt and white

tank on over my damp body, then put on my new suede fringe boots.

"You should just pull a no-show," Bianca says.

"And get fired?"

"So what?" she retorts.

"Well, I kind of like not being poor." I tear a brush through my dark blond hair even though I'd rather just get out of here—brushing isn't optional when you have as much wild curly hair as I do—then lean into the little locker mirror to apply mascara.

"I know . . . I bet it's because you secretly *love* working at that voodoo shop." She circles me, pretending to stir a cauldron.

For someone who claims that every single thing we do needs to be carefully calculated, that one misstep could thrust us back into loserdom, she sure likes to remind people about my quirky mom.

She affects a high-pitched, nasal voice "Eye of newt and toe of frog, tail of rat and hair of dog! Oh, and a pinch of Bianca's toenail clippings for good measure!" She throws her head back and cackles.

The locker room roars with laughter.

"God, your mom's crazy," Bianca says.

Oh no, she didn't just utter the C word. So what if I woke up at three a.m. to find Mom digging up the backyard by headlamp while chanting locating spells because her witchcraft bible was missing? That was one time! Six years ago! And lots of people practice witchcraft—hello, it's called Wicca. And so what if she thinks aliens exist? Eccentricity is practically a requirement to live in L.A.

But as much as I'm dying to do it, gouging Bianca's eyes out with my Maybelline Great Lash mascara brush probably won't improve the situation, so I laugh too.

"Well, have fun, loser." Bianca pokes me in the shoulder. "Call me later, okay?"

"Course." I send her a smile and sling my messenger bag over my shoulder, sliding on my favorite pair of oversized white shades.

But I let my smile fade as soon as my back is to the locker room, the heavy weight of disloyalty pressing on my shoulders. I tell myself that I'll make it up to Mom somehow. Maybe I'll stay late at the shop tonight. Maybe I'll make dinner. Hell, I'll even recite one of her spells with her, like she's always begging me to.

I exit through the gym's fire door (which the squad uses as a shortcut to the parking lot) and run into a brick wall of sticky, humid air carrying subtle notes of gardenia, jasmine, and weed, along with the not-so-subtle notes of pounding bass drums and honking horns from the start-stop traffic clogging the street. A pool of sweat forms instantly above my collarbone and my clothes start clinging to my body despite the ocean breeze carried from miles away. Which is to say, it's an average L.A. day.

I cut a path across the fresh-mown lawn of the football field toward the congested parking lot. It's not hard to spot my ancient Sunfire among all the shiny new cars. Driving Mom's castoff is only slightly less embarrassing than taking the bus would be.

"Indie!"

I glance over my shoulder and groan as I spot Paige lumbering across the field toward me, dwarfed under the violin case strapped across her back.

A more irritating and persistent neighbor I have yet to meet. Paige and I were friends for, like, three seconds way back in the day before Bianca came along, due to the whole same-age, lives-ten-steps-away thing. Our moms thought it was adorable when Paige would chase me around trying to get me to play with her, never realizing that maybe it was a sign. Now, at the age of sixteen, Paige is still chasing me around trying to get me to be friends with her. And it's still not cute.

I keep walking. Even if I had time for a chat, I wouldn't stop.

"Ind, wait up!"

I practically break into a jog.

Paige snatches my arm. "There you are." She gasps for air. "Didn't you hear me calling you?"

"No," I lie. "But I can't talk. I'm late for work." I pass an appraising eye from her mousy-brown bangs, which fall over thick-rimmed, leopard-print glasses, to her oversized band

T-shirt, pin-striped shorts, and unlaced Doc Martens, and decide she must actually be trying to look bad. There is no other explanation. It's no wonder Bianca says I can't afford to hang out with her.

She doesn't take the hint and skips along beside me, hiking the violin case over her skinny shoulder.

"So listen, I know reading's not cool and blah blah blah, but I just read the most fantastic book. Seriously, the best book ever. You have to borrow it. It's by this totally weirdo hippie guy but he's a genius, a genius, Ind. I totally thought of you when I read it."

The Sunfire has never looked so appealing. I rummage in my bag and produce my keys. "Great. It's just that I have to get to the shop right now. Otherwise I'd love to hear all about it." I open the driver's-side door.

"Actually, I was wondering if I could get a ride. My mom has a work meeting, and my new violin teacher is right by your mom's shop." She smiles sheepishly.

I sigh. Knowing Paige, she isn't going to give up easily. It'd probably be much less painful to just drive the girl and get it over with than to argue about it for twenty minutes in the parking lot. I look around to confirm no one's watching before saying, "Okay, get in."

"Sweet, thanks."

She takes an inordinate amount of time shoving her violin case into the backseat, before finally sinking into the passenger seat. I peel out of the parking lot into the insane afternoon traffic. Paige blathers on about this book—which admittedly seems pretty cool, the bits and pieces I catch of it—while my mind slips back to the scene in the locker room, to the way Devon's name slid over Bianca's tongue. It makes me sick, so of course I start imagining possible scenarios taking place at the restaurant right now: Bianca playfully hitting Devon's arm after he tells a joke, Bianca leaning across the table so Devon can get a good look at her cleavage, Bianca and Dev making out in a booth.

My stomach coils into a knot, and I have to remind myself that Devon would never cheat on me. He loves me. Even if he *is* an incurable flirt. Still, sometimes I wonder how much easier life would be if I just let Bianca have him.

But I don't really want that. Not when I think of Devon's characteristic lopsided grin. Not when I catch his scent on a passing breeze. Not when he throws his arm around me and his nearness makes my heart stutter.

"Indie?"

"Huh?" Twenty minutes must have passed without me saying a word, because we're suddenly surrounded by the vibrant-colored vintage shops, massive billboards, and palm trees of Melrose Avenue. Music and car horns pulse through the air; hordes of hipsters in bowler hats and funky shoes strut along the sidewalk as they chat loudly on their cell phones.

"Saturday. The barbecue. You're coming, right? Tiny

sloppy joes. So delicious. Lots of fun." Paige bites her lip, hands clasped in supplication. "Pleasepleaseplease?"

She looks so desperate for a yes that I'm hit with a feeling that is the opposite of good and rhymes with "rad." Which is dumb. Like Bianca says, it's Paige's own fault she doesn't take a hint. But maybe it's my fault too, I decide. If I were just more direct, if I told her how I felt, Bianca-style, without pulling any punches, I'm sure Paige wouldn't be offering up her mom's sloppy joes. It makes total sense. So why can't I do it?

"Fine, I'll come."

Paige blinks at me a bunch before growing a smile so wide I worry kids might try to kick a field goal in there. "You will?"

I shrug. "Yeah, sure, whatev—"

Before I can finish, a large, dark shape whizzes past the windshield and splats onto the pavement with a sickening thud. I slam on the brakes so hard we rocket against our seat belts.

Traffic around us sputters to a halt. Drivers emerge from their cars, and screams pierce the cacophony of the streets. Paige and I exchange wide-eyed glances, then unclick our seat belts and exit the car. As I cautiously edge around the nose of the Sunfire, the dark shape comes into view. My heart hammers in my chest.

It can't be what I think it is.

I slide my sunglasses up, and all the blood drains from my head.

"Oh my God!" Paige's fingernails dig into the skin on my arm. "Is that . . . ?"

I'm frozen in place, my breath lodged in my throat. I watch in mute horror as Paige takes careful steps up to the body that lies facedown on the sidewalk, limbs splayed at impossible angles.

2

Pedestrians flock around the body. I'm jostled left and right, but I can't stop staring at the pool of blood expanding beneath the man's worn leather coat. And I don't know why, but all I can think is that it's a hot day to be wearing leather.

A redheaded woman in a jogging suit crouches low and presses her fingers to the man's neck—a neck covered in tattoos. She nods, and two construction workers rush to help. As the man is flipped onto his back, a crumpled piece of paper tumbles out of his blood-soaked hand.

Only he's not a man.

There's so much blood—it drips from a wound under his hair, soaking his tangled black waves; it flows freely from his left ear, from his broken nose, from a gravelly laceration on his cheek; it coats the Ramones T-shirt that clings to his thin frame—but beneath the injuries is very clearly a seventeen-year-old—*maybe* eighteen-year-old—boy.

Someone screams, a high-pitched, strangled sound that rises above the other voices, the orders being called out, the wail of a siren.

I realize it's me.

"Out of the way, Indie." Paige pulls my arm to make way for the paramedics, who rush up with a stretcher. I stumble back but continue to stare at the boy's dark, vacant eyes.

One of the paramedics pounds on the boy's chest, landing his full weight onto him as he delivers CPR. But it doesn't matter. He's dead. They're not going to save him.

"Did anyone see what happened?" another paramedic asks. His words float around in my head, but I can't seem to grasp their meaning. It's like I'm watching a scene in a movie. This can't really be happening, not in real life.

"Did you see what happened?" Paige shakes my arm.

"Well?" the paramedic asks, suddenly staring at me.

I swallow hard and give a minute shake of my head.

"No, we didn't see anything, just . . . just him landing," Paige says. She tugs my arm again. "Come on. Let's give them some space."

That's when I see it again—the paper the guy held in his hand, lying crumpled next to the redheaded woman's feet. I snatch it up, stuffing it in the pocket of my skirt. Paige gives me a quizzical look but doesn't question me, just leads me back to the car. My legs are so unstable that I have to concentrate hard—one foot in front of the other—to make sure I don't collapse.

"I can't believe it," Paige says once I've managed to find a way out of the chaos of cars. The bloody scene fades into the distance, and the canvas awning of the Black Cat comes into view. "You okay, Ind? You don't look so good."

I shake my head to clear my thoughts. When I speak again, my throat feels scratchy and my voice comes out a rasp. "Yeah, I'm okay."

"You sure? Because you look really pale."

I keep thinking about the boy and the leather coat he wore even though it's over eighty degrees outside. Which is dumb, because he's obviously got bigger problems than overdressing for the weather. I use my forearm to wipe sweat from my brow.

"Are you okay to drive?" Paige asks.

I give her what I hope is a confident nod.

The hum of the engine takes over the silence.

"Think it was suicide?" Paige finally asks meekly, like she feels bad even suggesting it.

I don't have time to answer, because a car miraculously pulls out of the parking spot right in front of the shop, and I'm able to cut off a yellow Mustang to snag it. I could adopt a kid internationally for roughly what this spot will cost me, but it's worth not having to walk. I want to shake off Paige as quickly as possible so I can be alone and think.

"Thanks for the ride," Paige says. As we exit the car, I can't help noticing that we both crane our necks to see the site of the accident a few blocks down the street. But either they cleaned up quickly, or it was farther from the shop than I remembered, because there's no sign of the chaos of moments ago.

"Ind!"

I squint against the sun and spot Devon climbing out of his BMW a few cars behind me.

Well, this is super. Just great.

Devon jogs up the sidewalk, sun-kissed hair flopping around his tanned face.

"What are you doing here?" I ask as he nears.

"Why, you want me to go?" He gives me that crooked grin and slips his fingers in the belt loops of my skirt, playfully tugging me closer to him.

"No, I just thought . . . well, Bianca said you were going for burgers or something."

"The rest of the team went," he says, brushing a featherlight kiss onto my cheek. "I'd rather be with you."

His lips move to my mouth just as a double-decker bus drives past, blaring facts about Melrose Avenue through a loudspeaker to the tourists snapping pictures out the windows. I push against Devon's chest to stop him.

"Who cares about them," he says, dismissing the tourists with a wave.

"It's not that," I say.

"Then what?" He peppers my neck with kisses.

Paige clears her throat.

Devon's eyes flit to my neighbor, who is still standing awkwardly beside us because that's how she rolls.

"Who's your friend?" he asks.

"Paige Abernathy." She stretches a hand out. "From your fifth-period history class. And also from the last six years of school."

He shakes her hand and laughs.

"No, seriously," she says.

"Oh." Devon's cheeks get pink, and he scratches his head. "Uh, sorry about that. I don't know what to say—"

"Yeah, no big deal." She pushes her shoulders back. "I wouldn't notice me either if I were the captain of the football team."

This. Is. Too much.

"Okay!" I grab Devon's arm and tow him behind me. "Bye, Paige."

"Wait, what about what happened—"

"Sorry, have to go work now." I don't look back, but I know she's probably staring openmouthed as a fish as I retreat toward the shop.

"Wow, I feel terrible," Devon says out of the side of his

18

mouth. "I seriously didn't recognize that girl at all. How do you know her?"

"My neighbor," I say, leaving out the part about being friends once, long ago.

The bell above the door jingles as we enter the shop and are greeted by the aroma of Murphy Oil Soap and old books.

Mom looks over her shoulder from her perch on a stool in front of the bookcase, feather duster in hand. She's wearing a black blouse, a black-sequined skirt, ripped leggings, and approximately one ton of silver jewelry in the form of necklaces and bangles; as far as my mother's wardrobe goes, it's about the least embarrassing ensemble she could be wearing for an impromptu visit from Devon.

"Hey, Ms. Blackwood," Devon says.

"If it isn't Devon Mills! So great of you to visit." Mom hops off the stool and tosses the duster onto a stack of books, wiping her hands on her skirt. "And look, you've even brought my estranged daughter with you."

She crosses the small shop, heels clacking on the wood floors, but stops in her tracks when she gets a better look at me. Her gray eyes pass over every inch of my face, like she might find the answer to her question there. "What's wrong?"

"Nothing." I run my thumb under the strap of my bag.

Mom knows me too well to believe me, but she lets it go for now. "Okay . . . ," she says cautiously. "Well, I better get going. It's my turn to host the Wicca Society meeting and the house is a mess."

I cringe and refuse to meet Devon's eyes. He's been to the shop tons of times (in fact, he's intimately familiar with the storeroom), but I'm just as mindful of all the laughable things he's seeing now—the ritual candles, the silver chalices, the altar cloths, the pentacles that hang from the low ceiling—as the first time he came.

"Will I be okay leaving you two alone?" Mom asks, which makes Devon laugh and me turn forty-two shades of red. "I'm kidding, but, Indigo, could I speak with you for moment?"

Mom's eyes flash to Devon. He, unlike Paige, can take a hint, and pads off to the black cauldron on display in the center of the room.

Mom watches to make sure he's not paying attention, then leans in toward me. "I don't mind your boyfriend coming over, it's just . . ." She looks at Devon again. He has moved to the bookcase and is running his finger over the spines of the books.

"What, Mom?"

"Just don't let him near the book, okay?"

I don't have to ask what book she's referring to. *The Witch Hunter's Bible*. To me, it's just one of many weird books in the shop, but ever since Grandma gave it to Mom on her deathbed, Mom has been sort of obsessed with it— witness the backyard hole-digging incident—I know better than to be anything but completely serious when I answer her.

"No, Mom, I won't let him anywhere near the book, as I've told you already a billion times."

"I'm serious, Indigo. If that book gets into the wrong hands—"

"I said I won't. Jeez, what happened to the good old sex talk?"

"Ha-ha," Mom deadpans. But my answer has satisfied her. She shoulders her bag. "All right, then, you kids be good. I'll be back before late."

"Bye, Ms. Blackwood," Devon says, strolling over.

As soon as Mom leaves, Devon slackens his perfect posture. "There's some really screwed-up shit in this place, you know."

"Tell me about it," I say dryly, walking to the chair behind the counter.

Devon follows. He picks up a dagger from a nearby display and turns it over in his hands. "What's this for?"

I shrug, like I don't know exactly what it's for. Which I do. "Ceremonial tool. Or something like that."

He casually checks out the price tag and does a double take. "Two hundred dollars? Who would spend that much on some crappy old knife?"

"Any number of weirdos. It's L.A., remember?"

He laughs and puts the dagger back (in the wrong spot, I note), then leans his forearms on the counter and gives me a mischievous smile.

Most times I'd consider stealing from young children to snag a little more alone time with Devon, but right now I just wish he'd leave. I need to think, or whatever it is people do when they witness a death. But I'm guessing it's not suck face.

"I think the storeroom needs stocking," he says, waggling his eyebrows suggestively.

"We have that math test tomorrow," I say.

"And?" He leans across the counter and kisses me. I don't want to hear about how I never want to "do stuff" anymore for the next week, so I kiss him back for a good solid minute before pushing him away.

"*And* I don't want to fail. And you *can't* fail," I say, poking him in the chest, "or else you're not allowed to homecoming. Remember what your dad said?"

"If I didn't know any better, I'd say you didn't want to kiss me."

I roll my eyes. "Please. All I want to do is kiss you."

This earns me a grin, which unexpectedly blooms into a full-on smile.

"What?" I ask.

"How much do you love me?"

"Uh, tons . . . ," I say carefully.

"Like more than you ever thought possible, right?" He looks barely able to contain his glee.

"Sure. Now what's up?"

"Oh, nothing," he says, reaching into his back pocket.

"Simply that I got us these two front-row seats for the Jay-Z concert tomorrow." He brandishes two crisp blue tickets.

I know I'm supposed to react better than to blink at him a bunch—I know this because the huge smile wipes right off his face like he's just been doused with a bucket of ice-cold water.

"My dad got them off this investor he works with. The concert's been sold out for months. I thought you'd be excited." He scuffs the toe of his shoe against the floor.

"I *am* excited. really, I am. Just, what about the game tomorrow? Scouts are coming, and you know Bianca would send a lynch mob after me if I didn't show."

"It's not till after the game," he says. "We'd miss the opening bands, but they always suck anyway." He's in serious mope-mode now.

"Well, then it's perfect!" I say, forcing a cheery tone. "And I love you so much it's disgusting and should be illegal." I grab a handful of his shirt and pull him in for a deep kiss. When I feel absolved, I murmur "Thank you" against his mouth and then push him back across the counter. "Now get out of here."

He gives me a dazed smile. "I *should* get going. Told the guys to order for me. Jay-Z! Woo!" He drums his hands on the counter before turning to leave, rap lyrics accompanying him out of the store.

Sighing, I dig my hands into my pockets. The rough edges of crumpled-up paper catch my finger.

The note.

I pull it out and flatten the edges, which are stained with dried blood. What I see makes my breath catch in my throat.

The Black Cat. 290 Melrose Avenue.

The dead guy was coming to our shop.

3

I sit cross-legged at the kitchen table, mechanically eating a bowl of cereal while watching the tiny TV perched on the countertop. It's practically on mute, because for some reason that I suspect involves alcohol, Aunt Penny's asleep on our couch.

In the time I've spent not sleeping—obsessively flicking between local news stations, hoping to learn more about the death I witnessed—I've come to a couple of conclusions: one, the guy committed suicide, like Paige guessed, probably by jumping out a window; two, the note with Mom's shop's address was purely coincidental, and three, I'm a complete idiot for thinking otherwise.

Seriously, what does it matter if he visited the shop in the past or planned to visit in the future?

It doesn't. I'm an idiot. I'm talking Lloyd-and-Harry kind of dumb. But it's not surprising that I'd jump to radical conclusions, having been raised to believe aliens, witches, and vampires exist.

Still, I watch the news, hoping to find out more. You know. For closure.

"Hey, hon."

Mom strides into the kitchen wearing a threadbare bathrobe and slippers, with a virtual bird's nest of hair piled on top of her head. It's the closest to looking like a normal mom she'll get all day.

"Turn that down a bit," she says. "Aunt Penny's sleeping."

She pulls a pack of Virginia Slims from the carton she keeps in the freezer so they stay fresh—because aren't fresh cancer sticks what we all want?—then sinks into a chair across from me, lighting the cigarette pressed between her lips. Her eyes narrow on the TV as she exhales. "What, no MTV?"

I waft the smoke clouding around the kitchen table away from my face. "I thought you were quitting, Mom."

"I am. Next week. Now, are you going to tell me what's wrong or just keep trying to distract me? Because no daughter of mine watches the news."

"Distract you from what?" Aunt Penny stumbles into the kitchen. And such a hot mess I have not yet seen. Her hair, which last night was probably a beautiful updo of blond curls, slumps in a weird, frizzy bun next to her left ear, like even it has a hangover. Black makeup is smudged under her eyes, and her bandage dress rides so high up her thighs I can see panties.

"Whoa," I say. "What happened to you?"

"Bikini martinis," she says, falling into the seat next to me. "Let me give you a piece of advice: never have more than one—maybe two—sugary drinks a night, unless you want to puke your face off the next day."

"That's excellent advice for my teenage daughter," Mom says, cutting her a warning look.

Penny rolls her eyes, but when Mom's not looking, gives me a conspiratorial wink. Most people would assume that Mom and Penny don't get along well. They'd be wrong. Mom likes to pretend she's annoyed by Aunt Penny's carefree lifestyle, but everyone knows she loves being the responsible sister. Meanwhile, Aunt Penny likes to pretend she's annoyed by Mom's nagging, but everyone knows she loves having at least one person who cares about where she wakes up in the morning. It's the perfect relationship.

"So what's going on with you?" Penny asks, turning to me. "Boyfriend troubles?"

God, and for a minute there I thought I loved her.

"I don't know what you're talking about." I stir Cocoa Puffs around my bowl.

"Please," she says. "Did he cheat on you? I know an ex-UFC fighter who can kick his ass. Just say the word."

"Penny!" Mom cries.

"What? He'd deserve it if he cheated."

"No, it's not Devon," I interrupt.

"Bianca, then?" she asks. "She's been super bitchy lately. What's up with her?"

"I don't appreciate swearing in my household," Mom says, then addresses me. "I know you're not going to like this, but if Bianca's treating you badly again, I think I'm going to have to speak to her mother. Now, I know that's not cool and you have an image to uphold, but if she's going to keep giving you a hard time like this—"

"It's not Bianca," I say.

"Well, what is it, then?" Mom asks.

"Yeah, what is it?" Penny adds.

I look at the two of them, eagerly waiting for me to continue, and take a deep breath.

"It's, well . . . I saw something yesterday. When I was driving to the shop from school I saw . . . I saw someone die. He fell from, well, I don't know where, a rooftop or a window ledge, I guess. There was so much blood and his legs were definitely broken, and I didn't do anything, nothing at all, I just froze. This one lady, she checked for a pulse and then this paramedic did CPR, but it was useless—"

"Whoa, whoa, whoa," Mom interrupts. "Take a breath. What are you talking about, Indigo?"

"You saw this?" Penny asks, through the hand clapped over her mouth.

"And I didn't do anything to help." Tears well in my eyes so quickly I can't blink them back.

"Why didn't you tell me yesterday?" Mom stubs out her cigarette and rounds the table to kneel in front of me, taking my hands in hers.

I shrug. "I don't know. I guess I was embarrassed I didn't do anything."

"Oh, honey," Mom says, brushing my hair behind my ear.

"You hear about eight-year-olds doing CPR," I mutter.

"Yeah, and you want to know why you hear about eight-year-olds doing CPR?" Aunt Penny asks. "Because it's not normal. If it were normal it wouldn't make the news."

I think about this a moment, and decide I do love Aunt Penny after all. In fact, I feel so much better having talked about it that I have to wonder why I didn't say anything sooner.

"You know what the weirdest part is?" I continue. "The guy who died was holding a note with the address for the Black Cat on it."

Mom's kohl-rimmed eyes widen. I've said too much. Cue the *Twilight Zone* theme music.

"And with that, I'm out," Aunt Penny says, standing up. "It's been a slice. Great to see you, Ind; thanks for the crash pad, Sis." She gives Mom a wave, which Mom doesn't even register in her daze.

Awesome.

"It's a crazy coincidence," I say, hoping to derail Mom's

line of thought before this becomes a thing. "He must have been on the way to the shop or something."

"And then just decided to kill himself?" Mom's eyebrow arches up. "People don't usually make plans for the future when they're suicidal."

I shrug. "Okay, well, maybe he visited the shop earlier in the day, then."

Mom pauses as if to consider my theory. "Well, I guess that *is* possible. There have been several new customers in the shop the last few days, but it does seem strange." She rubs her chin in the absent way she does when her wheels are turning. "Could be jinn," she mumbles. "But why?"

Yes. I'm sure this is the work of genies.

I stand up and sling my bag over my shoulder.

Mom rises to her feet. "Wait. Where are you going?"

"School. And I'm already running late."

"Are you sure school's a good idea, sweetie? Maybe you should take a day off, relax a bit."

"Game day. Bianca would stroke out if I missed practice."

"The least I can do is cast a protection spell or a—"

"No, I'm fine, really. No circles or spells or anything, okay? I just want to go to school and get back to normal life. I really appreciate it, but can we talk more later? Please?" I walk around her, but she follows me to the door.

"Well, okay . . . but you call me if you change your mind and I'll come right home from the shop. And I'm going to put some thought into that death. Toy around with a few theories. Something tells me there's more to this story than meets the eye."

———•◦•———

All the way to school, my mind is preoccupied with Leather Jacket Guy. But once I arrive, I'm quickly swallowed by the stream of kids piling up the cement steps and through the double doors of Fairfield High, and it's hard to think of anything at all.

The corridors are an explosion of voices, laughter, and the metal-on-metal sound of lockers slamming closed; the familiarity is comforting, which is weird, because it's school.

The morning unfolds as it normally does. As usual, homeroom is so boring I consider plucking out my eyelashes for entertainment. As usual, Mrs. Davies has a breakdown when someone starts a spitball fight. As usual, a crowd gathers around Bianca before math class, hanging on every word as she muses about important topics such as the eating contest that took place between Devon and Jarrod at the In-N-Out yesterday and whether it's considered cheating that Jarrod puked afterward. As usual, the lunch bell rings at 11:45. I start to wonder if the death really happened, if maybe I had a psychotic break after practice yesterday.

I'm forced to pass Paige's table on the way to my reserved spot next to Bianca at the Pretty People table. Normally I make a point to check my messages on my cell phone, or chat with a friend, or be otherwise Very Busy so that Paige can't try to engage me in conversation. But I've got my tray of processed cafeteria food in hand and my cell phone is tucked in my purse, so I'm forced to pretend to see someone flagging me down and walk quickly toward my table, waiting for my name to be called out or for a hand to snag my arm. Luckily, I make it past the table without incident.

I risk a glance over my shoulder and find Paige in the middle of an animated conversation with Jessie Colburn, the new girl who transferred from Idaho or Nebraska or somewhere else similarly sucky. Paige whispers something in her ear and Jessie doubles over with laughter.

An unfamiliar part of my chest squeezes up into a ball. But I quickly shake off the feeling and force myself to keep moving toward my table, lest anyone notice I've paused in the middle of the caf like some sort of psycho.

It's really great Paige is making a friend, I tell myself. Maybe she'll finally leave me alone. And she could do worse than Jessie Colburn. She's very pretty, and if you count "I want to tap that ass" as a compliment, then at least half the football team agrees.

Bianca is so busy loudly recounting the story of the eating contest to the other squad members, who lean in intently as if (a) they haven't heard the story three times already, and (b) they really want to know exactly what color Jarrod's vomit was that she doesn't notice me slip into my spot next to her.

I peel the cellophane back from my caf sandwich, trying to block out Bianca's voice, but the puke talk filters in anyway, and a childhood memory plays out in my head. I find myself unexpectedly smiling.

"Hey, Bianca," I blurt out. "Remember that time my mom said that if we ate all our food we'd grow big and strong? And we thought it'd help us grow big boobs too, so we sat in my basement eating until we couldn't stop puking?"

Bianca cuts me a glare. "No, that doesn't ring a bell," she says through her teeth.

Now that it's out, I realize Bianca's probably mortified that I mentioned the memory that just moments before had me smiling. I should back off, but for some reason her denial inflames me. "Yeah, yeah," I say. "Remember it was just after your brother said some girls never grow boobs, and we were so scared we'd be those girls that we scarfed down that whole can of cake icing that was expired by a month?"

Bianca gives me her back and faces her audience again. "So *anyway,* as I was saying—"

The overhead speakers crackle, and Mrs. Malone's sharp voice comes over the intercom. "Would Indigo Blackwood and Paige Abernathy please report to my office? Thank you."

The cafeteria calls out *"Oooh"* in unison, like we're in third grade or something.

"Isn't that your weird neighbor who won't leave you alone?" Bianca asks. "What's going on?"

Great. I'll only hear about this for, oh, the next century.

I shrug noncommittally before getting up. Paige meets me in the middle of the cafeteria. Neither of us says a word on the way to the office, but tension radiates between us in waves. Cops. It has to be cops. We left the scene of an accident, after all. And maybe it wasn't a suicide. Maybe it was a murder. *And I took evidence!* I realize with alarm, remembering the note.

The secretary, Mrs. Fields, an approximately one-hundred-year-old woman with a puff of silver hair and round spectacles, glances up from a file she's reading as we approach.

"Ms. Blackwood and Ms. Abernathy?" she asks in her pinched little voice.

"Yes," I answer for the both of us.

"Right this way."

Mrs. Fields leads us to the principal's corner office, where, through the door's glazed window, I can just make out the silhouettes of three figures.

Mrs. Fields knocks on the door but doesn't wait before cracking it open. "They're here."

Mrs. Malone and two men I've never seen before swivel to face us.

If I'd run into them under any other circumstances, I'd never have guessed they were policemen. The taller of the two men wears his long, steel-wool hair slicked back in a ponytail that falls halfway down his back. His features—

from his pointed chin to his slender nose to his pale blue, slanting eyes—give him the appearance of a wolf. The other man, short and muscular compared with his partner, has what looks like a burn covering three-quarters of his hairless head and extending over his right eye, making it droop as though his face were melting. In fact, the only thing that looks policeman-like about the two of them is their sleek black suits.

"Thank you, Mrs. Malone," Mr. Wolf says to our principal, in such a way as to dismiss her.

Mrs. Malone applies a false smile I'm all too used to seeing around the halls of Fairfield High. "I'll just be right outside if you need anything." She shoots Paige and me a warning look before pulling the door closed behind her.

Mr. Wolf indicates for us to sit in the wooden chairs across from the big desk. After that, there's about thirty seconds when no one says a thing. Which doesn't seem like that long, but things start to get really awkward after the ten-second mark. Paige and I shift in our chairs as Mr. Wolf saunters over to Malone's desk and picks up a snow globe, turning it over in his hands. Scarface takes a seat in the principal's chair and thumps his boot-clad feet up on the desk, dry mud crumbling off the soles. He pulls a package of Marlboros out of the breast pocket of his suit, slides one out, and presses it between his lips.

Paige sits up straighter. "Hey, this school is nonsmoking."

"Paige!" I cry, incredulous. If I'm in trouble, the last thing I need is her getting me on their bad side.

The cop flicks his lighter. The cherry of the cigarette flames as he sucks in a breath, then exhales right in Paige's direction.

Paige wafts the smoke out of her face with dramatic arm-sweeping gestures. "I don't care who you are, you can't—"

"Excuse my partner's rudeness," Mr. Wolf says, now examining the snow globe close to his face. "You can dress him up, but you can't take him out. Know what I mean?"

Scarface laughs, a barking, unkind sound.

I haven't had many encounters with policemen in the past, but this isn't going down as I'd imagined.

"You girls saw something pretty frightening yesterday, didn't you?" Mr. Wolf sets down the snow globe and picks up a picture frame holding a photo of two blond children— probably Mrs. Malone's kids.

I'm about to answer when Paige cuts in. "How did you know that? I mean, we didn't leave our names with anyone, so how did you know where to find us?"

"Shut up, Paige," I say, elbowing her in the ribs.

"What? I'm just wondering. If he can blow smoke in my face, I can ask a question, right? And since I'm asking, you didn't tell us your names. Isn't that part of an interview?"

Mr. Wolf's thin lips curl up in an amused smile, revealing a row of crooked teeth. "We have ways of knowing . . .

things, Ms. Abernathy. Cute kids." He sets the picture frame down and starts ruffling through papers on the desk.

"You didn't answer my last question," Paige says.

"That's right," he says. "My name is . . ." He looks up, as if considering his response, and then levels his eyes on me. "Mr. Wolf."

A gasp falls out of my mouth.

"And this," he continues, giving me a knowing grin as he gestures to the other cop, "is my partner, Scarface."

My heart thrums like a bird in a cage, a cold damp slicking my palms. "H-how did you do that?"

"Do what?" Paige asks.

I can't say it aloud—that he's read my mind. It sounds too implausible. Too ridiculous. But it has to be true. That can't have been a coincidence.

"We're wasting time, Frederick," Scarface says.

"Shhh, I think I'm on to something here." Mr. Wolf, or Frederick, or whoever he is, rubs the stubble on his chin, assessing me.

Scarface removes his feet from the desk and sits up straight. "There are at least a dozen more people who saw Bishop die who still need to be dealt with."

Dealt with? What is *that* supposed to mean?

"Patience, Leo. Patience." Frederick drums his index finger on his chin, and Scarface/Leo crosses his arms like a child who's been put in time-out.

"They obviously don't know anything about the Bible," he mumbles.

For some stupid reason, Mom's tattered leather-bound book comes to mind. Suddenly Frederick leans in, close enough that he is just inches from my face.

"What is this book?" Spittle flies out the corner of his mouth with the force of his words.

Okay, so that settles it. He's definitely reading my mind. "Wh-what are you talking about?" I ask.

"That's it," Paige says. "I'm getting Mrs. Malone in here—" She starts to stand, but Leo bolts upright and points a finger at her. She stops so quickly it's as if he's pressed the pause button on the movie of her life.

"That's better," Leo says. "Now sit down, Paige."

She obeys.

"Paige?" I lean across my chair to get a better look at her. She stares straight ahead, her vacant eyes unblinking, her dainty features slackened like she's a stroke victim. Nauseating loops form in my stomach.

"Hey, this could be fun." Leo slicks his tongue over his teeth. "She's pretty cute, for a nerdy type, don't you think, Frederick?"

"Shut up, Leo." Frederick leans in, his breath rushing against my cheek. "Now tell me about this Bible."

I grip the chair so hard I wonder how the wood hasn't splintered. "What did you do to Paige?"

"Your friend will be fine if you answer my question. What

is this Bible? What does the cover say? And don't give me any more of this bullshit."

I swallow. Mom's warning streams through my mind. *If that book gets into the wrong hands . . .*

Then what? Mass hysteria? The earth implodes? Cats and dogs take over the world? I don't know—Mom never delved into specifics. But I get the impression that whatever it is wouldn't be good, just based on this guy's savage desire for it. Especially not with Mom at the shop, alone. "I—I don't know, it's just a regular Bible. I guess it just says 'Holy Bible' or something."

"Liar!" he yells, so loudly it makes my spine go ramrod straight. "Your mom's Bible is leather-bound and tattered. You said it yourself."

But I didn't say it—I thought it. My already racing heart speeds into Indy 500 territory.

I dart a glance at the door, wondering why no one has charged into the room. How can they not hear this?

Frederick grips my jaw with his long fingers and turns my head to face his. "Because we've made the room sound-proof. Simple incantation. They can't hear anything on the other side of that glass. You can scream at the top of your lungs but no one will come. Now, do you see your friend?" He turns my jaw so that I face Paige, then snaps it toward him again. "That is *the least* interesting thing we could do to her. If you don't start talking, we might have to change our minds."

I try to speak, but it's like I've swallowed a bucket of sand. Frederick breathes through his teeth, his patience visibly wearing thin.

"The Bible," I choke out, stumbling over my words. "It's an antique. It was passed down to my mom from my grandma, but it's just a regular Bible. Nothing of value, except to my family."

I hope what I've said will be enough to satisfy him, that I won't have to say more to implicate Mom at the shop.

His eyes narrow on mine. And then I realize he must be reading my mind right now. I remember a trick I once saw in an old horror movie, and think, *Brick wall, brick wall, brick wall.*

For about thirty seconds that feel like an eternity, Frederick and I engage in a staring contest, each of us waiting for the other to give. His jaw twitches, and I think he's going to hit me, but then he just laughs. "You're a stubborn one, aren't you?" He straightens and adjusts his suit jacket. "Leo, kill them both."

4

It makes no difference that Frederick said no one can hear us—I scream at the top of my lungs.

I scream until my lungs ache and my veins fill to bursting and my face is as hot as a furnace. I scream until I have no breath left and I can't scream anymore.

But no one comes.

"Done?" Frederick saunters in front of the desk, one shiny alligator shoe in front of the other. "As promised, no one can hear you. See, I'm not much of a liar, Indigo. That's something you'll learn about me. I may kill people for fun, but lying? That's something I'm strictly against."

Here I am, literally struggling to breathe, while Paige just stares ahead like an extra from *Night of the Living Dead*, completely oblivious that she's seconds away from death herself.

I dart a glance at the door again.

"Locked." Frederick leans against the desk and picks his teeth with a dirty fingernail. "Go ahead and try if you like."

I do like. The chair tips back as I jump up and bolt for the door. There are scuffling noises behind me.

"Just let her get it out of her system," Frederick says.

I wrench the knob from left to right.

No, no, no, how can it be locked from the inside? I pound on the door with both fists, rattling the wood in its frame. I can see Mrs. Malone's silhouette on the other side of the window, can actually hear her muffled small talk with Mrs. Fields, but they can't hear me. It's as if I don't exist. I let out an anguished groan and lean my forehead against the cool glass.

"Ready to start talking?" Frederick asks.

I whimper into the door.

"You're wasting my time, Indigo. Have a seat and we can start negotiations." A thump behind me indicates he has righted the tipped-over chair.

I don't see any other option, so I turn around. Frederick gives a nod of encouragement, his hand gripping the back of the chair. I stumble over somehow and slump back into it.

"Good girl," he says, patting me on the head. "Now tell me about the Bible."

I close my eyes and press my lips together to stop them from trembling, tasting the salt of fresh tears.

A shadow darkens the room. I open my eyes to find Frederick standing in front me, straightened to his full height. Slowly, he unbuttons his suit jacket. I don't take my eyes from him as he shrugs out of his jacket, revealing a crisp white button-down worn under one of those gun holsters that look like suspenders. My pulse races erratically. Frederick looks around for somewhere to put his jacket, before resting it on Paige's lap. When he faces me again, he seems to notice the focus of my attention.

"You don't know this about me," he says, walking slowly in front of my chair like a wolf stalking its prey. "But I'm something of a film buff. Isn't that right, Leo?"

Leo grunts.

"I usually stick to the classics, but there are a few modern films that I really enjoy. Take *Reservoir Dogs,* for example." He gestures to his apparatus, as if that explains why he's wearing it.

"Oh, come on," he says. "You've never seen *Reservoir Dogs*? Quentin Tarantino?" He clucks his tongue in admonishment, wagging a long finger at my nose. "You kids have no taste these days. Now, if you'd seen *Reservoir Dogs,* you'd know that it contains one of the best torture scenes in American cinema."

I'm suddenly so nauseated I could puke.

"Yes," Frederick continues. "Mr. Blonde cuts off this guy's

ear and douses him with gasoline. Can you imagine? Sonof-abitch would *sting*. But that's not even the best part. See, the best part comes before he cuts the ear off. Mr. Blonde dances around the garage, to that Stealers Wheel song—Leo, what's that song called?"

" 'Stuck in the Middle with You,' " Leo says in a bored tone, as if this is a performance he's played a part in many times before.

"Ah, that's right," Frederick says, a smile spreading across his face. "Great song. So, as I was saying, this Mr. Blonde character, he dances around the garage to 'Stuck in the Middle with You,' holding this straight razor. All the while this guy's bound to a chair and gagged. And Mr. Blonde wears a holster just like this one." He laughs self-deprecatingly, running a finger under the straps. "Kitschy, I know, but I like it."

Leo heaves a sigh.

Frederick starts pacing again, only to stop suddenly and face me. "Hey, I know! We can reenact the scene!" A huge smile lights up his face. He looks at his hand, and a straight blade appears there, the metal glinting in the harsh light of the office. "And look, I just happen to have props!"

"Okay!" I blurt out. "I'm ready to talk."

"Ahhh"—Frederick looks at Leo—"she's changed her mind!"

They both raise their hands, palms up, making mock-shocked faces at each other.

I pretend they haven't rattled me and push my shoulders back. "Promise me that if I tell you the truth, you'll let us go."

Frederick laughs. "Or I could just read your mind and kill you both anyway. Why should I make any promises? I've never been a promise-making kind of man, Indigo. And this goes back to my aversion to lying. I make a promise and I might have to break it. Then what am I but a dirty old liar? You see the problem, right?"

Suddenly I can't breathe. Because I just know that I'm not making it out of this office alive. I'm going to die. I'm going to have my ear cut off and be doused with gasoline and I'm going to die. I'll never eat another bowl of Cocoa Puffs, never cheer the Renegades on to a Friday-night win, never watch reruns of *Fringe* with Mom on a Sunday night, never feel Devon's lips brush against mine, never—

"Leo?" Frederick says. "Kill them."

"No!" I rush to stand in front of Paige. "The book really is a family heirloom—that part is true. But it's not a regular Bible." The words tumble out on top of each other in my hurry to stop him. "It's a witchcraft bible."

Frederick's lip twitches, but he is otherwise stock-still.

"It's just a bunch of stuff written in Latin," I continue, taking an instinctive step backward. "I don't even know what it means."

Frederick waves a hand toward Paige and me in a "go ahead" gesture.

I whip my head back and forth, looking between the two men, dread and fear competing for priority in my body. "You promised. Y-you said."

"I promised nothing," Frederick says. "Nonetheless, I don't think I'll kill you just yet. Leo, can I get a hand?"

Leo rises.

I back up farther, and my heels run into Paige's chair. "What are you doing?"

"Oh, don't worry," Leo says, taking purposefully slow strides toward me. "I won't erase *all* your memories. Just a day or so's worth. No big deal." A grin pulls up one side of his lips, the other frozen with scar tissue. He stops abruptly in front of me and points a crooked finger directly between my eyes, focusing a stare down the straight line of his raised arm. That's when I notice that his eyes are black. Not dark brown, but black. My heart skips a beat.

"You're scared now," Leo says. "But just think, in a few minutes you won't remember this whole mess. Not the dead body you saw in the street, not Frederick and me. Hell, not even what went on in this office." He winks, and a chill shudders through me.

Frederick starts for the door. "Make it quick. I haven't got all day."

I shield my face, tracking the sound of Frederick's footsteps across the room. The door opens, and a rush of noises—the hum of the paper copier, the squeak of rubber soles on lino-leum, the distant chatter of students—penetrates the quiet office. "Mrs. Malone, my partner is just wrapping things up with the girls—"

The door clicks shut, and the room is quiet again. And then everything goes white.

I blink my eyes and find myself sitting in a wooden chair across from a big mahogany desk. Sunlight slants in through half-cracked venetian blinds. Framed pictures of generic-looking blond children and a nameplate reading MRS. MALONE are on the desk, and the air is scented with middle-aged woman perfume.

All signs point to me being in the principal's office, yet I have no clue why I'm here. Or how I got here. Or why Paige is sitting next to me.

My heart races. Suddenly the hours of Internet research I conducted six years ago after the backyard hole-digging incident when Mom's Bible went missing come crashing back into my mind. From what I remember, most crazy diseases run in families. And what is happening now *most definitely* qualifies as crazy.

"Indie?" Paige says, leaning across to look at me, her forehead creased with concern.

A swoosh of air announces Mrs. Malone's entrance.

"Hello, girls. Sorry to keep you waiting." Mrs. Malone strides behind her desk, eyes peeled back in the permanently surprised expression she wears from too much Botox. She adjusts her pencil skirt before sitting in the big leather chair. She flips through a file. Pushes back the perfectly curled, dyed-red hair that frames her face. Taps the eraser end of a pencil on her desk.

"Did we do something wrong?" Paige prompts nervously.

"Wrong?" Mrs. Malone repeats, flipping through the file again.

My cell phone buzzes loudly in my purse. Dammit, I forgot to put it on silent. Mrs. Malone cuts me a disapproving glare and launches into an agonizingly boring fifteen-minute lecture on cell-phone use in school. When she finally excuses us just in time for the end-of-lunch bell to ring, I'm so relieved to get out of there that I don't piece together that she never did tell us why we were called to her office in the first place until I'm halfway down the hall. Like I would question her anyway, no matter how strange the whole affair. When you escape from the principal's office, you don't question your luck.

I decide I'm being paranoid, and wipe the entire unpleasant incident from my memory. It didn't happen. There.

Between my mental instability, getting my books from my locker, and a quick make-out sesh with Devon by the water fountain, I forget all about the missed call in Mrs. Malone's office until I'm deep in another agonizingly boring lecture in history class. I sneak a peek at the caller ID under my desk. Mom. I stow my phone away. She didn't call back, so it must not have been important.

5

The sun has edged behind the sycamores surrounding Fairfield High's football field, and floodlights pour artificial white light across the stadium. Despite the suffocating heat, the bleachers are already crammed with students showing their Renegade pride with painted faces, foam fingers, and clothing in blue and silver, our team colors. I can't fathom why anyone would willingly hang outside when there are air-conditioned entertainment options available, but hey, I might not mind the heat either if I didn't have to exercise vigorously in it.

Thankfully, my uniform allows for maximum air: just a scrap of blue pleats (I think they call it a skirt in some communities) over a pair of silver spankies, and a fitted black shell.

Coach Jenkins (or Carmen, as she insists we call her) has finally decided to put in some face time with the squad. I'd like to think it's because of her deep commitment to Fairfield High, cheerleading, and the betterment of the community, but the way she struts and preens in front of the football coach, combined with the fake knockers that hang out of her see-through white tank, is enough to put doubt into even the dumbest cheerleader's mind.

While Bianca bores everyone with the minutiae of Sebastian's life, I scan the bleachers for Mom—no matter how much I protest, she comes to all the games that take place outside the shop's business hours—but I don't find her. It registers that I still haven't called her back. Not the first time in the history of ever that I forgot to call Mom, but probably the first time it didn't prompt her to call me six more times until I finally answered.

"Blackwood!"

I snap back to the present. Shit, what were we supposed to be doing? Lunges? Basket tosses? Bianca cocks her head, wearing an expression almost as severe as her ponytail.

I look to the girls for a hint. Julia stands just a few steps behind Bianca, mirroring her pom-pommed-hands-on-hips pose. Thea's checking out something terribly interesting on her shoes, and the Amy/Ashley twins are retying their matching brunette ponytails. Thanks, guys!

"Sorry, got a little distracted," I say.

"Distracted?" Bianca spits. "Please tell me I misheard you."

I'm contemplating whether now's a good time to tell her where to shove her pom-poms when Carmen appears.

"Bianc*aaa*," Carmen singsongs.

Bianca jumps like she's been seared with a cattle prod. Carmen might be the most easygoing teacher at Fairfield High, but get on her bad side and prepare to have a strip torn off you.

"I leave you in charge for five minutes and everyone's standing around doing nothing?" She cocks an eyebrow (impressively high for someone else I suspect has taken a few Botox injections to the face).

Bianca exhales a short breath but for once is at a loss for words.

Which is perfect, because Carmen doesn't wait for her response. Foul mood forgotten, she turns on a high-wattage smile and spins to face the rest of the squad, striding in front of us with her hands clasped behind her back. "Well, don't you girls look gorge."

She launches into an inspirational pregame speech about precious high school memories and the importance of showing off our hot bods while we still have them, before spotting a friend and sprinting off toward the bleachers.

The outdoor speakers crackle.

"Thank you all for coming out to support the Fairfield High Renegades," Mrs. Malone announces, her normally stern voice brimming over with excitement.

Loud hoots and hollers ring out through the twilight.

"Game time is just five short minutes away. Until then, would everyone please give a warm round of applause to Fairfield High's varsity cheerleading team!"

"Great," Bianca says. "We didn't get to practice the basket toss again. Thanks, Blackwood." She trots off toward the center of the field, waving her silver pom-poms high in the air.

"Way to go, loser," Julia says over her shoulder before following Bianca. The rest of the girls trip over each other to catch up.

No one's looking, so I slip my bestie and her little sidekick the finger before getting into formation in the center of the field.

"Are you ready?" Bianca yells to the crowd. We clap.

> "We are the mighty Renegades,
> And we came here to win
> The other team don't stand a chance
> It's time to pack it in
> 'Cause we got the moves [cue suggestive writhing]
> And we came here to fight
> And everyone from east to west knows
> Renegades go all night! Renegades go all night!"

The crowd jumps to its feet and roars. We run to the sidelines, a springing mass of hair ribbons and silver pom-poms, as Mrs. Malone takes to the speakers again.

"And now, introducing the pride of our school, ranked eighth in the state and soon to be number one, the Fairfield High Renegades, led by captain Devon Mills!"

Devon sprints out and runs backward to face the bleachers, giving a two-fingered wave to the audience. The spectators yell and whistle and jump and generally make big fools of themselves, Coach Carmen being no exception. I feel a tug of pride in my chest and shake my pom-poms extra hard for my boyfriend while the rest of the team runs in behind Devon to a slightly subdued but still crazy reception.

I take this opportunity to hazard another glance at the bleachers to look for Mom, but something unusual catches my eye. While everyone else is on their feet cheering, there's one guy sitting—slouching would actually be a better word for it—at the end of the first row. And he's wearing leather. In seventy-five-degree weather!

He yawns, checks his watch, then starts scraping something from the bottom of his boot heel. Whoever it is he's here to watch is lucky to have such enthusiastic support.

The guy catches me staring. He raises a balled fist in a lame-cheerleader impression and yells, "Go, team!"

My mouth drops open. Is this guy serious?

A whistle blows. I reluctantly join in as Bianca leads another cheer.

"Defense, get physical
Get down, get hard, get mean

Defense, get physical
And block that other team!"

When I glance back at the guy, he's laughing. Laughing!
I want to bash the jerk over the head with my pom-poms.
If high school football's not your thing—and everything
from his stupid leather jacket to his messy black hair and tattoos tells me that it isn't—then why come at all? It's not like
he goes to Fairfield; I'd recognize a douche like him from
around the halls.

The crowd leaps to its feet.

A touchdown.

Teammates slap Devon on the back, and he sends me a
little wave from the end zone.

"Go, number nine!" I shout, and shake my pom-poms in
his direction.

A hoot of laughter from the bleachers rises above the cacophony of yelling and cheering, and I glance in that direction. At first the guy looks like he's trying to hold back,
but then he bursts into laughter again—a full-bellied, brace-
your-stomach fit—and I get the distinct impression he's
laughing at me.

"Get out there, girls!" Carmen shouts, shooing us onto
the field. "Cheer sixteen."

I swallow my irritation with our heckler as Bianca leads
our first touchdown cheer.

"The best at kicks
The best at passes
The other team
Can kiss our . . . !"

As the crowd shouts "asses," we turn around, bend over, and lift up our pleated skirts.

It's not like I particularly *enjoy* flashing my butt to half the school, but I've never really paid too much mind to it before. Now my face burns, and I won't look at the guy no matter how obvious and annoying his chortling is.

Carmen does excited little claps and jumps as we trot back to the sidelines. "Great job, Bianca."

Bianca smiles so wide at the compliment I think I see tonsils.

I don't look at the guy for the rest of the game, won't give him the satisfaction, even when he laughs so hard that other spectators tell him to shut up.

By the time the countdown clock reaches zero, darkness envelops the field and the Renegades are victorious. The football team ambushes Devon and lifts him above their heads. To say the crowd is happy would be an understatement of epic proportions.

It takes about three and a half minutes for the stadium to thin out after that. I know this because that's how long Devon gives me to change out of my uniform before we leave for the concert, and by the time I emerge from the girls' locker room, dressed in a black lace tank, a fluorescent pink micromini, sky-high black heels, and bright red lipstick, there's not a soul left in the bleachers. Everyone's converged on the parking lot to make plans for the night. Kids pile into cars. Music blares from open windows, sending vibrations across the earth that I can feel in my spine. Someone peels across the parking lot, and everyone whoops and cheers. The air crackles with positive energy.

"Hurry up!" Devon calls from across the lot, waving and hopping impatiently outside his silver BMW.

"I'm coming, I'm coming." I run as fast as I can in four-inch heels on loose gravel. Which is impressively fast, I must say.

I pass the rest of the squad and football team circled around Jarrod's car, which pumps techno music through the lot. They're still dressed in their uniforms, which they'll wear all night, if tonight is anything like past game nights; it's important to show our team pride around the city, Bianca says. Yeah, because what the citizens of Los Angeles can't get enough of is high school football.

"Hey," Jarrod calls to me. "You guys are coming to my house after the concert, right?"

"Course," I say. "Who *isn't* going?"

My answer elicits cheers from our friends. Jarrod better have some carpet cleaner handy, because his place is getting trashed tonight.

"Hey! Hey, you, Indiana, or whatever."

I spin around and find the leather jacket guy giving me a

wide smile. "Good, I thought I'd have to tackle, tackle, tackle you!" He mimics our cheer, a shit-eating grin on his face.

My friends must recognize our heckler too, because they circle around me.

"You know that guy?" Bianca hisses in my ear.

"No," I say, offended, then call over to him, "Hey, don't you have animals to torture behind a Dumpster or something?"

"Taking a break," he says without missing a beat.

"Want me to mess this guy up?" Jarrod asks.

Bianca pushes Jarrod back and marches in front of me to face the guy. "Look, I don't know who you think you are, but next time you chirp us during a game, we're getting you kicked out."

"Kicked out?" He claps his hand over his mouth. "You wouldn't!"

"You better watch how you talk to us," Jarrod says, taking a big, macho step closer.

"Indie, hurry up, we're gonna be late!" Devon calls.

"Look," Bianca says, catching Jarrod's arm, "as much as I'd love for you to get better acquainted, we have a party to go to, because we have, like, lives. Come on, guys. Don't waste your time on this loser."

"Are you all just gonna, like, let her boss you around like that?" Leather Jacket Guy says in a perfect Bianca impression.

The weirdo makes a valid point; I hate him slightly less.

But I'm running late, so I leave the petty, immature fighting to my friends.

"Finally," Devon says as I get inside the car. "Who were you talking to?"

"Some loser." I flip the vanity mirror down to check out my hair. It's a good thing I'm going to a concert where wild hair is acceptable, because it's Krazy with a capital *K*: about ninety percent frizz and ten percent curl.

"I don't like him," Devon says.

I flick him an incredulous look. "You can't seriously be jealous."

"I don't want you talking to him."

And I don't want my boyfriend telling me who to talk to. I normally wouldn't think twice before telling him exactly that, but we've been bickering too much lately. We need a good night.

Devon fiddles with the buttons on the dash until a Jay-Z song blasts through the speakers. "Yeah!" His head bobs in time with the music. "Hope he does this song tonight. It's wicked."

I smile and gaze out the window; the guy is gone. "Yeah, really wicked."

———◆———

Sweat collects in places I didn't know was possible. Beer is sloshed down the front of my tank top, which clings to my body like I'm an extra in some sort of *Girls Gone Wild* video. And I smell—bad.

Which all might be super embarrassing if twenty thousand other screaming Jay-Z fans weren't in the same exact situation as me.

"Having fun?" Devon yells into my ear.

And ow, that was loud, but I nod and smile, because I *am* having fun. Sure, rap's not my *favorite,* but it hardly matters when you've got floor tickets to the sold-out concert everyone in school's been talking about for ages. The energy in the stadium alone would be enough to make any rap hater have a good time. And Jay-Z hasn't even come out yet.

The lights dim suddenly, and a slow beat—not unlike the ones common in slasher movies—blasts through the speakers. The crowd hushes. Random images flash across giant screens set up in all corners of the building. Smoke billows from the very pores of the stage. An explosion sounds, eliciting gasps from the audience, and then floodlights pour blue light across the stage, and Jay-Z is there. The stadium erupts into savage cheers just as the first notes of his latest song begin.

Jay-Z strides across the stage—Jay-Z is right in front of me, holy crap, Jay-Z's red sneakers just walked past me!—and the crowd surges forward, so Devon and I get smushed up against the stage. Which would be totally painful if I weren't so freaking happy about being smushed up against my boyfriend at a Jay-Z concert. This is the best—*best*—night of my life.

So what if we hardly get to talk, and when we do get a chance, conversation is stilted and awkward like it never was before. And so what if at intermission we have to stand in line for approximately seventeen minutes to get a bottle of water, and then Devon doesn't even pay for mine. And really, I don't mind when Devon sees his football buddy, Ian, and runs off so they can smash their chests together in a testosterone-fueled greeting, then go on to badly sing Jay-Z lyrics for what feels like forever while I twiddle my thumbs by the concession stand.

Mere blips. I stand by my statement: best night of my life.

"Indigo!"

I search the packed lobby for the face belonging to the vaguely familiar voice calling my name. I do a double take when my eyes land on Leather Jacket Guy, leaning casually against a wall with his hands jammed in the pockets of his black pants. A chill ripples through me.

He followed me.

Leather pushes off the wall. For a moment I lose sight of his black waves among the sea of bodies crowding the lobby, and I panic. When he pops up again, it's nearly right in front of me.

I gasp, clapping a hand to my pounding heart. "Did you follow me?" I ask, trying to keep my eyes on him while simultaneously scanning the lobby for Devon.

"I'm here for the music," he answers.

I snort, despite my fear. One look at his smirk and I know he's lying.

"Does your mom know you're out this late?" he asks.

"Okay, getting creepy there, Leather Jacket Dude," I say. "Should I memorize your features for the police lineup now or later?"

"I'm just saying, it's late."

"And? I'm not twelve."

He shrugs. "Doesn't mean you shouldn't check in with your mom. Innocent suggestion here." With that, he gives me a little wave and disappears back into the crowd.

My throat goes dry. My missed phone call from Mom, the fact that she didn't call back, didn't show up to the game—something's wrong. really wrong. I frantically dig my phone out of my purse and punch in Mom's number.

It rings ten times before going to voice mail.

I try once more, but my luck doesn't get any better. Finally, I stow my phone and search for Devon. I spot his blond hair in a group of guys and cross the lobby to give his arm a violent shake. He glances at me before holding up the universal "one minute" signal. I shake him harder.

Releasing a heavy sigh, he reluctantly turns to me. "Ind, I was in the middle of—"

"I need to go home."

"Home? What are you talking about? Are you drunk?" He makes to turn back to his friends but I yank his arm.

"The guy from the football game you told me not to talk to, he was just here and he said some really creepy shit and now I'm worried about my mom."

"That guy was here?" he asks.

"Yeah, which you would have seen if you were paying any attention to me at all."

"Oh, come on—" he starts, but I cut him off because that argument can so wait.

"I think he followed me."

He puffs up his chest and scans the lobby. "You see him again, you tell me. I'll take care of it."

Seriously?

"That's great," I say. "But we have to go."

"Go? It's only intermission!"

I glare at him.

He wraps an arm around me and pulls me into him. "You can't seriously be suggesting we leave based on what some crazy guy said? I'm sure your mom's fine."

"I'm worried," I mumble. More like warble.

He kisses the top of my head. "We'll call the cops after the show and you can tell them all about the guy. Does that make you feel better?"

I consider this. He's probably right. I shouldn't take my cues from a wackjob. Mom is probably fine.

The sounds of warm-up drumming spill out from the auditorium, and we fight the crowd back to our front-row seats. Jay-Z takes the stage again, and the crowd erupts into cheers. But he hasn't even made it through his first song when I tap Devon on the shoulder. He bends slightly, without taking his transfixed gaze from the stage. "It doesn't!" I yell over the music.

He shakes his head, cupping a hand around his ear. "What?"

"I said it doesn't make me feel better!"

And then I go outside and hail a cab.

6

The drive from the Staples Center to my house is a blink in terms of L.A. time, but it feels like an eternity right now. Traffic moves painfully slowly. Every time I see the brake lights of the car in front of us flash, my chest tightens and I'm sure I'm having a coronary.

It doesn't help that the cabdriver insists on making small talk the entire way, in between obnoxiously smacking his gum and trying to kill us both with his insane driving. Was the concert any good? Did I hear Jay-Z's staying at the Chateau Marmont? Aren't I young to be out by myself? Did I hear Magnet is the latest celeb hangout?

I want to scream at him to shut up. The only thing that

stops me is the chance he might boot me if I insult him. Cabbies are weird like that.

I groan in despair.

God, why didn't Mom answer my calls? I flip through the most horrendous options like I'm going through a Rolodex. Car accident. Drive-by shooting. Heart attack. I dig my nails into my thighs so hard I'm sure I draw blood. Okay, it's probably none of those things. I'm probably being melodramatic. I'm sure it's just Aunt Penny having a crisis again. That's why Mom called—to tell me that the L.A. parking authority finally caught on to Penny's zillions of unpaid parking tickets, and Mom has to go save her sister's POS car from certain death at the impound lot. Or that she has to go talk Aunt Penny off a ledge after (gasp!) her latest douche of a boyfriend didn't work out. Or that Aunt Penny quit her cocktail waitress/personal assistant/makeup artist job because what she really wants to do is act, and she's not going to waste her time doing anything else.

I pull out my cell phone and punch in Aunt Penny's number. It rings six times before she picks up. Club music blares from the phone so loud I have to hold it away from my ear.

"Aunt Penny?"

"My favorite niece!" she yells. "What's up, girlie? One sec. *Vodka tonic. No, I said vodka tonic! Thanks.* Ugh, the bartenders are deaf here. So what's up?" Before I can answer, she erupts into laughter. The phone makes interference noises.

"Hello? Aunt Penny? It's important!" I yell.

Voices skip over the roar of the music, but none of them is Aunt Penny's.

I end the call.

So there goes my theory. Not that it made much sense to begin with—not that any of my theories make sense. A big piece is missing, and that piece is Leather Jacket Guy. How did he know about Mom? Who is he?

I blow out through pursed lips, trying to slow my racing heart.

Somehow, not much time has elapsed before we reach tree-lined Fuller Avenue. The cabbie practically inches past the gated three-story mansions, through the intersection at Waring, and down a few more blocks, until we finally reach the squat white bungalow with the sad little flower box under the picture window that I call home.

But Mom's car isn't here. It's after ten, and all the lights are off. She should be home.

"Change of plans," I say. "Two-ninety Melrose."

The cabbie throws the car in reverse. I start to think I really am having a heart attack as he navigates through traffic that only gets worse as prime bar hours approach.

But my muscles relax when we pull onto Melrose, and I spot the glint of moonlight on Mom's car, parked right in front of the shop. They tense up just as quickly, though, when we roll to a stop under the Black Cat's awning; darkness emanates from every window, yet the neon Open sign is on.

The cabbie twists to face me. Dispatch is barking orders through the radio. His lips move, but his words barely register.

I was in such a hurry to get here, and now I'm frozen, afraid to go inside for fear of what I'll find. A breeze sweeps through the open cab window and raises goose bumps on my exposed flesh. Night has finally chased away the suffocating heat of the day. I shove the nine hundred dollars I owe the cabbie at him before stepping outside. He gives me a wave and then peels off.

I'm alone in the dark. That's if you don't count the hoboes and knife-wielding crazies I'm sure are hiding in the shadows.

"Going in, or what?"

I jump so high I'd laugh if it were someone else besides me doing it, then whirl around to find the source of the voice.

Leather Jacket Guy leans against the stucco side of the fast-check-cashing place across the street, hands in the pockets of his black pants and one army-booted heel up against the wall. Signature pose, I guess.

"You? What are you doing here?"

Laughter rings out through the night. "Relax, I'm not going to attack you. Just pointing out that you might want to get inside. Lots of baddies in L.A. at night."

"Aren't you full of helpful hints," I say, backing up.

The light from a streetlamp etches shadows into his laugh lines and makes his smirk look sinister. He pushes off the wall.

"Don't come any closer." My voice comes out much shakier than I'd planned.

I climb up the steps, careful not to fully turn my back to him as I unlock the front door. Only it's not locked. My stomach churns. Mom would never leave the door unlocked after close. When eight p.m. strikes, it's the first thing she does.

Hands shaking, I push the door open. The little bell jingles as I enter, which, in the dark, sounds anything but inviting. I do a quick check to make sure the guy isn't going to try to push me inside the shop, and then hurry inside, slamming the door so hard it rattles the windows. I flip the dead bolt closed.

7

I'm afraid to flick on the lights, afraid of what I'll see. Then I hear Mom's moan and I can't turn them on fast enough. My hands fumble for the panel next to the door. I feel the cold plastic under my fingers and bash all the switches up.

I don't see her right away. Having adjusted to the dark, my eyes are seared even by the dim lighting of the shop, and I have to shield them from the candelabra. And then Mom moans again, and I find her.

The ceiling-high solid oak bookcase has been overturned, and underneath it is an absolute mountain of books. Mom's black-heeled boots poke out from underneath all the rubble. If it weren't for the cauldron on display in the center of the room, which caught one end of the bookcase, the whole thing would have landed on top of her. Would have killed her. And judging by the way the bookcase bows in the middle, an inch-deep crack splitting the center of the arc, it could still happen at any moment.

"In-Indigo?"

"Mom!" I snap from my trance and run to where she lies, falling to my knees and frantically pulling books off her. "Mom, what happened? Are you okay? Can you get up?"

Her head is steeped in the shadow of the bookcase, but it shakes minutely.

"I'm going to pull you out, okay?"

She moans as if to say "Don't touch me," but what else can I do? I can't leave her like this. What if the wood cracks while I wait for help to arrive?

I grab her by the ankles and use my weight to pull. I'm able to drag her out a few inches, but then her body snags taut, and she lets out a piercing cry.

"What? What's wrong?" I drop her legs and fall to my knees again.

"My arm," she mutters. "It's stuck."

"Oh God. Okay, um, if I lift the bookshelf will you be able to move it?"

No answer.

"Mom?"

"Okay," she says, her voice a harsh whisper.

"All right. This is going to be really heavy, and I'll only

be able to hold it up for a second, if that, so you'll have to move fast, okay?"

I widen my stance, brace my hands under the wood, and lift, lift, lift until my face turns hot and an artery pulses in my neck and my hands shake and I have to give up. It's not budging. I release my grip and massage the deep indents the bookcase left in my palms.

"I'm sorry, Mom. I can't do it." A sob escapes me and I fall to the floor. I've never felt more useless. "I'm calling nine-one-one, okay? Hang in there."

"Need a hand?"

I scuttle back like a crab. The guy from outside pokes his head into the shop.

"Stay back!" I yell. "I'm calling the cops."

"Could be a while before they get here." He pushes the door wider and leans against the frame, inspecting a chunky silver ring on his middle finger.

"Listen, creep, I don't know how you knew about my mom, but— Wait a minute, how did you get in here? I locked the dead bolt!"

"Look, you want my help or not? I'm not in the mood for dramatics."

I don't want his help. He's probably the reason Mom's under the bookcase in the first place. How could he have known she'd been hurt if he wasn't involved? But some part of me knows this doesn't quite make sense, because then why stick around? Why warn me at all, offer to help when the police could be on the way as we speak? And he's right. The cops could take a while to get here, and I can't risk that—not with that ominous crack in the bookcase.

"Okay, then. Guess I'm not needed, so I'll just—"

"Wait!" I push to my feet. "Help me lift this bookcase and then go away."

He laughs. "Now, there's an offer I can't refuse."

The floorboards creak under his feet as he nears, and holy shit, when did he get so tall? Not to mention the fact he obviously hasn't brushed his hair in at least a month and has a huge tattoo on his *neck*! Surely this is not the kind of guy I should be inviting to share small spaces with me. My heart races. What will I do if he attacks? I can't fight off a guy that big. Or any guy, for that matter.

He saunters around the wreck, scanning the mess.

I bite my nails. "Can you just do it, already? My mom's trapped under there."

"All right, all right." He shrugs off his leather jacket, revealing a sleeve of colorful tattoos on his right arm, then spreads his legs and grips the wood. And then he does something really strange, even for him. He closes his eyes and whispers something inaudible. I can't believe I wasted precious time on this weirdo. I snatch my cell phone out of my bag and dial 911.

"Hello, uh, hi. I need help. A bookcase fell over in my mom's shop and she's trapped. . . . Yes, she's breathing, but she can't get out and she's hurt. . . . Yes, it's the Black Cat on Mel—" Before I can finish my sentence, the guy's lifting the bookcase.

And making it look easy. I mean, he's got a deep crease in his brow and he's lifting slowly, as if it's a strain, but the muscles in his forearms aren't taut and his knuckles don't whiten a bit.

But that's crazy!

"Little help?" He nods toward Mom.

"I have to go. The Black Cat, two-ninety Melrose. Hurry!" I drop the phone and rush to grab Mom's ankles again. This time, I slide her out of the mess with only moderate effort, dragging her over the faux Turkish rug as far from the bookcase as I can before I have to give my muscles a break. When she's clear, the guy lowers the bookcase to its resting place on the cauldron. As soon as he does, the crack finally gives way. The bookcase lands on the pile of books with a boom that echoes through the room. A shudder runs through me at the thought of Mom under there just moments before.

"Mom, are you okay?" I kneel beside her and brush the matted hair from her eyes. She focuses her gaze on me, and smiles. I don't think I've ever been so happy to see her smile.

"I'm okay now," she says through labored breaths. "You're here."

I force a reassuring smile. "Your arm? Can you move it?"

She takes a breath and wiggles her fingers.

Okay. Everything's going to be okay.

"What happened?"

"I—I don't know." She swallows. "I was just dusting off the bookshelves, like usual, and then . . . I guess it must have just tipped over. I don't remember, really." Her eyes cloud over. "Must have hit my head pretty hard."

"Don't worry, Mom. An ambulance is on its way." I grip her hand, and she squeezes back.

And then I remember the guy. Sure, he just saved Mom and I should thank him, but first I need to find out how he knew what had happened to her. And then smack him for not helping her sooner.

But when I turn around, he's not there. He's not anywhere I can see, and there aren't a lot of hiding spots in the small shop. "One minute, Mom."

I drop her hand and race to the open front door, peering down either side of the street to make it official.

He's gone.

8

Mom sits propped against a wall with a mug of cocoa in her hands. She refused to get into the ambulance, even though the paramedics practically begged her to get her arm checked out. Mom *hates* hospitals. Plus, she says her arm is fine, just a little sore. Right. Even though it looks like she got in a fight with a meat tenderizer and lost. Her head's okay too. Just a bit of a headache. And so what if her knees buckle when she tries to stand too long? Who needs to walk anyway?

So the ambulance took off, and we're left with one police officer, who takes pictures of the damage, and another (I've dubbed him Chief Wiggum) who interviews Mom.

"So, let's go over this again, Mrs. Black—"

"It's Ms.," Mom interrupts. "I'm not married." She gives him a weak smile. I thank God she's in a bad mood and that he's not cute; otherwise she might recount the tale of Dad leaving when I was three—or, in her words, being abducted because of his knowledge of the CIA. Seriously.

"Okay, Ms. Blackwood. You say the last thing you remember is dusting the bookshelf?"

"Yes. Like I said before, I don't know what happened after that. Just that I woke up and was underneath the bookcase. Did you know that thing weighs over three hundred pounds? Lucky it got caught on the cauldron or I'd be dead."

"Yes, you mentioned that," the officer says.

Like three times. I think he's worried about head trauma. I know it's just normal Mom.

"You don't remember anyone coming into the shop? Even earlier? Someone acting strange?" He tips his head forward, urging her to speak.

"No." She grips the mug tighter. "No one unusual. Well, except for the boy who helped lift the bookcase. The one Indigo was telling you about."

Or partially telling him about. I left out the bit where he knew Mom was hurt. The last thing I need right now is to get Mom worked up with conspiracy theories. I've got big plans to fill the officer in on the rest of the story when Mom's out of earshot.

"I thank you for your patience, ma'am," Chief Wiggum

says, "but just a few more questions. You say there's nothing missing that you're aware of? Nothing of value that someone would want to steal?"

Mom sighs.

"I'm sorry to ask so many times, it's just that . . . well, I probably shouldn't tell you this, but we've seen a lot of cases like this in the last few weeks. Blackouts. Memory loss. It'd really help us out if you could think hard on this one."

Lots of blackouts? I dart my gaze to Mom, and sure enough, she's rubbing her chin. Great.

"What's this about blackouts?" She sets down her mug and leans forward.

Wiggum clears his throat. "Look, I really shouldn't have said anything. If you could just let me know if anything is missing."

Mom looks around the shop. "Everything looks just like it normally does. Well, except for the booksh—" She straightens, her skin turning pale.

"What, Mom?"

"The book," she whispers.

"What's that, ma'am?" Wiggum asks, pen hovering over notepad.

"Indie?" Mom says, pleading with her eyes.

She can't be serious. Just who does she think would break into her shop to steal a crusty old book? But I can't exactly say that, not after what she just went through.

"I'll check," I say, reluctantly climbing to my feet.

❧ 77 ❧

This sucks. This really, really sucks.

The attic access is at the rear of the shop. It's a tiny, unfinished space with exposed insulation for walls and a low ceiling. And I hate it. It's dark and creepy and I don't care if my fear is immature. Mom knows about my aversion to the attic and makes a point of not asking me to go up, but when it comes to the book, she can be pretty unreasonable.

I jump up, grab the chain that hangs from the ceiling, and pull the stairs to the ground.

"Hurry, Indie," Mom calls.

"I'm hurrying." I grip the sides of the ladderlike stairs and look up into the black-hole opening.

Okay, just do it. Just get it over with.

I climb the rungs with slow, purposeful steps until I'm surrounded by black and the only thing I can see is the circle of light from the floor beneath me. The scent of dust and cardboard envelops me, and my heart thrums so fast I can't distinguish one beat from the next. This is the worst part—walking in utter darkness to the light that hangs from the ceiling in the center of the room.

Sucking in a breath, I run across the attic, claw around in the air for the chain, and pull. I gasp as the low-wattage lightbulb flicks on, despite the fact that everything looks as it normally does—boxes, boxes, and more boxes, lined high against every wall. Aside from them and some cobwebs, the only other thing up here is an antique table that Mom bought at a yard sale but is too small to do anything useful except hold her ashtray. Which, I note, has about half a dozen cigarette butts smushed inside.

I tut under my breath. I should have known better than to think Mom would really quit this time. I walk over and pick one up. Marlboros? Weird. Mom's been smoking Virginia Slims ever since I can remember. I drop the cigarette back into the ashtray.

"Is it there?" Mom's worried voice carries up the stairs.

"I'm looking," I answer, and it makes me feel a bit better, somehow, to speak loudly up here. Like I'm claiming the room. Like the shadows aren't hiding ax murderers.

I push aside boxes until I see the access panel in the faded wood floorboards. Dropping to my knees in front of it, I edge my nails under the wood and lift. When the plank comes free, I toss it aside with a clatter and peer inside.

Nothing.

"What?" I frantically swipe my hands along the inner walls of the space, even though I can clearly see the shoe-box-sized hole is empty. How can the book be gone?

"Indigo, are you all right?" Mom calls.

I sweep my forearm across my brow. Upsetting Mom is the last thing I want to do right now—the last thing I ever want to do—but really, what other option do I have? I go to the stairs.

"Are you sure you didn't misplace it?" I call down.

"Yes, I'm sure. It's not there?" There's panic in her voice. "Check again. It has to be there."

My legs shake as I descend the rungs.

"Indie, didn't you hear me? I said to check again, please, it's really important that—"

"It's not there, Mom." My tone has an air of finality.

"What's missing?" The officer poises his pen over his notepad.

I look to Mom for an answer.

"Just a family heirloom," she says after a delay. Then she clucks her tongue. "And you know what? How silly of me. I forgot I took it home the other night. Sorry to alarm you, Officer."

His brow creases.

"You know," Mom says, rubbing her arm, "this arm is actually starting to really bother me. I think I'll have my daughter drive me to the hospital now."

"Oh, sure, just a few more—"

She climbs to her feet, wincing in pain, and practically pushes the officer and his photo-taking partner out of the shop.

The minute they're gone—really gone, as in "Mom watched from the window to make sure they drove away" gone—she makes a limping run for the attic to confirm my news.

"Like I'd miss a book in there," I call up as she bangs around boxes upstairs. "Mom, be careful—your arm."

She doesn't even dignify that with a response.

I fully expected her to be enraged, but when she comes

downstairs, her face is streaked with tears, and her eyes, which are normally a bright, vibrant gray, now look like two big voids.

"Oh, Mom." I pull her to my chest, and she lets out a sob that rattles her body. Warning bells go off in my head. Mom went off the deep end the last time the Bible went missing, and it wasn't even gone that long before she found it right where she left it, in a shoe box in her closet. I don't want to think about what might happen if we never get it back. I imagine padded rooms. Needle jabs by mean nurses. There might even be drooling involved.

I brush hair that clings to her wet cheeks away from her face.

"I think I know where it is," I say.

"Y-you do?" Mom asks, hope filling her cloudy eyes.

Okay, so that's a lie. But one thing is clear as I take in the fragile state of my mother: I have to find this book. And I do at least have *one* clue to go on: Leather Jacket Guy. He knows something, if he didn't actually take the book himself. All I have to do is find him.

"I'm going to get the Bible back, Mom. I promise."

9

So, slight problem with that plan: I have absolutely no clue where to start.

There are over three million people in Los Angeles. The Staples Center seats twenty thousand; Dodger Stadium holds fifty-six thousand. Finding someone in L.A., especially if they don't want to be found, is like finding a needle in a haystack. Or, as Mom would say, like bailing out a battleship with a bucket.

But I've promised Mom, and I'm almost certain that, if I weren't planning to sneak out just as soon as she falls asleep, she'd be in support of my plan. In support of anything that means finding the Bible.

I set Mom up with a live stream of *Fringe*, Season Four—so confusing it's sure to lull her to sleep.

"You have everything you need? A refill on the tea, maybe?" I hike my thumb toward the kitchen.

"I'm not an invalid, Indie."

"Don't be ridiculous. You need to rest." I take her half-empty cup to the kitchen.

"Just, maybe one more thing?" she calls to my back. And the way she says it—guiltily—lets me know she wants her cigarettes.

"Seriously?" I answer. But I'm already going to the freezer.

"Thanks, doll! I'll quit just as soon as I'm feeling better."

"Yeah, yeah." A blast of cold air hits my face as I open the freezer. I grab a pack of cigarettes from the carton and pad back to the living room. "Virginia Slims? What happened to the Marlboros?"

Mom's brows draw together. "Marlboros? What are you talking about?"

I remember the Marlboro butts in the shop's attic, and my spine tingles.

"What, honey?"

"Oh, nothing."

Two cups of tea and three cigarettes later, and Mom's sawing logs.

So now I'm sitting in the front seat of the Sunfire, the engine vibrating beneath me, gripping the steering wheel as I stare at our house in the headlights.

Hours pass. Or maybe minutes.

I *could* trawl the area around the shop and look for Leather Jacket Guy, talk to some people, maybe see if anyone saw him or which direction he went. I tap my fingers on the steering wheel. It's a pretty solid plan, the only real plan I can see. So why can't I move?

It *definitely* isn't because I'm scared. Nope. Not possible. I'm not afraid of the dark, and it isn't like hundreds of hoboes will jump on the hood of my car if I dare slip below fifty on Melrose at night—probably. I can handle this by myself.

But just for fun, I run through the options of friends I can enlist for help.

Bianca?

I bark a laugh. That's a good joke. "Hey, Bianca, can you please leave this fun party to help me find my mom's witchcraft Bible?" Yeah. Not likely.

There's Devon. . . .

I remember his helpfulness tonight and groan, sinking my fingers deep into my hair. Nope, Devon is out too. None of my friends can help me. Not unless the emergency is of the fashion or hair variety.

For some weird reason, Paige flashes into my head.

Paige is a nice girl, if annoying, and she comes with the bonus that she's not the gossiping type. Plus I bet she's the only person in L.A. without plans on a Friday night.

The more I think about it, the more it seems like a fantastic idea. Sure, some people might say I'm "using" her, but those people just don't have the complex understanding of human behavior that I do.

I exit the car, and with a handful of pebbles collected from the edge of the driveway, scamper through the narrow space between our houses until I stare up at Paige's bedroom window. It's higher than I expected, and my first throw misses by a wide margin. But on my second attempt, I hear the rock *tink* against the glass. I throw a second pebble, and then a third, for good measure.

Then I wait, wringing my hands as I pace in the tall grass. What could be taking her so long? Is she trying to prove a point or something? Or maybe she fell asleep with her iPod headphones on. Yeah, I bet that's it.

I cup my hands around my mouth and whisper-yell, "Paige! Paige, it's me. Open the window."

I lose patience when she doesn't answer immediately, and resort to actual yelling. A light flicks on in her room, and relief floods my body. A moment later the window slides up and a familiar face peers down at me. Only it's not Paige's.

"Indigo, is that you? It's after midnight. What are you doing?" Mrs. Abernathy squints down at me, her usually perfect bob pulled up in curlers on the top of her head.

I think about diving behind a bush, but it's too late. She's seen me. So I wave up at the confused woman leaning over the window ledge. "I'm sorry I woke you, Mrs. Abernathy. I was just trying to wake Paige up. I'm having a . . . a boy emergency."

My cheeks flood with heat, and I'm glad of the dark so she can't see the telltale signs of the lie on my face.

"Oh. Well, I'm very sorry, but Paige isn't home."

I blink up at her, the words not registering. "What do you mean she's not home?"

"Paige is spending the night at a friend's house." The way she says it is almost like an apology, and suddenly I couldn't feel more pathetic, standing under Paige's window in the dark while she's off having a good time somewhere else.

"Jessie Colburn's?" I guess.

"Yes, that's the one. Very sweet girl."

"I'm sure." Tears prick my eyes. Of course she has a friend now. Of course she has plans. What did I think, that I could push and push her away and she'd always be there, waiting for me in case I ever got bored of Bianca?

"I'm sorry, Indie," Mrs. Abernathy says. "If you need to talk to someone you're welcome to come inside."

I take a deep breath so my voice doesn't shake when I speak. "Thanks, but that's okay."

I trudge back to the car, idling in the driveway, and sink into the front seat. For a moment I'm resigned to doing this thing on my own, but then I give myself a hard shake. This is not the Indigo that I know and love. I won't give up that easily. So Paige made a friend? Jessie's got nothing on me.

I throw the car into reverse and peel down the street. In minutes I'm parked up on the curb across from the Colburn residence, a huge Spanish-style home on North Vista. At least, I'm pretty sure it's her house. Only so much confidence can be placed in gossip from the hallways at school.

I text Paige:

> Come outside

A minute later:

> *I'm not home. Is something wrong? It's late.*

> I know. I'm outside Jessie's. Hurry.

I watch the quiet house for signs of life. No light flicks on inside, but a moment later the front door edges open, and Paige cautiously pokes her head outside.

I wave her over in big, impatient gestures.

She pulls her sweater up on her shoulders and crosses the street.

"Indie? What's going on?" She probably thinks someone died. Which is just about the only good reason for doing what I'm doing.

I take a deep breath. "It's my mom's Bible. Someone stole it and she's freaking out."

Paige blinks at me. "Her Bible? And this couldn't wait until the morning?"

I exhale. "No, it can't wait. It's really important to her. Like, vital."

Paige shakes her head. "Where's Bianca? Why isn't *she* helping you?"

Oh. It's like that now? You'd think the girl would recognize a bone when one was being thrown.

"Because I didn't ask her," I retort. "I asked *you*."

She shifts from foot to foot. "Well, can't you call the cops or something?"

I don't believe this is happening. "I did. They can't help." I realize how small my voice has become. Paige must too, because her shoulders soften and she glances behind her at the house.

"I can't just leave."

"Why not? You're always trying to get us to hang out, and I'm sure Jessie would understand." I regret the words as soon as they're out of my mouth. I sound jealous. Which I'm *so* not.

"It's just a shitty thing to do," Paige says.

Yeah, it's shitty, I want to say. So what? But of course Paige doesn't treat her friends this way. She probably bakes Jessie cupcakes when she's had a bad day or something. I nod and shift the car into drive.

Paige sighs. "Just give me a minute to talk to Jessie."

A stupid grin spreads across my face. Paige rolls her eyes before sprinting off across the street.

Minutes later she's shuffling back to the car, this time with a giant duffel bag slung over her shoulder. She dumps the bag on the backseat before climbing into the passenger side.

"I hope you're happy. I had to make up a lie so she'd let me off the hook. I hate lying."

"Thanks, Paige. I mean it." I smile across at her.

"Yeah, whatever." Her reflection gazes out the window.

Somehow I thought she'd be happier about this.

A few minutes pass in silence, and I don't know what to say to cut through the awkward tension.

Luckily, Paige finally speaks. "So what happened, anyway? It sounds pretty crazy."

I heave a relieved sigh. And suddenly words are spilling out of my mouth faster than I can organize my thoughts. "The Bible, it went missing and Mom's going crazy. I said I'd find it, but I have no clue where to start. See, Mom had this accident and she blacked out. And there was this guy, and he lifted the shelf off her, but he was at the game too, and he knew about my mom being hurt, which is, like, really, really weird, right? And now—"

"Stop," Paige interrupts. "What. On earth. Are you talking about?"

I deflate.

"Tell me what happened," Paige says, clapping her hand on my shoulder. "And start from the beginning."

I fill her in on the history of the Bible and the events of the night. And it feels good—really good, actually—to get it all off my chest.

When I'm finished, Paige lapses into a deep silence. I can practically see the gears shifting in her head. "Okay, so we have to search the area around the shop," she finally says. "When you lose something, you're supposed to retrace your steps. Same thing for people, right?"

I smile. "That's just what I had in mind."

Silence once again takes over the car. But it's a comfortable silence now.

"You got a text." Paige picks up my cell from the dash, but I yank it from her before she can see anything.

Devon's sent me no fewer than a dozen texts since the concert. They started out nice: where u at? cant believe you left. Then: is everything ok? As the night progressed there was: thinking of you :) And my favorite: this party sucks without you. That one made me smile, even if I currently hated him for not leaving the concert with me. A few beers later came: wht r u wearng? :P And how can I forget: i'm hrny.

Nice.

"Well, aren't you going to see who it is?" Paige asks.

"Illegal to text and drive," I say.

"Uh, yeah, I guess."

We slog through the insane bar-hour traffic. The sidewalks pulse with people, and lines several blocks wide of girls dressed in six-inch heels and miniskirts snake outside clubs wedged between nail salons and all-night check-cashing joints. Car horns, thumping basses, and sirens fill the thick night air, and neon lights brighten the inky sky.

We circle the area of Melrose Avenue where the shop is located, then every main and side street from La Cienega to North Highland, craning our necks to scan every man, woman, and child we pass. Nothing. Not one person remotely resembling Leather Jacket Guy. It's not like I had much hope to begin with, but now it's becoming increasingly clear we aren't going to find him.

My phone buzzes for the zillionth time in ten minutes.

"I guess we must be the only people not at Jarrod's party tonight, huh?"

Paige's arms are loosely hugging her drawn-up knees as she stares at the whirring L.A. landscape outside the window. A realization strikes: I've always thought Paige secretly wanted to go to our parties, that she was just pretending she'd rather curl up on the couch with *Atlas Shrugged* on a Friday night because she wasn't invited. It didn't make sense to me that she didn't want to be popular. But she never cared.

My phone stops buzzing, only to restart a millisecond later. Unease flutters in my stomach.

When I left the concert, I was sure I'd never talk to Devon again and not lose a wink of sleep over it. But now? I'm not so sure. Devon could have brought anyone in the world to that concert and he chose me, only to have me ditch him halfway through. And sure, his prioritizing leaves a bit to be desired, but could I really blame the guy for not wanting to run out of the place based on the word of some freaky stranger in leather? I probably would have done the same thing in his shoes.

I'm suddenly desperate to see him.

"Would you mind if we made a quick stop at the party?" I ask.

Paige rolls her eyes. "God, tell me you're not serious."

"You don't have to come in," I say.

Actually, it would be perfect if she didn't. Hanging out with Paige at a party? Social suicide. Not to mention the fact that Bianca would kill me. Like, actual death would happen.

"So what you're asking," Paige says carefully, "is would I mind waiting in the car while you check up on your boyfriend?"

Yes!

"No! Of course not. You're totally welcome to come in. And I'm not checking up on him."

"Whatever." Paige absently swipes her bangs from in front of her glasses. "We've already done this street."

I look around and see that she's right. We've pretty much covered every drivable inch of the Fairfax district, and now we're going over the same ground. I signal right and pull the car over onto the side of the road. "So what now? Where would a guy like him hang out?"

"What about bars? We could try Johnny's or the Griffin."

"Good, but it's not like we can get in."

"So what? We can hang around outside and wait for him to come out."

"I guess, but what—"

Fingers tap on the window. Paige and I let out blood-curdling screams.

"Need some help?" The guy—Leather Jacket Guy—bends in front of the driver's-side window, a smirk playing on his lips.

"Lock the doors!" Paige yells.

I scramble to locate the button in the dark. And the whole time I'm panicking, dude's just giving me the same infuriating smile.

"Drive, Ind! Get the hell out of here!" Paige shakes my arm.

But wasn't I just looking for him? It seemed like such a great plan until only a quarter-inch of glass separated me from a potential psycho.

"What are you doing? Step on the gas before this weirdo busts out a gun or something." Panic cracks Paige's normally steady tone.

I guess now's as good a time as any to roll the window down.

"What the hell is wrong with you?" Paige clambers over me to try to halt my hand.

"It's him, Paige," I say, trying my best to keep anxiety from showing in my voice.

"Oh, I like the way you say that," the guy says. "Makes me sound all mysterious."

Paige obviously hasn't heard me. "Are you on drugs or something? Get this window up, now!"

I push her back into the seat with alarming force. She cowers against the door.

"Sorry, it's just you weren't listening. I said it's the guy"—I gesture to him—"the guy from the shop."

Paige swallows. "Oh. Okay. Uh . . ."

I feel the same way. Now that I've found him—or did he find me?—I have no clue what to do next.

"Is there a problem?" he asks, playing innocent.

Hundreds of questions trip over each other to get out of me.

"Okay," the guy says. "I'll guess, then. Flat tire? Out of gas? Feminine issues? It's feminine issues, isn't it?"

Ugh. This guy is seriously disturbed. "Why are you following me? And my mom—how'd you know? Did you have something to do with it?"

"Do *you* think I had something to do with it?" He braces his hands on the roof of the car, and a slice of bare stomach shows from under his T-shirt's hem. And great—he's caught me looking, and now his stupid grin couldn't be any wider.

I avert my eyes from his midsection and consider his question. "No," I say finally, recalling the help he gave me.

He laughs. "And they say cheerleaders are brain-dead."

I choose to ignore his jab. "Tell me how you knew, then, if you weren't there."

"I didn't say I wasn't there." He rocks back on his heels, and a breeze flutters the edge of his T-shirt.

Don't. Look. At his stomach. "Would you stop playing

games?" I yell. And it's decided: yelling at him feels pretty good. "What do you know about the book?"

"You know, I don't think I've ever seen a cheerleader go so crazy over a book before."

Not "What book?" And suddenly I know without a shadow of a doubt that he knows about the Bible. I clench my jaw, nostrils flaring. "You listen to me. I'm *going* to get that book back. Whatever it takes."

"Maybe we should just call the cops," Paige says.

Like he's going to stick around long enough for them to arrest him. And for what? I have no proof of anything. It's my word against his.

I unlock the door.

"Indie. What are you—"

I step outside and slam the door behind me. "Look." I take a page out of Bianca's playbook and poke him in the chest. "I'm not going to ask—"

And holy crap, I forgot how tall he is. This plan seems much less sound now that I'm face to sternum with a giant. What did I think, that I was going to beat the truth out of him? Perform a citizen's arrest?

"You were saying?" His dark eyebrows pull up as though with concern, but his deep-set eyes flash with amusement.

I swallow.

"Go on, I'm intrigued." He waves a hand adorned with chipped black nail polish and a chunky silver ring, as if to say "Continue."

"Who are you?" I ask, my tone considerably kinder than before. "I mean, what's your name?" I give him a wide smile, but from the look in his eyes, it's more alarming than alluring, so I pull it back a few notches. What the hell—I scrunch up my hair at the roots, throw in a tip of my head so my hair tumbles in front of my eyes, bite my lip. This has got to work—guys are so simple.

"You're kidding me, right?" he says.

"What?" I ask innocently, but I can feel myself blushing.

"I'll tell you my name, but not because of your little bimbo act. Maybe Quarterback Jack would fall for that sort of stuff, but not me."

My mouth drops open.

"Oh, don't be too offended. You're cute and whatever. I just like a girl with a bit more going on up here." He taps his temple.

"I'm plenty smart, jerkwad. I've got the third-highest GPA at my high school. And FYI, I would *never* be interested in a guy like—"

"Third-highest, huh? And I bet Blanca is first, right?"

"It's *Bianca*. And— Ugh! Why am I arguing with you? I don't even know you!"

He smiles, placing a hand on his chest. "It's Bishop. Nice to meet you."

"Bishop," I repeat.

"That's what I said." He leans back against the side of the car.

"Okay." I cross my arms over my chest. "So what's your last name?"

"Haven't got a last name," he says.

"Who are you, Pink? Everyone has one."

"Not me."

I shield my face with my hand so he doesn't see the tears of frustration welling in my eyes.

"Come on, Ind." Paige tugs on my arm. "This is stupid. He's not going to tell us anything."

I give him my back, because great, I'm crying.

"Oh, come on, don't do that," he says.

"Do what?" Super. My stupid voice just cracked.

He sighs. "All right, then. I'll tell you everything."

I glance over to see the smirk on his face that'll confirm he's lying, but for once he's stone-faced.

Maybe he isn't such a jerk after all.

"Just don't do *that* anymore," he says, gesturing to my tear-tracked face. "It's terribly unattractive, and I do hate to be seen with unattractive girls. Bad for the reputation, you know?"

My anger surges back full force. "Just tell me what you know, already."

"Seriously, can you clean that up?" He circles a finger at my face.

"God, you're a—"

"Jerk? I know. So listen, you have to take me somewhere private if I'm going to tell you anything."

"Absolutely not." Sorry, buddy, but I've seen that episode

of *Oprah*. "Never let them take you to a second location" is, like, Rule #1 of foiling predators.

"Why not?" he says. "Too busy driving around looking for me?"

I huff. "Actually, we were just about to go to a party, thank you very much."

"Awesome, except a party isn't exactly private. Unless it's a party for two." He winks at me.

Ew.

I cross my arms. "As much as I love that mental image, can you please quit playing games and tell me what you know already?"

"Sure," he says. "As soon as we go someplace private."

"You've *got* to know that I'm smarter than that."

He starts to walk away, and I panic. If he leaves now, I may never see him again. And then all hope of finding the Bible will be lost. It'd ruin Mom. Completely destroy her.

"Wait!" I call out.

He spins.

I heave a sigh. Sweet Jesus, I can't believe I'm doing this. "Fine. I'll go with you. But we have to stop somewhere first."

For a few seconds, both Paige and Bishop stare at me like I've just sprouted a second head. But before I have time to think about the dangerous situation I've just gotten myself into, Bishop yells, "Shotgun!" and skids across the hood of the car to land in front of the passenger-side door.

Sorry, Oprah.

10

Bishop is already adjusting the passenger seat to accommodate his long legs before I can even get into the car.

"No way." I settle into the driver's seat. "Paige rides up front."

"She doesn't care. Look, she's already in the back." He swivels in the seat to face Paige. "You don't care, right?"

Paige snaps the buckle of her seat belt. "It's fine."

I purse my lips. But actually, it's probably better not to have my back turned to him. And I have to say, he looks much less intimidating with his legs all smushed up like he's riding in a clown car.

"So where's this party at?" He rubs his hands together.

I start the car. "You'll see when we get there."

"Oh, like a surprise. How fun."

I glance at Paige in the rearview mirror. She catches my eye and gives me a look that distinctly says "What the hell have you gotten me into?" I quickly turn my focus back to the road. I don't know what to tell her. Sorry, I wasn't really thinking straight? My apologies if he hacks out our innards with a rusty pocketknife?

I *could* drop her off at home, or even back at Jessie's house, but the truth is I don't want to be alone with this guy, even if the drive is less than ten minutes. Guess I've grown rather fond of my innards.

"Got any tunes?" Bishop reaches for the dial on the radio. He skips from station to station.

"Would you quit that?" I ask.

"Got Sirius? An iPod? A CD, even?" He opens the glove compartment and rummages inside.

I slap his hand away. "Do you mind?"

"What?"

"Don't touch anything, okay? Just sit there and be quiet."

He snorts, but miraculously, he obeys.

That's when I notice how incredibly deserted Los Angeles has become. I mean, we do pass cars, but the traffic is about an eighth of what it usually is, and only the occasional upstairs light is on inside the houses lining North Highland. I glance at the clock on the dash and find that it's after three in the morning. A thought strikes me: what if the party is over? It wouldn't be uncommon for the cops to bust up one of Jarrod's rockers.

But my fears are quickly dispelled when I take a right onto Lorraine Boulevard. Vehicles parked end to end line the narrow street, and even though Jarrod's house is blocks away, the faint bass of club music pounds above the hum of the Sunfire's engine.

"Windsor Square!" Bishop says. "You never told me this was a wine-and-appetizer party."

I get lucky and find a spot only a block from Jarrod's massive Tudor house. If I squint, I can even see the silhouettes of bodies moving in the backlit windows.

I cut the engine, and Bishop unfastens his seat belt.

"Come on," he says. "I'm sure there's plenty of bruschetta to go around. No need to be shy."

"Ha-ha," I deadpan.

"Oh, right." Bishop nods sagely. "Forgot you flashed your ass to half of Los Angeles earlier. Not shy at all."

I smack him on the arm, and he laughs.

"You go ahead, Bishop," Paige says. "We'll meet up with you in a minute."

Bishop narrows his eyes.

"Girl talk," she explains.

Paige? Girl talk? I almost burst out laughing, but Bishop just shrugs.

"Whatever. More Jäger for me." He hops out of the car and saunters up the sidewalk, disappearing into Jarrod's house.

Oh God. Here it comes.

"Care to explain to me *what the hell* is going on?" Paige asks.

I swivel in the seat to face her. "I'm giving him what he wants, okay?"

"Yeah, right. Of course. Good idea." She barks a laugh, neurotically bobbing her crossed leg so that the whole car rocks.

"Paige—"

"Have you lost your mind?" she interrupts. "You've just chauffeured some crazy dude to a party where all your friends are."

When she says it like that, it does sound pretty off the rails.

"We're not staying long," I reason.

She sears me with a look.

I sigh, facing forward again.

The sounds of the party come into focus. I wonder what Devon is doing at this moment, how he's going to react when he sees me. My nerves stretch tight, and I tap my fingers on the steering wheel.

"Well, it's obviously too late to leave now," I say, breaking the silence.

"Is it?" Paige asks incredulously.

"I should at least get Bishop out of there. What if he's murdering people or something?"

Okay, probably not the best argument.

"Look," I say, facing her again. "I'm just going to go in quickly and check on things and then we'll leave, okay?"

She rolls her eyes, as if she was expecting something like this to happen, and then pulls out her phone.

"What are you doing?" I ask.

"Texting Jessie."

"Why?"

"Because she wanted an update on your dog, if you must know." She taps at the screen.

"Dog? What dog?"

"Your dog is dying," she says without looking up.

"I don't have a dog."

She glances up. "Oh, would you prefer I'd told her the truth?" She takes my horrified expression as an answer and returns to her typing. "Didn't think so. He's not going to make it, by the way. Poor Tripod. really should have laid off the thongs. But they were his favorite, and it wasn't his fault you kept your underwear lying around the house all the time."

What the . . . ? I try to snatch the phone from Paige, but she pulls it close to her chest and grins. When the hell did she get so snarky? I watch, annoyed, as Paige taps away at her phone. She better not open her mouth about this at school.

I start to open the car door, but something niggles at the

back of my mind, stopping me from leaving. I try to push the concern back, but it just shoves itself forward again, refusing to be ignored. Dammit. I swing around to face Paige again. "You can't stay out here alone. Bishop might come back."

"So what?" she says, but I can tell by the pause in her typing that she's considering what I've said.

"You're right," I say. "You can probably handle Bishop alone. You can run fast, right? His legs are freakishly long, though." I tap my chin with my finger. "You could always scream? Except that it might be hard to hear you over the noise of the party."

Paige wrinkles up her nose at me, but she stows her phone in her purse and unbuckles her seat belt. I resist the urge to smile. And Bishop said cheerleaders aren't smart.

Except that maybe he's right. Because wasn't this—the social suicide of being seen at a party with Paige—what I was *just* trying to avoid?

I give Paige an appraisal as we walk toward the house. She's wearing a pair of ripped boyfriend jeans and a fitted wifebeater. It's actually a good look on her. She should probably consider wearing her pj's out more often.

We climb the spotlit steps that lead to the doors, which are framed with neatly trimmed bushes.

I open the doors and— Holy crap. How has this party not been busted up by the cops yet? The living room is crammed full of three hundred of Jarrod's closest friends, a sea of bodies jumping, writhing, and swaying to the music that thumps from huge speakers set up in all corners of the room. There are red plastic cups *everywhere,* and a couple is practically doing it on the couch. Not to mention the air reeks of vomit. Jarrod's neighbors must be out of town. Or in a really, really forgiving mood.

"Indie!" Some guy I vaguely recognize from the football team wraps his arm around my neck (really, it's like a choke hold), sloshing his drink down the front of my shirt. "Hey, everyone! Indie made it!"

The party erupts into cheering and whistling, and I can't help but smile, despite smelling even more like a whiskey distillery than when I left the concert. The guy finally lets go of my neck and stumbles off to join a group of guys doing shots at the minibar.

"Be right back," I say to Paige. She leaps back from a drunken girl who nearly stumbles into her. And just like that, my fear of being seen with Paige vanishes entirely, because I'm now confident that if anyone saw us come in together, they won't remember tomorrow.

I push through the crowd, toward the kitchen, craning my neck to look for Devon's floppy blond waves. I finally arrive there with only two new scents (vodka and beer) added to my shirt.

And what the hell is this? Bishop leans against the stainless steel fridge, hands in his pockets, while no fewer than four girls circle him. Two I don't recognize, but the other two are the Amy/Ashley twins. One touches his arm while the other bats her eyelashes at him. Have they been passing around hallucinogens at this party?

I scrutinize Bishop more closely. Longish hair, tattoos, leather—I guess he *is* good-looking. I mean, if I were drunk I might find him good-looking. In a bad-boy, poser kind of way.

He gives me a two-fingered salute, then goes back to flirting with the girls.

I suppose it's good he's not killing anyone. And why should I care what the stupid Amy/Ashley twins do? I don't. There.

I turn away and spot Jarrod's red hair over the top of a crowd of people near the keg.

"Jarrod!" I call out.

"Indie! Come do a keg stand." He wobbles, holding out the black hose attached to the keg.

"Um, no thanks. Have you seen Devon around?"

He shrugs. "Nah. Hey, Andrew, wanna do a keg s-stand?"

Some guy stumbles up from behind me, and then Jarrod's helping to hold up his legs.

I will never understand keg stands.

I check the dining room and sitting room without any luck, then go upstairs. It's less crowded, but I still have to flatten myself against the wall to maneuver down the wide hallway. I pass the first bedroom—and seriously, who doesn't close the door? Shielding my eyes from the writhing mass of skin on the bed, I continue down the hall. There's a line at least a dozen people long coming from one door, which I guess is the bathroom. The next room I find is an office, which is surprisingly empty. That leaves only one room left. Down this wing, anyway.

I give the door a little tap, then crack it open. It's dark, but moonlight slants in through the open windows and onto the king-sized four-poster. The sheets are rumpled over two bodies, which shift at the sound of me entering.

"Sorry!" I start to close the door.

"Indie?"

My breath hitches. Bianca? For some reason, instead of cowering, I throw the door open.

Bianca sits up, drawing the covers over her bare chest. I can't see her face, just that her perfect hair is mussed.

"I'm so sorry," she says.

"Sorry? Sorry for what?" I take a step into the room.

And that's when I see the blond hair pressed against the pillow next to Bianca.

Devon.

11

I stumble back a few steps, turn, and run. People swear and complain as I charge through the crowd, back down-stairs, and through the living room, but I couldn't care less right now. I just need to get out. I need space. I need *air*.

Paige calls my name somewhere behind me, but I don't stop. I don't stop when I stumble out the front doors into the thick night air. I don't stop when Paige runs up be-hind me, begging me to wait. I don't stop until I reach the car, and even then I don't want to slow down. Not really. Because then I'll have to face what I just saw—Devon and Bianca. In bed. Together.

I brace my hands on the pockmarked hood of the Sunfire to keep from crumpling to my knees.

"Ind, wait up!" Paige jogs up to the car, gulping for air. "What's going on?"

Good question.

"I think you missed your true calling," Bishop says, hiking his pants up as he saunters over. "The Renegades could really use you on offense."

"Not funny," Paige says, wrapping an arm around me.

I haven't had a single drink, and yet I've never felt closer to puking.

Devon and Bianca? I mean, sure, she flirted with him, and yeah, he flirted back, but I always thought that was as far as it went. I thought he loved me. I thought she was my best friend.

But I should have seen it coming. She's Bianca—she always gets what she wants. And he's got a dick.

"Shit, are you crying again?" Bishop asks.

"No." But when I touch my cheek my fingers come away wet. I turn my back to him.

"Come, now," he says. "Is it because they ran out of bruschetta?"

"Still not funny." Paige pats my back and shushes me, which makes me feel about five. "Are you going to tell me what happened?"

I shake my head.

Bishop comes around the car and paces in front of me. "Ten bucks it's about Quarterback Jack."

I cover my face with my hands.

"Oh shit," Bishop says. "I was just joking."

"Why are you still here?" Paige yells, and then she's talking to me in her calming voice again. "Is it something Bianca did? Want me to punch her in the face?"

I look at her through laced fingers.

"Just kidding," she says gently. "The ovaries."

I let out a tiny laugh, and Paige hugs me closer.

"Okay, so we're all done, then?" Bishop kind of hops in one spot and refuses to make eye contact with me.

I swipe my hands over my cheeks and take a shaky breath. This is stupid. There are much bigger and more pressing things for me to worry about right now. Like Mom, and the Bible, and school, and, I don't know, world hunger. So what if Bianca and I have a lifetime of memories? If she knows me better than any one person should be allowed to know another? If I can hardly think of a single childhood memory that she wasn't a part of?

And he's just one stupid guy. One stupid guy I wasted the past eight months of my life on. Who cares about his lopsided smile and his clear blue eyes? And so what if he smells like apples and soap, and after being near him I can catch his scent on my clothes for hours afterward and it makes my stomach flutter like there are a million little tap dancers inside me?

My face crumples up again and out comes a fresh wave of sobs.

"Oh, come on," Bishop says. "He's obviously really stupid if he'd choose that chick over you."

"Shut up," I mumble.

"I mean it," he says. "She's so obvious. Blond hair, big tits. It's really lame. Even if her tits are pretty nice."

I groan.

"I'm kidding! They're just mediocre."

"Screw off already," I say.

He sighs. "Okay, forget about those guys. You're much better off without them. Trust me."

"Yeah," Paige says cautiously, obviously reluctant to agree with him about anything. "He's right."

I straighten, not because I believe any of the crap they're feeding me, but because I'm sick of being the token crying girl at the party.

"Right then, so we're all done?" Bishop claps his hands. "Good. Been a little anxious to get on with the next portion of the evening."

"Really?" I ask. "You looked pretty comfortable with Amy back there."

"Jealous?"

"Yeah. Right." I wipe my nose on my arm. "So listen— I'm tired. I want to go home. It's time for you to talk."

"I will. Once you take me to the Hollywood sign."

"What the . . ." I pinch the bridge of my nose. "No, no Hollywood sign."

"Well, okay, Mount Lukens, then, but I thought the sign would be—"

"No! We're not going anywhere, okay? I'm sick of—"

"Look. You want answers, I'm ready to give them to you"—he glances at Paige—"and your little friend here, I guess. But we're going to need privacy."

"And the only place to get privacy is at the Hollywood sign?" I shake my head hard. "Abso-freaking-lutely not."

"You okay to drive or should I?" he asks.

I jump in front of him before he can open the driver's-side door. "Wait a minute, here. We're not driving to some remote wooded area so you can kill us both and then leave our remains for animals to eat."

He pulls a disgusted face. "You're a sick woman, Indigo."

"That *was* pretty gross," Paige agrees.

"I'd be sure to bury your remains where no animal would ever find them," Bishop says.

Paige gasps, which makes Bishop burst into laughter.

"Kidding! Now can we get on with this?" He places a hand over his heart. "I promise not to kill you."

"Why should I bother?" I ask. "Why not just drive you right to the police station and tell them I have the guy who broke into Mom's shop?"

"This again? You don't think I did that, or you would've called the cops ages ago. Now let's go. We're wasting time."

"Ind!"

My spine straightens. I look over the hood of the car and

see Devon pulling his shirt over his head as he stumbles down Jarrod's front steps.

"Ind, wait, I can explain."

"Let me guess," Bishop says. "You were just trying to jump over her and couldn't quite make it." He laughs, and Paige slaps him so hard he grabs at his arm.

I grapple for the door handle and slip into the front seat, gunning the engine. Bishop and Paige scramble to get inside the car before I peel away. Devon calls my name, but I don't stop. I don't even look in the rearview mirror.

12

Somewhere between Wilshire and Franklin, I notice that the faster the wind slaps hair across my face and the more blurred the palm trees bordering the road become, the easier it is to block thoughts of Devon and Bianca from my mind. The speedometer needle vibrates around eighty miles per hour. I'd go faster if my throwback of a car would allow it.

"Mind slowing down?" Paige asks from the backseat. "I think I'm going to vomit." One glance in the rearview mirror tells me she isn't exaggerating: her pale skin has turned a sickly shade of green, and she's clutching the Oh Shit handle like a life preserver. Bishop, on the other hand, is slouching in his seat, tapping out some secret tune no one else can hear on his thighs.

"It's all right." He looks out the window. "She's just pulling a Bella."

"A what?"

"A Bella. You know—guy does you wrong, so you punish him by practically killing yourself."

"What?" I bark a laugh. "That is *so* not what I'm doing."

"Whatever you say, boss." He starts up his stupid drumming again. I'm beginning to feel homicidal.

But even though he's majorly wrong, I lay off the gas a bit. For Paige's sake.

Soon, I'm navigating the Sunfire along the narrow, two-lane street that winds up around the Hollywood Hills. On the left are the stupid-big homes of the stupid-rich-and-famous, interspersed with a bunch of eroded rock and grass and trees. And on the right is the guardrail that stops motorists from careering to their fiery deaths, all overlooking a beautiful view of Los Angeles.

"Okay, we're here." I slide the car into park in front of the gate at the end of Deronda. "Start talking."

"Hold on, now." Bishop climbs out of the car.

"This is as close as we can get," I call out the open window. "Service road. Hello?"

He takes off up the hill and disappears into the dark.

It would be dumb to get out of the car. Worse than dumb:

idiotic. But I've come this far already, and I can't imagine the grocery list of bad decisions I've made to this point being for nothing. I turn off the car and unfasten my seat belt.

"You're really going out there?" Paige asks, but she's unfastening her seat belt too.

"Well, I'm not just going to let him get away, am I?"

"Nooo," she says, throwing as much sarcasm into one word as humanly possible, "you definitely want to run *toward* the ax murderer."

I ignore her and jog after Bishop, brush needles clawing at my ankles as I struggle to find my footing on the loose gravel.

"Bishop!" I hiss into the dark. "It's against the law to hike to the sign." Like I'd hike to it right now even if it weren't illegal. Without the lights of the city, we're boxed in by an eerie darkness that would make a field mouse feel claustrophobic. Plus, there are mountain lions, and rattlesnakes, and rough brush, and a zillion other reasons to stay in the car. And did I mention it's illegal?

"Hello!" Paige calls. "Security cameras, motion sensors, razor-wire fence?" She sighs. "This is stupid, Ind. I'm going back to the car."

"Over here."

I can't tell where Bishop's voice came from. It sounded like it was above me, but that's obviously impossible. I squint into the dark and scan the silhouettes of trees and bushes that jut out from the rocks.

"Here," Bishop says.

I startle. Because, yes, his voice definitely came from above me. Holding my breath, I look up, and—holy freaking crap—Bishop is ten feet in the air, his moonlit back floating against the dark night sky. I scream and scrabble backward, bumping into Paige.

"Oh my God, oh my God, oh my God." Paige's fingernails dig into my arm. "What the hell *is* he?"

Even in the dark, I can see the smirk on Bishop's face. Somehow, it stops me from running. He can't really be flying. This *has* to be a trick. I swipe my hand under his army boots—nothing. I squint into the darkness, looking for a tree or a rope or, I don't know, *anything* to explain what I'm seeing. Which is Bishop. Very clearly. Flying. And making it look easy, hands jammed into his pockets like it's no big deal.

"Come on." Paige yanks on my arm, trying to get me to run with her, but I pull free and root myself in place. I don't claim to be a medical professional or anything, but it *can't* be healthy for my heart to clang this way in my chest, for my head to drain of blood, and for me to breathe so fast and hard that I feel the stretch of every single alveoli in my lungs.

"No patrolman tonight," Bishop says. "I checked."

Fear grips its talons around my throat, making my words come out too high. "Oh good," I say. "Because *that's* obviously what I'm worried about right now."

Bishop's laughter chimes through the night.

117

"I don't like this, Ind!" Paige cries. "What is he? Some sort of freak?" Her voice vibrates like she's about to have a nervous breakdown. "I'm going back."

I try to grab her arm, but she slips from my grasp and runs a few steps.

"You have to come with me," Paige pleads. "Your mom wouldn't want this."

If that's what she believes, then she doesn't know my mom at all. I'm so close to answers. "You can go back if you want." My hands shake as I fish in my bag for my keys and toss them to her; she misses, and they jangle to the ground in front of her feet. "Go back to Jessie's. I'll find my way home."

Paige picks up the keys. She glances behind her like she's about to bolt, then lets out a frustrated groan. "Like I'd leave you with *him*."

"Great," Bishop says brightly. "So are we going up, or what?"

"Up where?" I ask.

"To the sign." He gestures behind him. "It's why we came here, right?"

"Right. Stupid me. Care to tell me *how the hell you're flying*?"

"Of course, since you asked so nicely. Once we get up there."

"We?" I say.

"Yeah. Don't worry, I froze the security system. We'll get up no problem."

"We?" I repeat. "Just how are *we* going to get up there? If you hadn't noticed, Paige and I can't fly."

"I'll take you, obviously. Even though you have a major attitude problem."

"No way." Paige backs up. "Uh-uh. No chance in hell. Not happening."

"You won't drop me?" I ask.

"You can't be serious," Paige says. "Ind, no. You're coming with me. We're going home and we're calling the cops and telling them there's a nuthouse inmate on the loose."

"Paige, I'm doing this. It's too important." I fasten my curls back into a ponytail, then nod to Bishop and hold my arms out to the side to show him I'm ready to be picked up.

Bishop touches down lightly. I wave for him to hurry up before common sense (or the fact that I probably reek and shouldn't let a boy get close to me) makes me go with Paige's plan instead. He bends and scoops me up, one arm under my knees and another around my waist, like I weigh about twelve pounds instead of ten times that. He's so close that his breath rushes against my ear, and the little hairs on the back of my neck stand on end. For the first time since we got out here, I'm grateful for the darkness, because he can't see how furiously I'm blushing. Which is insane. He's flying! He could be a vampire or a demon or any manner of paranormal creatures, for all I know. And I'm blushing? There's something fundamentally wrong with me. If it turns out that I'm crazy, I blame Devon and Bianca for pushing me over the edge.

I look forward and clear my throat. "Okay, let's get this over with."

Paige passes in front of us, wringing her hands and mumbling under her breath.

I try to ignore her, even though her babble is really making me question my decision. But then it's too late. We're flying.

And it's nothing like I imagined flying might feel. I mean, I never really put much thought into the matter, but I guess I just expected there to be some sort of effort involved when defying the laws of gravity. Instead, we lift from the ground with ease, as if flying were child's play, and hover twenty feet above the ground as Paige cranes her neck to watch us.

"You okay?" she yells.

My heart races, but I manage to nod and yell down an affirmative. This is all right. I can do this.

"Ready?" Bishop asks.

I swallow. "Just be careful, okay?"

"Hold on tight." A smirk plays on his lips.

Yeah, right, perv.

We dart through the air so fast my heart leaps into my throat. I cling to his neck and press against his chest—his surprisingly hard chest for a skinny guy—wind slapping my cheeks and raising goose bumps on my arms. Yep, I'm going to die, I decide. I've just gone and killed myself. But just as I wonder why my life isn't flashing before my eyes, the wind stops and tendrils of hair that have pulled loose from my ponytail fall around my face.

"Open your eyes," Bishop says, laughter in his voice. But I don't. I can't. "Am I going to have to peel you off me?" he asks.

Ugh.

I wrench one eye open. And great—there's no chance of my heart going back where it's supposed to be anytime soon.

I must have been dreaming to think Bishop would land on some safe, flat surface. When I look down, I find that he's perching on the inches-wide metal scaffolding of the Hollywood sign's letter *W*. Even in the pale light of the moon, I can see the jutting edges of the rocks some fifty feet below that await my fall.

"Relax." Bishop gives me a little shake.

"No way, man." I cling to him even tighter. "You'll have to pry my cold, dead hands off you before I loosen my grip."

He chuckles, and I really, really don't like the way the sound bounces us around. I grip him around the neck so hard I wonder how he's not losing consciousness.

"Look out there." He nods to indicate the view, apparently not at all bothered by my choke hold.

I take a two-second break from considering how it will

feel to land on the pointy rocks to look at the view. The city of Los Angeles spreads out before us, a landscape alive with trees and lakes and houses built on lush, rolling hilltops. Beyond that, skyscrapers reach into the black of night, winking light and illuminating everything in the horizon with a whitish haze.

"So, what do you think?"

"I think . . ." Well, that it's beautiful. Also, that I don't want to die. "I think you need to put me on solid ground before you're dry-cleaning vomit off your leather jacket."

Bishop's face screws up. "You're a classy lady . . . but your wish is my command." He steps off the edge of the scaffolding. And suddenly we're falling. My stomach drops into my shoes, wind burning my face like no chemical peel could.

Only at the last second, as we're just feet from the ground, does Bishop engage whatever flying ability he has, and we float the rest of the way down. As soon as my feet hit soil, my legs buckle, and I stagger to my knees.

I swore after the second time I cried in front of Bishop in the less than twenty-four hours I've known him that it would be the last, but now hot tears well in my eyes.

"You . . ." I don't hesitate before lunging at him. I catch him by surprise, and he topples backward with a thud. I deliver two-fisted punches to his chest. "Don't. You. *Ever*. Do. That. Again."

I don't know what I thought would happen—maybe that

he'd cry out in pain or just plain cry—but instead he gives me this infuriating smirk, as if a toddler were trying to beat him up and it's too darn *cute*.

"Go on," he says. "I like it rough."

Double ugh! I'm suddenly acutely aware that I'm straddling him—wearing a micromini and heels, no less—and I can't roll off him fast enough.

"You're sick, you know." I push my hair back from my face, panting for air.

He sits up and brushes gravel from his pants.

A breeze rattles the supports of the sign and ripples through the coastal sage scrub that dots the mountaintop. My ragged breathing is audible over it all.

"Sorry," he says.

I turn my face away so I can discreetly wipe my cheeks.

"Aw, don't be mad." He pokes me in the shoulder.

I can't say anything or I will break down. So instead I take big, deep breaths and wait until I get control of myself. Bishop, for once, doesn't say anything annoying, just fiddles with the zipper on his jacket in some sort of quiet understanding.

"How do you do it?" I finally ask. "Fly?"

He shrugs—a whole-body gesture. "Magic."

"Magic?" I repeat.

"What? You think there's some more logical explanation I'm hiding from you? A rocket pack in my jeans or something?"

"Okay, so what are you, then? You know, since normal people can't fly."

"A warlock," he says without missing a beat.

I search his face in the dark, but there's no humor there.

"Okay. . . ." It's a lame thing to say, but really, what *should* I say when someone tells me he's a warlock? Twelve years in the public school system have left me unprepared for a situation like this.

"That's it?" he asks. "You harass me for information all night and that's all you want to know?"

"No, that's not it," I say. I press my fingers to my temples. "There are a million things I want to know. Like, okay, how'd you know about my mom being hurt? And *The Witch Hunter's Bible*—do you know who took it? And did you use magical powers to lift that bookcase off her? Because it didn't even look like you were trying and that thing's super heavy—I should know, I tried to lift it myself and it didn't budge. And how'd you know to find me at the game? I mean, however you knew that Mom got hurt, how'd you know I was her daughter and that you'd find me at the game? And back on Melrose with Paige, were you following me? And do you by any chance smoke Marlboros?"

Bishop doesn't appear even slightly alarmed that I'm now out of breath again. He smiles and leans back on his elbows, legs stretched out in front of him. "I guessed she was hurt because I sensed something was off, the Bible was stolen by members of the Priory—Frederick and Leo, if you found

Marlboros around; Leo's a chain-smoker. No, there were no magical powers involved in me lifting that bookcase, just six feet three inches of pure, unapologetic muscle"—he winks—"and I knew to find you at the game because I followed you, and I guess that answers your last question too."

Frederick and Leo? The Priory? He's been *following* me? It's too much for my brain to handle. "Are you, like, a junkie or something? Please tell me you're a junkie."

He laughs. "Okay, why do you want me to be a junkie now?"

"I don't know. Because then maybe all this would make a little bit of sense. I could put all this"—I whirl my finger in the air—"down to a drug-induced mania or something. I've seen this sort of thing on *Intervention*. You know that episode with the girl who snuffs computer duster? She got so screwed up and was saying the weirdest shit. Please tell me you snuff computer duster."

"Um, I snuff computer duster?"

I cover my face with my hands and groan.

"Not this again," Bishop says.

I shoot him a look. "Oh, I'm sorry. Am I not handling the news that you've been stalking me as well as you'd hoped?"

He grins.

"And why are you following me? That's pretty creepy, you know."

"Thought you'd never ask," he says. "I was sent by the Family. They're a group of the most powerful witches and warlocks in existence. They govern the rest of us regular joes. Make the rules, enforce the rules, intimidate—you know, that sort of stuff."

"Uh, okay, why?"

"Because," he says, sitting up and wiping dirt off his palms, "witches come into their powers on their two hundredth full moon. And since you have witches in your family, there's a chance that you could be one too. Can't have some newbie coming into her powers and accidentally blowing our cover not knowing what's going on. And then there's the more important issue of my taking the Bible back to headquarters."

Witches in my family? I rub the slow throb starting in my temples. "So let's pretend I don't think you're crazy. What 'moon' am I at now?"

"One ninety-nine," he says matter-of-factly.

I shake my head. "So you're telling me that on the next full moon, I'm going to turn into a witch."

"Yes." He nods solemnly. "You'll grow a hooknose with a hairy mole at the end, and your hair will turn gray and frizzy—or more frizzy, rather—and your back will grow a hump any camel would envy, and—"

"Be serious for once."

He laughs. "You won't *turn* into anything. You'll just have access to powers you didn't before."

"On the next full moon."

"On the next full moon. *Maybe*."

I look up into the sky, where the moon floats against the star-studded canvas of night. I can't believe I was ever disloyal enough to Mom to worry, even secretly, that Bianca was right about her. That she was crazy. But the fact that she officially isn't, that witches exist and the Bible really is a centuries-old relic, is the one glimmer of light in all this darkness. "So my mom's a witch too? I mean, she's been saying that since I was a baby, but she's a real witch?"

He shakes his head, then picks up a handful of stones and starts throwing them over the rock ledge. They land with a distant *plink* that reminds me of just how high up we are.

"I don't get it," I say. "How can I be a witch but not my mom?"

"Maybe a witch," he corrects, "and your mom just got unlucky in the gene department."

"Hey! Don't talk about her like that."

"I wasn't being rude," he says. "The gene for witches and warlocks is recessive."

I stare at him. This sounds vaguely familiar. We covered genetics in Mrs. Crawley's biology class last year.

"Oh, come on, Third-Highest GPA. Every witch and warlock has two copies of the gene for magic: one inherited from the mother and one from the father. Each copy can be either dominant or recessive. You need two recessive genes to be a witch. Your grandmother was a witch, so we know she carried two recessive genes. Your grandfather was human but a carrier of the recessive gene. So your mom had a fifty percent chance, at best, of becoming a witch."

My grandma was a witch. What else don't I know about my own family? Is Aunt Penny a witch too? I almost laugh at the thought. Aunt Penny's made it abundantly clear what she thinks about witchcraft. Besides, if she were a witch, surely she would make life a little easier on herself. Erase a few bills. Conjure a few outfits. A mansion to live in instead of a puny one-bedroom apartment shared with three other girls.

"So what are my chances?" I ask.

"Depends," he answers. "The Family hasn't told me much about your dad. Just that he . . ." Bishop trails off and scratches his nose.

"Left," I finish for him. "Don't worry. I'm not all touchy about that, but it's cute you thought I'd be."

He shrugs. "Well, you know . . ."

"So, I have a zero to fifty percent chance is what you're telling me?"

Bishop nods. "Wow, I'm impressed."

I guess I retained more from biology that I thought. "So what is this Priory you mentioned? And what's all this got to do with Mom's book?"

"Ah, now we're getting to the good stuff." Bishop crosses his legs, as if preparing for a *long* story. "Where the Family is the governing body for witches, the Priory is the governing body for sorcerers. And like most powerful parties, they absolutely hate each other and always have. It only got—"

"Wait," I say, holding up a finger. "What's the difference between witches and sorcerers?"

"Essentially," he says, "not much. Both can perform magic—some the same, some different. Sorcerers can't fly, for example. But witches have to learn their magic, where with sorcerers it's just this innate thing."

"So then why do they hate each other?" I ask.

He shrugs. "Who knows?" Perhaps sensing I think his answer is totally lame, he asks, "You want to hear my theory?"

I nod.

"They're jealous."

I cock an eyebrow.

"Seriously. They're envious of what we're capable of. They want all the power for themselves."

I consider this.

"Anyway," he says, "that's all beside the point. This hatred between the Family and the Priory only got worse after a witch killed one of the Priory leaders way back when for who knows what reason. The Priory retaliated by trying to kill every witch on the planet."

A cold feeling hollows out my stomach. They killed witches? And I might be a witch? If he didn't have my attention before with all the flying stuff, he definitely has it now. I scoot forward.

"They did a pretty good job too. Thousands and thousands of witches died. After a while, some inventive witch cast this spell—the most powerful spell in history—whereby any sorcerer who kills a witch is instantly drained of power. They can't perform magic or read minds or . . . anything, really. They're just regular humans. A pretty good deterrent for a bunch of greedy-ass, power-hungry bastards. So this worked well for a while—I mean, yeah, there was still hatred and infighting and the usual political stuff, but at least no one was killed." He pauses, twirling the ring on his finger. I lean forward in anticipation. "Until *The Witch Hunter's Bible*. Some sorcerer figured out a ritual to get around the witch's protection spell so that a sorcerer could kill a witch and keep his powers intact. A complicated ritual, but he laid it all out in the Bible. Witch genocide ensued, yada yada yada, until finally, a witch got her hands on the Bible. She tried to burn it, but lo and behold, it can't be destroyed. Some kind of protection spell. So since then it's been hidden here, there, and everywhere, never staying in one place for much longer than a few decades or so, and never, ever at the house of anyone important because it'd be too obvious. Lately it's been hanging out at your place."

I scowl at him.

He ignores me and continues. "But somewhere along my travels I noticed I was being followed. I could never get close enough to the shop to get the Bible because every time I did—bam!—Frederick and Leo were there, with some newbie sorcerer in tow. Finally I got sick of it and confronted them, and, uh, it didn't end well. This led to that, and I guess they got the Bible."

"But why were they following you?" I ask.

"They've been tailing any witch sent on a Family mission. I guess it worked out for them this time, because I led them right to the Bible."

We grow quiet. In our silence crickets chirp, bullfrogs ribbit, and somewhere close, a coyote howls. It's like the world's volume control was turned down just for the story, and now it's been cranked back to normal level.

"So that's it?" Bishop asks. "No more questions?"

I glance at him, and he rakes back the black waves that have fallen in front of his face. It's a feminine gesture, yet he obviously doesn't care, and somehow his self-confidence makes it very masculine. He couldn't be more different from Devon, I realize, who cares infinitely about what people think of him.

I guess I've scrutinized Bishop for too long, because he gets this unreadable expression on his face and starts throwing pebbles down the mountain again.

"Just one more question," I say. "Why Betty Boop?"

Moonlight accentuates the crinkles around his eyes as he smirks. "Ah, so you've been checking me out, huh?"

My cheeks flush. "It's on your neck, idiot. I didn't have to look too hard."

He rubs the cartoon character tattoo poking above the collar of his T-shirt. "Why not Betty? She's pretty hot."

"Yeah, but like, permanently-on-your-body hot? And on your neck too? Aren't you going to regret that when you're, like, a seventy-year-old man in a nursing home?"

He laughs. "Nah. I regret nothing. But I'm glad we're having this conversation. Very important topic to cover, right up there with our impending death."

Maybe he meant to scare me with that last comment, but I ignore him. "Okay, but does she have to be naked?"

He raises an eyebrow, giving me a knowing look. I guess one *would* have to be looking pretty closely to know she was naked, since her boobs are pretty well hidden by his jacket's collar.

"What?" I say defensively. "I saw it when you picked me up."

He nods, grinning.

"Couldn't she be wearing a cute little bikini or something?"

He laughs. "I didn't think you were such a prude, Indigo. Last I recall—"

"God, if you bring up that ass-flashing thing one more time I'm going to—"

"What?" He leans across me so that he's just inches from my face, and his dark eyes stare into mine. "What are you going to do to me?"

I pause for way, way too long, so that when I say, "Ugh! You are such a creep," it doesn't come out genuine at all.

Which, apparently, is hilarious to him.

"So what now?" I ask, and I really don't have to force an irritated tone this time.

His laughter finally ebbs. "Good question. Track down your boyfriend and beat him with sticks?"

"Very funny," I say. But guilt presses on my shoulders like an anvil—Paige has been alone down there for ages; I should have suggested we go back long ago. Actually, I shouldn't have left her to begin with. Shouldn't have dragged her into this whole mess.

I push to my feet. "We better get back—"

Before I can finish my sentence, the lights of the city— the entire city, from the homes on Mulholland to the sky-scrapers as far as the eye can see—dim, flicker, then glow anew.

"Holy crap." I swing around to face Bishop. "Did you see that?"

Bishop sits up straight just as a bolt of lightning brightens the sky, which is suddenly thick with low-hanging clouds. His eyes grow wide, and he chews the nail of his thumb as he looks out at the city. In the short time I've known him, I've never seen him look anything but irritatingly cool, calm, and collected, and I don't like it. I *definitely* don't like it.

"What? What's wrong?" I ask.

He swallows. "They're here."

"Who's here?"

Bishop scoops me up without any warning.

"What the— Do you mind? Put me down!" I push against his chest.

He doesn't argue, just grips me tighter. We lift into the air, and I get that butterfly-in-stomach feeling that happens when you fall from a height. Only this time, as we fly, I cling to him a little less maniacally, like I'm some kind of seasoned flier now. I even keep my eyes open, though I won't look down.

"What's going on?" I yell over the wind.

"The Family's coming for me."

"What do you mean, coming for you?" I yell. "You didn't do anything wrong."

He lets out a humorless laugh. "Doesn't matter to them."

The name "the Family" conjured up all sorts of warm, fuzzy feelings in me, but right now, the way Bishop's face is set in hard, uncompromising lines, like the fear of God has been put into him, I'm questioning my previous assumptions.

"I was supposed to bring the Bible back to headquarters, and now it's in the enemy's hands," Bishop says, like he plucked my question right out of my mind. "Our whole race is at risk of genocide."

Bishop lowers to the ground just feet from the Sunfire. The driver's-side door flings open, and Paige runs up to me. "Thank God! I was just about to call the police." She hugs me so hard I can barely breathe.

Bishop's in the air again before I can protest.

"Wait!" I cry out. "Where are you going?"

He looks across the horizon. Something wet drips on my head—it's raining.

"I have to go."

"Go where?"

"Don't worry," he says. "They want me. Now listen, Indie, this is important: secrecy at all costs, okay?" He gives me a pointed look.

I nod. "But what about the Priory?"

"They have the book. They have no reason to come after you now."

"When will I see you again?" I ask, because apparently I have no dignity left.

"Never," he says. "Good luck."

13

Paige sets the steaming kettle onto a pot holder on the coffee table. I don't know why she bothers, since no one touches it or any of the Dream Puffs she put out for a snack. A cookie—no matter how strawberry- and cream-filled and delicious—is just not going to help after what I've had to reveal. But for as long as Paige has been my next-door neighbor, she's been like this: trying to be helpful even when there's nothing she can *really* do to make things better. I guess it's a nice quality in a person. I mean, she didn't leave me at the Hollywood sign like most people would have if they'd been dragged from their warm beds in the middle of the night, only to be ditched on a dark, deserted mountaintop.

Mom draws her knees up to her chest, which makes her look as fragile as a bird. "This is all so . . . wow. So, let me get this straight: we find out . . . we find out if you're a witch in three days?"

I nod. Only my mom would skip over the whole "sneaking out and jaunting aimlessly around L.A. with a strange boy" bit to seriously zero in on the part where I tell her I might be a witch. "According to this Bishop guy, anyway. Who knows what to believe?"

"*I* believe it." She stares into her lap without seeing. "I just . . . *feel* it."

The grandfather clock in the dining room ticks away the seconds of silence.

"Sugar?" Paige poises a spoon over the sugar bowl.

Mom shakes her head. "Black is fine. Thank you, Paigey." The corners of her lips twitch as she forces a smile and accepts the cup Paige proffers. She slurps a tiny sip, then sets the cup down on the table.

"So, Ind . . ." Mom still won't look up as she picks invisible lint off the patchwork quilt covering her legs. "Did this Bishop say anything about why I didn't know almost any of this? I mean, except that the Bible was important, this is all new to me." Her voice hitches, and she laughs to cover it up.

My cheeks grow hot. All this time I'd been thinking about myself, and I never even stopped to think what this would mean to Mom. Her own mother was a witch, and

-❈ 137 ❈-

somehow I was the one to recount her family history to her. She should have known. She should have been the one to tell me.

Her eyes glisten, and my heart is ripped from my chest. And there's nothing, nothing I can do. I have no idea why she wasn't told.

"No big deal." Mom gives me a tiny smile. "Must be a witch-only kind of thing. At least she gave me the Bible. You know, trusted me to protect it. That means a lot."

She breaks down, sobbing. I pull her into a hug, taking in her scent—a combination of Pantene Curly Hair Series, Chantilly perfume, cigarettes, and something else uniquely Mom. "I'm sure there's a good reason, Mom. There has to be."

Paige shifts on the love seat opposite us as Mom releases deep, shuddery sobs.

"You could be in danger," Mom says between gulps for air. "And it's all my fault."

"What?" I draw back to get a good look at her face.

"The Bible," she says. "It was my job to—"

"And you were unconscious," I interrupt. "And those were superpowerful sorcerers. A human would be no match for them. You shouldn't feel bad."

She gives a minute shake of her head.

"Seriously," I continue, "it's the Family's fault for not coming for the Bible sooner, after Grandma died, when you had no way to protect it." I can't believe that, in just hours,

I've gone from a nonbeliever to casually name-dropping the Family in conversation.

"Does seem a little strange," Mom mutters.

"Exactly." I sling my arm back around her shoulders.

"I just . . ."

"What?" I ask.

She sighs. "Well, I just wish that I could coach you through all this. I don't know anything about this type of stuff. Wicca and this, they're completely different ball games. I mean, flying?" She lets out a hopeless laugh.

"Don't worry," I say. "Bishop said he'll show me the ropes if I turn."

At my lie, Paige shoots me a look, which I put down with a discreet throat-cutting gesture. Mom doesn't need anything else to worry about right now. And anyway, the full moon's three days away. Lots of time to plan something between now and then.

"Plus," I add, "Bishop said there's nothing to worry about. The ball's out of our court. We just need to get back to normal life."

"Normal life?" Mom repeats.

"Yep. Starting now. I'm going upstairs because the sun is coming up and going to bed at sunrise is *so* not normal."

Mom seems to realize, for the first time, that dawn has filtered in through the half-drawn venetian blinds, illuminating the Mexican-knickknack-filled living room with soft pink light.

"I guess," she says, and we all push to our feet.

Paige lets herself out, and Mom concedes to let me guide her upstairs.

Even though I've been up for more than twenty-four hours, I didn't once feel tired. How could I? But now, with Mom safe and asleep in the next room, I fall into a coma as soon as my head hits the pillow.

When I wake up, I'm sure of at least two things. One is that the sun has already set. The other is that I've slept way, way too long, and now will suffer all night with a massive sleep headache. My phone beeps, reminding me of a third thing—that I've missed about forty calls. Half from Devon, and about as many from Paige. And that brings up a big, huge thing that I'm *not* sure of: what the hell happened last night.

There was something in there about witches and sorcerers and Devon screwing my best friend and people wanting to kill me. And Bishop. But none of that seems real now; it's like some nightmare that will fade away once I'm fully awake.

I open my first text message. It's from Devon: plz answer, u have to hear me out.

So I guess that part was real. My stomach clenches. I vaguely remember not caring about it all last night when I was with Bishop, but Bishop's not here now. In fact, he never will be again, if I can believe anything he's said. Tears blur my vision. As if on cue, my cell phone starts buzzing in my hand, and a picture of Devon—my favorite picture of him, sweaty and smiling in his football jersey after the game against Beverly Hills High—flashes onto the screen. My chest contracts painfully, and my thumb hovers over the keypad before I finally press Ignore.

There's a knock on my door. Mom pokes her head inside without waiting for a response.

"Just wanted to let you know I put leftovers from the barbecue in the fridge," she says.

Barbecue? Shit—the barbecue Paige invited me to. The one I promised I'd attend. I cross to my window and crack the blinds. It's dark, the barbecue cover is on, and her backyard is conspicuously devoid of party guests. Shit, shit, shit.

So, Paige sticks by my side even after I've treated her like complete crap, conceding to be dragged along on one suicide mission after the next, and I can't even bother to amble next door for a stupid sloppy joe? I suck. Big-time.

I want to climb back into my warm bed, hide under my duvet, and cry until the world becomes a less cruel place to live, or until high school graduation. Whichever comes first.

So that's what I do.

14

Mom has to literally drag me out of bed on Monday morning. She shovels Cocoa Puffs into my mouth and even goes so far as to try to dress me in this hideous last-season tracksuit she dug out of the dregs of my closet. I snap out of it long enough to throw on jeans and a tank top instead.

I'm almost out the door when I decide that a little makeup wouldn't hurt. And what the hell, why not wear some cute sunglasses and those wedge sandals I bought last week? I mean, just because my boyfriend cheated on me, my best friend betrayed me, Bishop deserted me, I might be a witch, and evil sorcerers could try to kill me with the Bible they stole from my family doesn't mean I can't look good, right?

I sling my messenger bag over my shoulder and venture outside for the first time in days.

It should be raining. That's how it works, right? Bad day / rain? Well, I guess L.A. didn't get the memo, because the sun sits high in a cloudless blue sky. A warm breeze flutters the fronds of the palm trees along Melrose Avenue, and at a stoplight I swear I hear birds (birds in L.A.!) chirping a tune eerily similar to "Walking on Sunshine." And it's just so, I don't know, uplifting, that I get to thinking that today might not be as bad as I thought.

But my feet haven't even passed through the doors of Fairfield High when the staring starts. And by staring, I mean necks practically snapping as people trip over each other to get a look at me. My cheeks burn under my oversized sunglasses. I mean, I knew people were talking about me. After ripping apart Bianca's collage of us, I deleted all my pictures of her and Devon from Instagram and Facebook. And while doing that, I couldn't help but notice the one topic that everyone couldn't stop talking about: me. I also couldn't help noticing how many times Bianca and Devon mentioned how sick they were after the party, because they were *sooo* drunk. Yeah, sure. But all that's beside the point—doesn't anyone have anything better to do than analyze my life?

Tilting my chin up, I march into the school like a zillion eyes aren't following me. And the fake confidence actually works. I find myself thinking, *Who cares? This'll all blow over.*

But my attitude only lasts until I reach my locker. I'm unloading my next-period textbooks when I hear my name. I look over my shoulder, and when I do, I find the Amy/Ashley twins whispering from their post by the water fountain. They look away once they realize I've heard them, which just confirms that they are in fact talking about me. And that's when I lose it. My blood turns cold even as my pulse races. Sure, we're not exactly best friends, and yeah, I've snickered along when Bianca mocked their style choices, but where is the squad loyalty?

I'm considering putting my newfound offensive tackle to use when one of them—God knows which—breaks apart from the other and walks over to me. I stand, shoulders pushed back, prepared to deliver a scathing retort should she (a) deny she was just talking about me, or (b) bring up the party.

"Hey, Indie." Amy/Ashley smiles brightly, then glances behind her as if to confirm with her twin she's doing okay. Seriously, get an independent brain cell. "So I was just wondering . . . you know that guy you were with at the party? Is he, like, single?" Her cheeks flush pink, and she giggles.

Bishop? She's asking me about Bishop right now?

It's so totally not what I expected to hear that I'm shocked into silence. She shifts her weight from foot to foot and starts wringing her hands. "I mean, I saw you guys leave together, but I figured you were just friends, you know, because of Devon"—her entire face goes the color of a ripe tomato—"but if you're together or something, I totally understand."

"No," I say quickly. "So not together."

"Oh!" She exhales, looks behind her, and gives her sister the thumbs-up. "So, you wouldn't, like, mind if I went for him?"

"Mind?" And I guess I must have said it a little more tersely than I'd intended, because Amy/Ashley's eyes couldn't be rounder.

Get a grip, Indie. Who cares? "Not at all." I smile wide for proof of my lack of interest in Bishop. "Please, have at him. Little warning, though."

She nods eagerly and leans forward so I can whisper in her ear. "He's really into the Betty Boop stuff."

Her eyebrows knit. "Like, what do you mean?"

"You know, dress-up, role-playing . . . he's pretty kinky like that."

"Really?" She smiles and lets out this delighted little laugh.

So not the reaction I was going for. I huff and walk around her.

"But wait," she calls after me, "I need his number!"

As I take my seat in homeroom and wait for class to start, I realize that I haven't seen Bianca yet. Which is weird. Bianca has this way of making her presence known. Hope blooms in my heart that maybe, just maybe, a bus struck her on the way to school. The thought alone makes listening to Mrs. Davies at eight-thirty in the morning slightly bearable.

Biology is uneventful, but the next period is math. I couldn't be more grateful when the spot next to mine—

which might as well be reserved with a little Bianca place card—remains empty after the bell rings. But that's when my luck runs out.

Devon jogs into class ten minutes into the lesson. He sends me one of his trademark lopsided smiles, and my heart gives a painful thump in my chest. I bury my scorching face in my notebook under the pressure of twenty-eight stares.

Apparently the universe hates me, because today is also the day we start trigonometry, and Mr. Lloyd is so lost in sine-cosine heaven that he doesn't notice Devon stealing away from his spot at the back of the class approximately every three minutes. I won't even look at my ex as he whispers (and by whispers, I mean talks in a slightly less booming baritone than usual) all these excuses and apologies: Not his fault. He was drunk. Seriously, why don't I just look at him? I'm the one who's been acting so weird lately. Don't eight months together mean anything? He loves me.

You know, the typical cheating-douche-bag kind of stuff.

I stare straight ahead, even when the urge to punch him is almost unbearable.

The lunch bell rings.

It's only once I'm in the cafeteria, piling my plate high with carbs as the heat of hundreds of stares bore into my back, that I realize today would have totally been a good day to eat out. But it's too late now. They've seen me. And the only thing more humiliating than having your boyfriend cheat on you with your best friend would be to take your tray into the hallway to eat.

I'm almost at the lip of the dining room entrance when, at the last minute, I lop off half the mountain of mashed potatoes. (I don't want people thinking I'm eating my feelings—it has absolutely nothing to do with stalling.) And then I make my way to the Pretty People table. With each step, the din of the cafeteria quiets further. I pretend not to notice, though all the while my heart's clanging so hard it hurts. Devon is in his usual spot next to Jarrod at the end of the table, but I refuse to look in his direction, just focus on taking steady, even breaths, on making sure my hands don't shake as I lower my tray to the table and take a seat.

And it is *more* than awkward the way everyone refuses to make eye contact with me, as if they're just far too pre-occupied with their trays of cafeteria food. Everyone except Julia. She holds her head high with this irritatingly satisfied smile on her face. I pretend it doesn't bother me, because that's what she wants. The girl would probably die and go to heaven if she could steal my spot next to Bianca.

After a few painful minutes, the clatter of dishes and peals of laughter return to a normal decibel. When the guys at the end of the table start loudly talking about their NFL fantasy draft, Thea takes one for the team and leans across the table.

"Indie, are you, like, okay? I saw you run out of the party. You looked pretty upset."

On cue, the rest of the girls edge in to hear my response.

I look around at the fake-concerned faces and come danger-ously close to crying. Because I realize I have no friends. The only real friend I have is sitting over at the loser table eating french fries with Jessie Colburn.

A hush falls over the cafeteria. At first I think, *What now? Do I have mashed potatoes on my chin?* but when I look up I find that no one's watching me. They're all looking at Bianca as she walks toward our table. I almost don't recognize her. She's sporting a pair of big sunglasses, which would be strange enough since we're *inside*, but she's also wearing a sweat suit. Okay, so it's a supercute sweat suit that hugs her shapely body, and since her hair is perfectly styled and her face applied, she pretty much rocks the look, but still. It's a sweat suit. And it's Bianca.

She falls into the seat next to mine, and it's so dramatic that it cannot be natural. She pulls off her sunglasses and gives me a sheepish smile. Or at least, that's what she's trying for. It sort of looks like she's constipated.

"Are you still not talking to me?" she asks carefully. "Be-cause you didn't return any of my calls . . ." She looks into her lap, but her eyes shift to gauge my reaction.

There are a few ways this can go down.

OPTION ONE:
Me: You're a nasty little bitch, Bianca. Now come here so I can drag you around the cafeteria by your cheap extensions!

Option Two:

Me: What calls, Bianca? I got three texts from you. *Three!* Which might as well be none. After nine years of friendship, I think I deserve a little more than that. [Followed by a breakdown (and I'm not a cute crier, as Bishop can attest).]

Option Three:

Me: You don't know this, Bianca, but I've recently discovered I may be a witch. So I'd watch out a few days from now. You may receive an unpleasant surprise in the form of whiteheads and cellulite.

When I look around the table, I find that everyone's waiting with bated breath to see how I will react to Bianca's sort-of apology, and I know that I'm going to have to go with Option Four.

I turn to Bianca. She blinks her big eyes at me, waiting for a response.

I think about the nine years of friendship we shared, from the first grade, when we were completely inseparable, right up until last year, when it was so painfully obvious we were drifting apart. I think about the Pretty People Club and cheerleading and my reserved table at lunch and all the parties, and of how hard we worked to get to this place on the social ladder—and suddenly I couldn't be more tired of it all. The worst part is that I've known our friendship was over for a long time. I just didn't want it to be true. And if I really think about it, it's the same thing with Devon. It's like I was just waiting for them to screw up because I wasn't brave enough to end things on my own. Or didn't know how to do it.

But suddenly it's very clear what I have to do.

I pick up my tray.

"Where are you going?" Bianca asks.

A low murmur runs through the cafeteria. My heart beats so hard I'm sure everyone can hear it as I walk across the dining hall, but it's not because I'm scared I'm making the wrong choice. Not at all. I know even before I thunk my tray down next to Paige's that I'll never regret it.

15

Somehow, when I imagined the big moment when I'd learn the truth about whether or not I was a witch, it didn't take place at home with my mom on a Monday night.

"Should we light candles?" Mom leans forward as she sits cross-legged on my bed.

"We're not doing a séance." I give the carpet a two-second break from the tread I'm wearing in it to crack the blinds and look out the window. The sun has edged behind the mansions on our street, bathing the sky in the pinks and oranges of sunset. It won't be long before those colors fade to the inky black of night. Before the moon comes out.

"What do you think is going to happen?" Mom asks.

"Nothing—I told you. We really don't have to make a big deal out of this. It's not like the sky's going to break apart or fireworks will start or something."

"I know," Mom says, waving a hand to dismiss my comment. "But it *is* a big deal. Coming into your powers is a momentous occasion."

"*Maybe* coming into my powers," I correct her. "There's only a fifty percent chance, at best."

Mom's about to argue with me when, downstairs, a knock on the door interrupts her. We exchange confused looks.

I trail behind her to the door, flattening what I can of my frizzy curls. One can never be too prepared when suddenly single.

She opens the door.

"Hi, Ms. Blackwood." Paige smiles shyly at Mom. "Hope I'm not barging in or anything. I brought candles."

"How thoughtful!" Mom throws the door wide open. "Look, Ind. Paige is here."

Paige clutches the candles in front of her and rocks up on the balls of her feet, making a point of not looking at me.

"I see that, Mom. Hi, Paige," I say.

"Hey." Paige directs a tight smile at me.

Mom looks from Paige to me. It's not unusual for Paige to drop by unannounced, but it's definitely unusual for me not to make some lame excuse and run for cover upstairs. Mom knows enough not to ask, though, instead muttering something about putting on a pot of coffee and bustling out of the room.

When I sat with Paige today in the cafeteria, she acted totally normal. She gave me a smile and introduced me to Jessie, which I was sure meant I didn't owe her any further apologies for the years of mistreatment and sudden convenient timing of my change of heart. Or something. But apparently that's not enough.

"So, um," I start. "Thanks for letting me sit with you and, you know, not making a big deal about it. And I'm sorry I haven't exactly been . . ." I trail off, unable to find the words to sum up everything I'm sorry for, and okay, hoping she'll interrupt my apology so I don't have to get into mortifying specifics. "Things have been weird the last . . . few years," I finally stammer.

Crickets. Actual crickets are chirping. I continue.

"But I should have made time to hang out with you more—"

"More?"

"At all, no matter how much homework Mrs. Davies assigned, or how hectic it was balancing cheerleading and work, and no matter how little sleep I got, I should definitely have made the time. And I should have come to the barbeque, even with the whole revelation I might be a witch and the Devon and Bianca thing . . ."

She rolls her eyes.

Even *I* know that was a shitty apology. I'm about to start over when she holds up a hand to stop me. "It's okay."

I blink at her. "It is?"

She nods. "You've had a bad week. I know you're sorry, even if you suck at admitting it. That's what counts."

I give her a grateful smile.

"And I know you're going to be different now. I can tell."

Okay, so there was a bit of a threat in her tone, but still. It's much more than I deserve. I'll take what I can get.

We walk into the kitchen and nab spots on opposite sides of the table.

"Whatcha watching, Ms. Blackwood?" Paige asks, slipping back into her old cheery ways.

Mom has paused mid–spooning out coffee grinds and is staring at the TV on the counter. "Oh, nothing," she says, fumbling with the remote until the screen goes dark. "It's a double double, right, Paige?" Her back is to me now.

"What's going on, Mom?"

"Hmm?" She shoves the filter into the coffee machine. "It's a double double, right? I can't seem to remember. . . ."

I cross to the counter and flick the TV on.

A newscaster who has clearly never met a bottle of hair gel he didn't like stands in front of the Getty. Yellow crime scene tape blocks off the entrance, and uniform-clad police officers chat near the doors.

"For those of you who've just tuned in," the newscaster says, *"we're reporting live from in front of the Getty Center in*

Brentwood, where officials say at least thirty people simultane-
ously lost consciousness. When they awoke, hours had passed,
and they had no memory of what happened. At this time, Getty
representatives say it doesn't appear as if anything has been
stolen, but they are conducting a thorough investigation into
the matter as we speak. This is just the latest in a string of
what police say are bizarre incidents occurring throughout the
city. . . ."

All the blood drains from my head, and I feel faint. Chief
Wiggum's words the night the Bible went missing reverber-
ate in my head. Blackouts. Memory loss. It's the Priory—it
has to be.

"Oh, sweetie." Mom reaches past me and turns off
the TV.

"Do you know what this means?" I ask.

The percolator bubbles and spits in the background.

"This isn't just dangerous for witches," I say. "It's blackouts now, but what next? After they kill all the witches and
they can do whatever they want? Just think of what this
means!"

"I know," Mom says to the linoleum, before shooting her
focus back up to me. "Look, I've been thinking. Maybe if I
talk to the girls at the next meeting—"

"No!" I cry out. "Mom, no one can know about this. Not
the Wicca Society, not Aunt Penny, no one."

"All right." She raises a hand. "It was just an idea."

A very bad idea, I want to say. There is no way any good

would come of the public finding out about witches. Hello, Salem witch trials, anyone? But she's just trying to help.

"It's getting dark," I say. We all look out the patio doors at the twilight that descends over the backyard.

Paige holds up the candles. "Lighter?"

Candles bathe my bedroom in flickering yellow light, casting ominous shadows that look like trees across the forest-green walls of my room. Paige sits on the bed, cradling a cup of coffee in her lap, while Mom stands vigil at the window. Me, I'm perched on the end of my computer desk, feet resting on the wooden chair that is so uncomfortable I sit in it only when I'm really serious about homework and don't want to fall asleep.

"Well, there it is." Mom draws the blinds all the way up so I can see the fat yellow moon sitting high against the black sky.

"Yep. There it is." I slap my hands on my thighs.

"Feel any different?" Paige asks.

I do a little inventory of myself. Ten fingers? Check. Ten toes? Check. Absolutely ridiculous Afro of curls? Check. "Nope. Everything's just as I left it."

"Think you should try some magic or something?" Paige asks.

I laugh. "Like what? I don't know any spells."

She shrugs. "Maybe try to fly, like Bishop."

I shake my head. "I don't know how to—"

"Well, that's because you haven't tried," Mom interrupts.

I let Mom drag me off the desk to the center of the room. She backs up, and now both she and Paige look at me as if enough staring will lift me right off the ground.

"Try," Paige urges.

I couldn't feel sillier if I were wearing a clown costume, but I do as I'm told and widen my stance, closing my eyes and reaching around inside for whatever magic I might have. After a couple of seconds have passed, I blink one eye open to check on my progress, only to find that my feet are still firmly planted on the floor.

"You're not trying," Paige whines, fingers twined together in front of her.

"Yes I am!"

"Say something," Mom urges. She's pressed against Paige, mirroring her anxious pose.

"Like what?"

"Like a spell or something."

I raise my eyebrows. "News flash: I don't know any spells."

"Well, what happened to Bishop showing you the ropes?" Mom asks.

"That's *if* I become a witch, Mom." I close my eyes so she won't see I'm lying. "No reason to come by if I'm not, which is obviously the case."

"Just try!" Paige and Mom cry together.

I sigh. "Okay, okay." I take slow, measured breaths through my nose and concentrate on making my body listen. *I'm weightless, I'm lifting from the ground, I'm flying.*

"Fly!" I say, and feel endlessly stupid for it. But from the sounds of their clapping, Mom and Paige seemed pleased with my efforts, so I go on. "Fly, fly, fly!"

I crack one eye open. Still nothing. I close my eyes again. "Oh, God of, uh, the earth"—I lift my palms up—"please, pretty please, can I fly?"

I open my eyes and—yep, not flying. An emotion bearing an uncanny resemblance to disappointment mixed with embarrassment falls over me.

"Forget it." I let my arms drop to my sides. "I'm clearly not a witch."

"You don't know that," Paige says, but she doesn't sound very convincing. "Maybe you just need to learn some spells or something."

"Oh, sweet pea . . ." Mom strides up to me and wraps an arm around my deflated shoulders.

"Hello?" I say. "What's with everyone? Remember the news? I'm not going to die at the hands of evil sorcerers. This is a good thing."

Mom hugs me tighter. Dammit, why does she always see through me?

"You're right," Mom says. "Any other time I'd say being a witch is a blessing, but right now it would be too dangerous. We're all glad you're safe."

"Good," I say, a little too quickly. "Now I need to shower for school tomorrow."

They exchange a knowing glance before Paige blows out her candles. "Yeah, I guess I should start my English paper."

Mom pats my back. "I'll be in the kitchen if you need me."

I wait until after their footsteps have retreated down the stairs and the front door clicks shut before I escape into the bathroom to begin my usual nighttime hair ritual—wash, condition, attempt to pass a comb through the poodle growing on my head, consider chopping it all off, then eventually wrestle the last knot out, and reconsider the drastic haircut—and though it feels strange to be doing something so normal after such a bizarre couple of days, it also feels kind of good. Like tonight is the start of my new life.

Mom must be feeling really bad for me, because I'm in the bathroom for what feels like forever and she doesn't knock on the door twenty times to ask when I'm coming out or to remind me that it's late and it's a school night.

I wrap a towel around my midsection and open the door, releasing a wave of steam.

"Done!" I yell down to Mom.

She doesn't answer.

I shrug and cross the hall to my bedroom, flicking on the light.

Weird—my window is open. A breeze flutters the curtains and makes goose bumps rise on my bare skin. *Looks like I'm going to have to have another "my room is my business" conversation with Mom,* I think as I pad across the soft carpet.

I muscle the old window down, and my breath catches in my throat. A man is reflected in the glass.

16

I whirl around, gripping the towel tight over my chest. "Who are you?"

The man smiles, but with his row of crooked teeth, it looks anything but friendly. "I've been called Mr. Wolf." He takes three big steps forward, so that I'm backed against the window, and extends a hand. "But I also go by the name of Frederick."

"Stop right there or I'll scream!"

He laughs. "Relax, Indigo."

I could stand naked in the middle of Melrose Avenue on a Saturday afternoon and not feel more exposed than I do right now in this thin towel. "Wh-who are you and how do you know my name?"

"And why am I in your room?" His eyebrow arches.

I brace my arms tighter over my chest to secure the towel.

Frederick grins. "Don't worry, you're not my type."

He strides in the other direction, so I see the gray ponytail that falls down the back of his black suit jacket. My mouth has gone dry, and I can hardly think past the sound of my heartbeat pounding in my ears.

"Now, let's talk about what you've done." Frederick turns, regarding me with slanted blue eyes.

I wet my papery lips. "I—I don't know what you're talking about."

"I think you know exactly what I'm talking about." He stops in front of a corkboard covered with photos, cards, and every other item of junk I can never think of where to put, and leans in to inspect something. "*Twilight*?" he asks, full of disgust as he fingers old theater stubs.

I look at my open bedroom door. If I make a run for it, I can probably get out before he's even—the door slams shut, and I gasp. He hasn't moved an inch, and the door closed. The door closed on its own.

"You—you're Frederick, from the Priory," I stammer.

"And now that we've established the basics," Frederick says without turning, "why don't you tell me what you know. This can very simple, Indigo. You've put a spell on the Bible"—he runs his finger over a photo of Mom and me from the year I had my birthday at American Girl, before violently ripping it out from under the tack that holds it in place—"that prevents it from being opened."

I swallow what feels like a whole fist in my throat. "You obviously don't know what you're talking about, because I'm not a witch, and I don't know any spells."

"Really?" Frederick says. "Then tell me how a spell came to protect the Bible that is in your possession? It wasn't your mother. It wasn't your aunt. So who was it, then? The family cat?"

I race through my brain for an answer to his question. "My grandma! It must have been my grandma. She was a witch."

He shakes his head. "This spell is new, Indigo, within the last few years. Strong and unbreakable. You know, this was so much easier when I could just pluck what I needed right out of your head."

I swallow my rising panic at his nonsensical words. "But even if I was a witch, it's only my two hundredth moon tonight. I couldn't have possibly put a spell on the Bible before it went missing. Think about it! It makes sense!"

His jaw hardens, and I can see why he said he's called Mr. Wolf. He looks at me like he's considering ripping me to shreds with his bare teeth.

He takes slow steps toward me, fanning the picture in front of his face. "You know what? I think you're lying. I think you know a lot more than you're admitting."

I back up, but my heels run into the baseboards and I can't go any farther. The window—I could go out the window. And what? Fall two stories and break a few bones?

He leans in so close I can see every little hair he missed shaving, the plaque etched over his gumline, the cracks around his mouth. I push farther back and touch the window.

He cocks his head.

"I'm not a witch." Tears well in my eyes. "I don't know how to help you."

Frederick takes a deep breath through his nose, his jaw tense as granite, and straightens to his full height. And then he rips the photo of Mom and me in half, letting the pieces flutter to the floor. "I thought you might behave this way. Good thing I've come prepared. Leo?"

The bedroom door bursts open. Mom stumbles in, a scarred man with a shaved head and dangerous black eyes behind her, pushing her forward with a knife held to her throat.

"Mom!" I try to skirt around Frederick, but he holds a hand up, and I smack into an invisible wall. "Let me out!" I slam my palms against the barrier, but all it does is ripple the air in front of me. Mom's round eyes flit around the room, mascara running down her cheeks. And there's nothing I can do. A terrified cry escapes me.

"I tried to warn you," Frederick says. "Perhaps you'd like to be a little more forthcoming now?" He takes measured steps around the force field to where Mom stands, each step making my heart race faster.

"Stay away from her!" I scream.

Frederick grins and reaches up to tuck flyaway hairs behind Mom's ears. She flinches, and I renew my efforts trying to knock away the invisible wall.

"This can all stop, Indigo." Frederick locks eyes with me. "Just break the spell on the Bible, and we'll let your mom go."

"I told you, I don't know how to break any spells."

Frederick tuts under his breath and, without breaking eye contact with me, waves a hand. Leo pushes Mom forward, a grin pulling up just the left side of his face, the other made immovable by scars. His left eye blinks unnaturally, the effect grating on the nerves in my stomach.

"No, no, no! Please, I'll do anything, just leave her alone." Tears spill down my cheeks.

Mom reaches out a hand to me. "It's okay, Ind—" But her words are garbled when Leo presses the knife harder against her throat.

"I'm afraid you leave me no choice." Frederick walks to the window and pulls it wide open. Cool air pours inside.

"What are you doing? Come back. Take me instead! Leave my mom alone." My breaths come in hiccupping gulps.

Leo pushes Mom forward, and she stumbles into Frederick. Mom tries to run, but he snags her by the collar of her shirt and yanks her backward. She yelps, clawing helplessly at the air. No magic involved, just brutal violence.

"Well, what will it be, Indigo?" Frederick has one boot-clad foot up on the window ledge, a long arm snaked around Mom's middle.

"I can learn the spell. Just give me some time, please. As soon as I figure it out I'll break it. I just need a little time."

Frederick nods, and I think I've finally said the right thing.

"And you'll get your mother back just as soon as you do." He climbs onto the ledge. I don't even have time to say goodbye before he hops out the window, Mom flapping like a rag doll in his grip. Leo climbs up next and, with a final wave to me, jumps out after them.

17

Panic surges through me. They've got Mom. Evil sorcerers have got Mom, and I'm trapped in some invisible mime-box.

Even though it's been nothing but a waste of energy so far, I start to pound my fists against the wall. But this time I don't meet resistance, and I stumble forward.

What the . . . ?

But I don't spare more than two seconds to consider my turn of luck before I'm at the window ledge, wildly searching left and right, up and down, for a sign of which way they've gone. Nothing. Not the scuffing of footsteps retreating down Fuller Avenue. Not the shriek of car tires against pavement. Not even a distant speck in the moonlit sky.

She's gone.

My heart knots up as if someone's squeezing it, wringing it out like a wet dishrag. *What do I do?*

I thrash through the pile of untouched homework and old dishes on the computer desk until I find the house phone. My hands tremble as I dial 9, but I stop there, because what will I tell the police? Two sorcerers just stole into my room and kidnapped my mom, and they won't give her back until I unlock the secret spell that binds *The Witch Hunter's Bible*? Yeah, I'm sure that'd go over real well.

I smash the phone against the wall, sending springs and batteries flying over my bed, and start pacing my room. Mom needs me—I've got to think of something, anything. But what? I'm not a witch. If I am, I must be the crappiest witch on the planet. I couldn't do a thing to help Mom. I let out an anguished groan.

I need help. That much is clear.

I don't waste time scrolling through the options. There's only one person I can trust who will know what to do.

I throw on the first clothes I stumble across and fly down the stairs and out the front door. Only when I get outside and see that all the lights are off inside Paige's house do I remember that it was after eleven when Paige left, and that was ages ago. I can't just knock on the front door, unless I want to explain all of this to Mr. and Mrs. Abernathy. No thank you—straitjackets do nothing for my figure.

I could call, but I'm already outside. Plus, let's be honest:

it's not like I haven't done this before. And so, stumbling over the unwound garden hose, I tiptoe around the side of their house until I'm standing beneath Paige's window.

"Paige!" I stage-whisper. "Paige, it's Indie."

I wait only a second before I start feeling around on the ground for a rock to throw at her window.

"Bit of break and enter?"

I shriek and scuttle backward from the dark figure leaning against Paige's house.

"Bishop?"

"You expecting another ridiculously handsome man to appear right now?"

"Oh, Bishop, thank God it's you!" I push to my feet and plow into his chest, wrapping my arms around his middle and holding on to him like he might disappear at any moment.

"Uh, okay." He laughs, then pats my back. "Not exactly what I was expecting, but I'll take it. Shall we find a bedroom, or is here good for you?"

"They came, Bishop." I pull back so I can look at him. Aside from serious five-o'clock shadow and a slouchy knit hat he sports despite the heat, he looks just like he did the last time I saw him: all height and leather and tattoos. "They wanted me to break some spell on the Bible," I continue, "but I couldn't because I'm not a witch, but they wouldn't listen to me, so then they kidnapped Mom at knifepoint, and I have to find her, Bishop. I love her so much, even though it might not seem like it at times. But she can be so frustrating, you know? But I do love her—"

"Whoa, what? The Priory was here?"

The window above us cracks open, and Paige pokes her head out. "Indie, is that you?"

"Why are you here?" I ask Bishop. "Did you know about the Priory coming after me?"

"How would I know about that?" he asks defensively. "I only just got released from headquarters."

"What's going on down there?" Paige asks. "Is that Bishop with you?"

"Whatever, how do we get her back?" I ask.

"Well, since you asked," he answers, "here's what we'll do. First we'll drive to the sorcerers' lair. Then we'll knock on the front door and we'll simply ask if they'd be so kind as to give your mother back. I'm sure they'll be very reasonable."

I cut him an icy glare.

"Look, I'm sorry if I'm being rude, but I don't think you're getting the gravity of this situation. I'm just one person. Who knows how many they've got down here."

"Well, don't you have any warlock friends? And what about the Family? Why not get them to help us?"

"No, I haven't got any friends, and you're forgetting that I just barely escaped headquarters after losing the Bible. The Family isn't very likely to want to do me favors at the moment. And that's not to mention the fact that they don't care about your mom." I gasp, but he shrugs. "I'm sorry, but they don't. They're worried about the lives of thousands of witches and warlocks; they don't have time to save one human."

"But the Bible! Won't they want to get it back? Those guys have it."

"You mean, won't they want to run into a group of sorcerers with centuries of pent-up anger ready to explode at any moment? Sorcerers who've just discovered the secret means to kill them? Yeah—no. They're busy building an army, planning defensive tactics, et cetera, et cetera."

Tears of frustration well in my eyes.

"Hello!" Paige calls down. "Anyone care to tell me what's going on? Is your mom in trouble or something, Indie?"

"Hold on. So what then, Bishop? You're saying that it's useless?" My voice cracks, and I don't even care that I'm crying again. I don't think I'll care about anything until I get Mom back.

"I didn't say useless," Bishop corrects. "I said it wouldn't be easy. And since you're not getting any help from the Family, you've got to master your magic, and fast. Most witches take months to get any good at this stuff, but we obviously haven't got that much time."

"I told you: I'm not a witch."

"And how do you know that? Just because you don't know how to use your magic doesn't mean it's not there."

"Told you so," Paige says, leaning out the window.

I let this sink in. "So let me get this straight: you're suggesting we practice magic before going after my mom?"

"Finally! I was starting to think you ride the short bus to school."

"You're the stupid one if you think we have time to just sit around and practice. They took my mom. They had a *knife* to her throat. What are you not getting?"

"What *you're* not getting, Indigo, is that if we go in there unprepared, you—if not both of us—will die."

I groan and scrunch my hands into the roots of my hair. "Just tell me where they took her then. I'll do this myself if you won't help."

"And why do you assume I know where they are?"

"Tell me, Bishop." I slam a hand against his chest as hard as I can, and it's as if I've just punched a cinder block.

He doesn't even have the decency to pretend I've hurt him. "You'll kill yourself."

"Fine, then, I'll kill myself." I massage my aching wrist. "Where are they?"

"You're serious?"

"Yes! I don't know how to make myself more clear to you."

He sighs. "Fine. Get your car keys."

"Where are we going?" Paige suddenly stands between our houses, backlit in the circle of light cast from our front porches.

"Oh no." Bishop shakes his head. "She's not coming. It's enough to have one liability, let alone two."

Paige huffs. "I'm glad you think so highly of us."

He skirts around Paige, heading toward the driveway. When he reaches the driver's-side door, he bounces on his toes like a boxer, waiting for us normal-limbed people to catch up. But when I enter the light, his bouncing comes to a stop and his jaw twitches, his eyes passing down my legs. I become aware that I'm wearing a pair of cotton shorts that could double as underwear in a pinch, and a holey T-shirt.

"They're pajamas, perv." I say.

He nods in appreciation. "Car keys?"

"What for? We aren't flying there?"

"No, we aren't flying. Why do you think I took you to the Hollywood sign the other night? No one can know about us. And I said she's not coming." He flicks his hand toward Paige in a dismissive gesture.

"Yes I am." Paige places a balled fist on her hip and locks eyes with Bishop, giving him a death stare that would put Bianca's to shame. "If Indie's in danger, I'm going to help."

"Okay, sure. You're coming. What do I care if you die? I don't. There we go. Car keys, Ind?"

I give Paige a grateful smile before running inside to snag the keys from the hook by the door. When I return, Bishop is holding out his hands to catch the keys.

"Dream on, buddy." I push past him and slip into the driver's seat.

The engine turns over as Paige buckles her seat belt and Bishop wedges himself into the tiny passenger seat. "Where to?" I ask.

"The Chinese Theatre," Bishop answers.

"The Chinese frickin' Theatre?" Paige says. And that pretty much sums up how I feel about it too.

"Yes." Bishop cranes his neck to look back at Paige, dark eyebrows pulled up underneath the brim of his hat. "Is that not a good enough place for you to die?"

Paige does an impression of him yapping.

"Why there?" I ask, reversing out of the driveway. "This isn't like last time, is it? Traipsing around the city for no good reason at all, just to amuse you at the expense of everyone else? Because we don't have time for that crap."

"Listen to you." Bishop adjusts his seat to accommodate his freakishly long legs. "You'd think I wasn't doing you a favor or something."

I shake my head. "God, I'm so glad to have you back, you know, because you are just *so* pleasant to be around."

"Oh, come on. I was just joking." Bishop pokes my shoulder.

I don't respond. I'm *so* not in the mood for this.

"Hey, I have a great idea," he says brightly. "Let's paint each other's nails, bust out some magazine quizzes, and make this a real girl party!" He takes a chunk of my hair and starts braiding it. I knock his hand away.

He rests back against his seat, muttering under his breath.

I only the catch the last words: "be such a stick-in-the-mud all the time."

"Yes, well, when someone kidnaps your mom and you have no clue if she's dead or alive and being tortured in a cellar somewhere, then we'll see what kind of mood you're in."

"My mother is dead," he says, his tone flat and even.

I glance over and pray, pray, pray that I see humor in his face, but he stares straight ahead, his expression hard and inflexible.

"Oh God." I rub my temple. "I'm sorry. I didn't mean—"

"It's fine."

"No, it's not fine. I shouldn't have—"

"I said it's fine. Now we're even." He gives me a half smile. But rather than comfort me, it leaves me with a grating sensation, like a mosquito buzzing around my head that I can't swat away.

I squint at his face, studying everything from his intensely dark eyes to the caterpillar brows drawn over them to the tiny lines around his mouth that make him look so much older than a teenager, and finally, to the slick waves that frame his sculpted jaw.

"Ind, watch out!" Paige screams.

A horn honks and white light fills the car. I crank the steering wheel to the right, bringing us safely back over the yellow line. A car speeds past, its driver yelling obscenities out the window.

"Maybe he *should* drive," Paige mutters.

"I knew we kept her around for a reason," Bishop says.

I glance at him again, sidelong this time so I can still watch the road. "How old are you?"

"Eighteen," he answers. "Why?"

I glance at him after verifying a Mack truck isn't going to slam into us. "Where did you go to high school?"

"Nowhere you'd know." He clicks the radio on. "Not in L.A."

"What, was it some Hogwarts-type school?"

"No, it was a regular high school."

"Then try me. I passed geography."

He laughs. "Okay. Roosevelt High, San Antonio, Texas. Heard of it?"

"Texas? But you don't have an accent."

"Because I lived in California until I was sixteen and a bit."

"Where?"

"Rancho Santa Margarita."

"Why'd you move?"

"Because my mom died and I was sent to live with my uncle."

I lapse into silence as I consider his responses.

"Done with the inquisition?" he asks, shining his ring on his pants. "My answers have pleased you?"

"What's with that thing?"

"This?" he says, holding up his hand so that his ring—the

chunky type with deep grooves etched into heavy metal that boys wear when they want to accessorize and still appear manly—glints in the moonlight. I notice that the grooves spell out the number two in Roman numerals.

"What's the two about?" I ask.

He shrugs. "Family heirloom. Anything else?"

It's an omission, at the very least, but I don't bother pushing the issue because I can tell he's not going to talk. Also, I don't care.

"Do I know you from somewhere?"

"Um, yeah. The shop, the party, the Hollywood sign, just now at your house—"

"Before that, I mean."

He rubs his forehead. "God, now I feel bad. I slept with you, didn't I? Oh, this is terribly embarrassing. This happens sometimes, you know. But it's just so hard to remember all the faces, all the names—"

"Very funny," I say. "You look really familiar."

"Actually, Ind, he kind of looks like that Kyle Loza guy," Paige pipes up from the backseat. "Indie used to have the biggest crush on this BMXer who was on that spin-off of *The Hills*."

"I did not!" I snap.

"You are aware my bedroom faces yours, right? I saw the poster."

Bishop laughs and pats me on the arm. "It's okay, Indie. I completely understand."

I shake off his hand. "Can we all not be having such a great time right now? My mom's in trouble, remember?"

Paige sinks back into her seat, as Bishop mumbles apologies.

We're quiet the rest of the drive. Only after we pass the Hollywood and Highland Center parking garage does Bishop pipe up again.

"What are you doing?" he asks, twisting around to watch the parking garage disappear behind us.

"What? You wanted me to park there?"

"Unless you want to pay the eight-hundred-dollar fine for parking in a red zone."

This is not a conversation I thought I'd be having on the way to save Mom from evil sorcerers. I circle the block until I'm back at Hollywood and Highland.

The garage stares back at me in the glare of my headlights, and a cold shiver passes through me. I've never been a huge fan of creepy underground parking garages, but under these circumstances, as we slip into its darkened mouth, it feels as though we're entering the maw of some predatory animal.

But even though it's so late it can almost be called early, I'm happy to note there are still a good number of cars inside, and even a few people in club clothes marching toward the escalators to street level. It makes me feel a bit better, though I'm not sure why.

"I don't get it," I say, steering the Sunfire beneath the low ceiling and artificial track lighting of the garage. "Why here? There are tons of people around." I slip the car into a spot and kill the engine.

"Exactly." Bishop opens the car door and steps out.

Am I supposed to know what that means? I twist to look at Paige. She raises her hands, palms up, and shrugs.

I run after Bishop, and Paige follows suit.

"Okay, think about it," he says, his footsteps echoing in the garage. "You're a sorcerer. You're away from home, out of your comfort zone without your sorcerer friends to help you, and every witch on the planet is hunting you. What better place to keep a hostage, or say, really important book, than in plain sight?"

"Still don't get it," I say.

"Because," he continues, "there's nothing witches value more than secrecy. The last time the public found out about our existence it didn't exactly end well. No witch would risk exposure by confronting a sorcerer in so public a place as the Chinese Theatre."

"Or the Getty," I mumble, remembering the news report. My footsteps sputter to a halt as I consider this, Paige stopping next to me.

"Right. They've been hopping around from one L.A. landmark to another for weeks, never staying in the same place for long."

"So what's the plan?" I call to Bishop's back.

"What plan?" he answers without turning. "I'm the one who said we shouldn't come here unprepared." He steps onto the escalator. We scramble to follow him, lest we be left alone in the garage.

"Sorry for thinking you might have some brilliant idea," I pant, out of breath. "You know, since you're supposed to be a warlock." I cross my arms and glare at him. Which, I have to say, is much less effective when you're gliding slowly up an escalator to instrumental soft-rock music.

Bishop laughs. "You know, your mean face is pretty sexy."

Ugh.

"Okay, I have an idea," Paige says.

I take a reluctant pause from considering how best to maim and injure Bishop to look at Paige.

"Okay," she says. "Bishop, you use your little magic thingy to get inside. Check out the situation, and then report back to us so we can come up with another plan."

Bishop shakes his head and tucks his hair under his hat. "Fantastic. So look, if you're not coming, then you might want to hang back."

I huff, the neon of Hollywood Boulevard coming into view over the lip of the escalator. "So what are you suggesting, that we wait in the car?"

He steps off the escalator and turns to face me. "Yes, that's exactly what I'm suggesting. But you're perfectly welcome to follow me." A smirk plays on his lips. He gives me a little wave before vanishing into thin air.

18

I've lived in Los Angeles my whole life and have never been inside the Chinese Theatre. Outside is another story. I've driven or walked past it zillions of times, taken pictures of celebrities' footprints and handprints on the Walk of Fame, and camped out across the street, hoping to catch a glimpse of Katy Perry at the premiere of her 3-D movie.

But I've never been inside. Which seems dumb, because it's an L.A. freaking landmark! Either there's been a huge line for tickets, or the movie I wanted to see sold out, or Bianca wanted to see something playing at another theater. I don't know, but I'm slapping myself for it now. If I knew the layout of the place—the battlefield, as it were—rescuing

Mom would be that much easier. And I would have to rely on Bishop that much less.

Paige and I lean over the dash and scan the garage for signs of Bishop.

"Maybe he didn't go inside," I say. "Maybe he just got mad at us and left."

Paige shakes her head, bangs shuffling over the rims of her glasses. "He wouldn't do that."

"Why not? He took off before."

"But your mom wasn't in danger."

"What does he care about my mom?"

"He cares about *you*, obviously, or he wouldn't have come back."

I snort. "Oh yeah, he *really* cares about me."

"Has it escaped your notice that the two of you have done nothing but flirt since the minute you met?"

I laugh. "You obviously don't know what flirting is. We're *fighting*. Big difference."

"God, are you really that blind? It's like in kindergarten when a boy pulls a girl's hair. He likes you."

I shake my head. "No way. And in any case, he's a jerk. I would never be interested in him."

It's her turn to laugh.

"He's completely not my type, Paige. He wears leather. He looks like he hasn't washed his hair in weeks. He's wearing a freaking beret!"

"It's not a beret, it's a beanie. A slouchy beanie. And you know it's sexy."

"Sexy?" I draw back to get a better look at her. "You can't be serious."

She shrugs.

"What, do you have a crush on him now or something?"

"Why, would that bother you?" She cocks her head, waiting for my reply.

My mouth opens and closes before I get a handle on what I should say. "No! Not at all. If you like him, go for it."

She doesn't look convinced. I change topics.

"What could be taking him so long?"

Paige looks out the window at the shadowy corners of the garage. "Getting the layout of the place, I guess."

Neither of us mentions the idea that maybe he's been caught, even though we're both obviously thinking it.

A group of clubgoers totter around the corner, talking and laughing loudly. We edge up in our seats to look for Bishop, because there are scantily clad girls involved and it's entirely possible he got distracted. But he's not there.

"Should we check on him?" I ask.

"Yeah, no. If Bishop can't get in and out safely, we most definitely won't be able to."

Before I can argue, something lands on the roof of the car with a jarring thud.

We shriek, instinctively ducking. Metal crunches overhead,

and then two shiny alligator shoes step onto the hood. My heart races, adrenaline surging through my veins.

The feet hop off the hood. Frederick bends next to the driver's-side door, his face just centimeters from mine. His mouth curves into a menacing smile.

"Drive!" Paige yells.

I fumble with the keys, unable to break eye contact with Frederick. But the car won't start. The engine doesn't even attempt to turn over.

"It won't start!" I cry.

"Try harder."

"I *am* trying! It's not working."

Frederick circles around the front of the car, knocking out a tune on the hood.

As Frederick nears Paige's side, she inches back against me so that she's practically in my lap.

I catch sight of the group of clubgoers a few car lengths' down, and for a fleeting moment hope flares up inside me that they'll help, or at the very least, run for help—but they don't move. A girl holds a camera out and her friends all huddle for a picture, but they're just as frozen as if I were looking at a photograph. No one's going to come. No one's going to help us.

"Now this is just getting silly," Frederick says, his voice muted by the quarter-inch of glass between us. I can hardly hear him above the sound of my heartbeat.

He circles around the car again, and Paige and I crane our

necks to follow his movements. He nears my window and bends low, regarding me with icy blue eyes.

"I just want my mom back," I manage.

"Oh, don't you worry," he says. "She's in good company. You might know him, actually. A little brat by the name of Bishop. They've been great support for each other. And you know, support is very important when you've . . ." He trails off, then waves his hand. "Well, better not get into specifics."

A sob escapes me, a sick sense of foreboding clamping down on my chest.

"But then I got to thinking. You know, it's not very fair for them to have all the fun." He smiles to reveal a row of crooked, decaying teeth, then braces his hands on the hood of the car.

The rocking starts gently, like the tremor of a small car as a semi whooshes past on the interstate. A spider of dread climbs up my spine. Paige and I exchange wide-eyed stares, and the spider becomes a big, hairy tarantula. Frederick quickly picks up momentum, and the car rocks hard from left to right, knocking Paige and me against each other and the windows, then is suspended on two wheels for mere seconds before crashing down hard in the other direction. My head smashes against the window, and a searing pain shoots through my skull. White spots dance in my vision. I feebly brace my arms, trying to stop some of the impact, some of the pain.

But then the rocking stops.

My first thought is that someone's saved us. But when my eyes adjust, Frederick is still there, walking in front of the car, taking slow, purposeful steps as if he's got all the time in the world. He locks eyes with me and tips his head to the side, one thumb under his chin as he taps an index finger on his lips. And that's when I realize something: he's not going to kill me. Even if killing me wouldn't bleed him of his powers, he wouldn't do it. He's going to keep me alive until he gets what he wants. But Paige? He has no reason to keep her alive.

"Should we make a run for it?" Paige asks between gasps for air.

I swallow. "On the count of three"—I drop my voice to barely a whisper—"you go left and I'll go right."

"What? No way." Paige clings to my arm.

"It's the only way either of us has a chance." *It's the only way* you *have a chance.* I squeeze her clammy, shaking hand.

She nods, biting down on her lips as tears stream over her pale cheeks.

"Good luck."

Frederick moves in my peripheral vision. Time's up for mushy moments.

We scramble to open the doors, and without another glance at each other, dash across the garage in opposite directions.

"Indigo, what sort of way is this to treat your old pal?"

Frederick says, his lilting voice sending a chill rippling through me. But his voice is distant now, like he hasn't moved. Like he's letting me run. Which should make me feel relieved, but instead it just makes me wonder what he's got up his sleeve. If he's going to go after Paige instead of me.

But I can't turn back now. Because if I can just make it upstairs to street level, maybe there'll be people there who can help. He can't have frozen all of Los Angeles.

I careen around a corner and make a mad dash for the escalator, leaping the moving stairs two at a time. My chest burns with every gulp for air, adrenaline pushing me forward like an Olympic sprinter. Hollywood Boulevard comes into view. I jump onto the street and blindly hang a right. That's when I spot them: people. Moving, living, unfrozen people, milling around outside the Hard Rock Cafe. Sure, the women wear miniskirts and six-inch heels and the men sport shirts unbuttoned to reveal waxed chests, but they're *people*. They can help me. My heart pounds so hard I think it might break free and make a run for it if my pesky rib cage weren't getting in the way.

I run toward them. "Help! Help me!"

Heads spin in my direction, and I notice their eyes: red, burning, demented. As if on cue, they surge toward me like zombies in some cheap horror film, shrieking and frothing at the mouth, flailing their arms in their desperation to reach me. Behind them is Frederick, leaning against the huge windows of the bar, casually pushing back his cuticles.

I stumble backward and run. I run past the Dolby Theatre. Past a Starbucks. Past a knockoff Madame Tussauds wax museum. I run so hard and fast over the stars of Hollywood Boulevard that sweat breaks out in beads on my lip, and my chest burns, and my muscles ache with lactic acid buildup.

The tip of my shoe catches in a crack in the pavement, and I pitch forward. I hold my hands out against my fall, thudding hard against the ground. Shrieks and moans and the clacking of heels draw nearer. I push myself up, gravel stinging my palms, and run for my life. Exhaustion weights my every step, but I don't dare stop, don't dare slow my frantic pace. And just when I think I can't possibly make my legs move anymore, that I'm going to have to find somewhere to hide until I regain energy, I realize that the sounds of pursuit have stopped. I slow to a jog and wheel around. No one is there.

Relief floods me. I did it!

"Spot of tea?"

I yelp and spin around. Frederick is seated at an outdoor bistro table across the street.

Shit, crap, shit.

I dart down the street, across four lanes of halted traffic. Around a car with a driver paused in the action of applying her lipstick in the rearview mirror. Around a black Escalade that must hold a celebrity, based on the sheer number of people pointing cameras outside their car windows at it. I veer onto Las Palmas, careful to stay in the light so that Frederick can't jump out at me from any more dark corners.

A streetlamp crashes down inches from my face, inches from flattening me. It hammers the earth so hard I jump three feet into the air. A firework of sparks rain down from the exposed cables.

"Just break the spell, Indigo. It's that easy." I look up. Frederick sits on a window ledge five stories above me, swinging his legs like a kid in a too-big chair.

I whirl around and bolt in the only direction left: a dark, narrow alley.

One hand on the cool wall and the other clawing the air in front of me, I move into the dark. Moonlight fractures a patch of graffitied stucco and the overflowing Dumpster beneath it, and absolutely nothing else. The reek of garbage and sweat clogging my nostrils would be enough to make me gag if I didn't have other reasons to want to puke, and a steady, syrupy drip sounds from somewhere just ahead. I slow my steps, despite everything, for fear of what I might smack into in the dark.

Footsteps thud on the pavement behind me, echoing against the walls. My mouth turns dry and parched. What does Frederick have in store for me this time? Rabid dogs? Buildings collapsing onto me, burying me under a ton of brick? I sob, because I know I can't keep running forever. It's pointless. This ends when he wants it to end.

Steeling myself with a big breath, I turn to face Frederick. "I'm ready."

"Really, now? And what on earth changed your mind?" He laughs, his sharp nose and open mouth backlit by the streetlights.

I swallow the cry of fear bubbling up inside me. "I-if you take me to the book, I'll break the spell."

He stops laughing now and tips his head to the side, as if to judge whether I'm serious. And then he disappears—vanishes before my very eyes.

Before I can even whirl around to look for him, his breath warms my neck as he leans over my shoulder. I scream, but the sound is muffled when his long, cold fingers clamp around my neck.

19

My heels skid along the pavement as Frederick drags me down Hollywood Boulevard. Drags me by the neck, like a little boy might drag a stuffed animal that's become floppy from overuse. Blood fills my head and my face turns hot, a jackhammer of a pulse pounding in my forehead. I tear uselessly at the hands cutting off my air supply, my breath coming in frantic wheezes, my vision turning black at the edges.

When my feet slide across the cement slabs where stars actually left their hand- and footprints, I know we're back at the forecourt of the Chinese Theatre. The familiar red pagoda with its copper roof, massive dragon stamped across the front, and two lion-dog statues standing sentinel at the entrance, comes into view, upside down.

Once we're through the gilded doors of the theater, Frederick tosses me into the lobby. I stumble forward, gasping for air and touching the grooves along my neck where I still feel his fingers.

My throat burns like I've swallowed fire, but I can breathe. Once I establish that, I take a look around.

If people I care about weren't about to die, I might be impressed by what I see on my first time inside the Chinese Theatre. There's none of the tacky, popcorn-littered carpeting, loud arcade games, and bright track lighting typical of most movie theaters. While there *is* a concession stand that emits a concentrated popcorn scent, this lobby boasts elaborate Chinese murals, imposing red columns, and a massive, ornate chandelier hanging over the top of a red-and-gold dragon-themed carpet.

But Mom isn't here, and neither is Bishop. Paige, I can only hope, ran far and fast when Frederick came after me.

I spot dim light seeping under a set of doors at the end of the hall.

"Go on."

I look over my shoulder. Frederick nods in the direction of the light. "I hear there's a good show playing." His lips slide into a grin.

Dread pinches up my stomach, growing stronger with each step I take nearer to the light. I don't want to know what's behind the door, but at the same time, I desperately *need* to know. My mind whirls, my every organ working in overdrive. And suddenly I'm there, my shaking hands pressed against the wood. Holding my breath, I push the double doors open.

The theater is massive. Thousands of bright red seats fill the auditorium, facing a red velvet curtain. Still more Chinese murals stretch across the walls, and dotted along them are intricately carved stone pillars with small lanterns hanging between them. Another colossal chandelier hangs from the ceiling, and from the ceiling's center bursts even more painted dragons.

But still no Mom, still no Bishop.

I get the disturbing feeling that this is a fake-out. But then the curtains draw open, and there they are. At least kind of.

A video of Mom and Bishop is on the screen. They're in a pitch-black room with only a spotlight shining on them, and they sit side by side, acres of thick rope tying them to wooden chairs, and rags stuffed in their mouths. Mom's eyes flit around the darkness, sweat tracks shining on her forehead. Only Bishop's expression, a perfect cross between bored and annoyed, stops me from having a full-on, get-the-paddles heart attack.

I don't know whether to be horrified by the position they're in, or relieved that they're not dead, or upset that they're not actually in this room so that I can do something to help. A million emotions play tug-of-war with my heart.

Mom looks at me. It's such a focused look that I wonder if she actually sees me. If maybe there's some two-way-video thing happening.

Mom screams into the rag in her mouth, squirming frantically in her chair. And I'm *sure* she's screaming my name. When I look at Bishop, he's looking at me too. Yep, they can definitely see me.

"At least they're not dead." Frederick's breath touches my cheek, and I jump high even as I shiver. "You seemed to like them," he continues, "so I did you a kindness."

A kindness? I turn his words over, trying to figure out what he means. I look between him and the screen, where Mom rocks hard against her chair, trying to topple it over.

"If you ask me, being inside a movie is the *best* possible life. Others may disagree."

And then it hits me: they're not in another location, being filmed while they're tortured. They're actually *inside* the screen.

"Remember those books where you get to choose what happens next?" He strokes his chin, as if deep in thought. "Oh yes—*Choose Your Own Adventure*. See, this is just like that. We get to decide what happens next. How exciting is that?"

I want to scream, to sob, to fall into the fetal position and rock until it all goes away. But I can't let Mom see that I'm terrified. She's got enough to worry about right now.

"How about let them go?" I ask, my voice cracking with fear.

Frederick gives a full-bellied laugh and wags a finger at me. "Good one. See, I was thinking more along the lines of tigers. Tigers are fun, no?"

The low rumble of a growl fills the theater.

"Oh no. No, no, no!" I run down the aisle to the screen, but that makes it even worse, because I get a close-up of the tiger's snarled lip, of the drool sliding down its razor-sharp teeth, of the slanted green eyes assessing its meal.

The tiger stalks up to Bishop and sniffs his ear. Bishop flinches, but I can't tell if it's because he's scared or because the tiger's whiskers are poking into his face. The tiger slinks up to Mom next. Mom draws back against her chair and closes her eyes tight, tears streaming down her face. The same throaty rumble vibrates the white fur on the tiger's chest, and Mom whimpers into the rag.

"Let them go!" I yell.

"As soon as you break the spell," Frederick answers.

I look at the screen again and let out an anguished cry.

"See, I had a feeling you were lying back there in the alley. That's why I brought you here. Thought I might be able to convince you . . . by other means."

I take a deep breath and turn to face him. "Look, I told you I don't know how to break the spell, but I'll learn, I swear. I'll stay here until I figure it out. Just let them go."

He shakes his head. "Not good enough."

Mom's muffled screams fill the auditorium. I spin around just in time to see the tiger's paw clawing the air. Trails of crimson slip down Mom's cheek in three perfect lines.

"Oh God. Mom!" A sob breaks free of my throat, and I cry—the ugly kind of cry you do only when no one's watching, or when you just don't care anymore.

Frederick's behind me again, patting my back. "Don't worry. I figure I'll just have him gnaw off an arm, maybe a leg. Wouldn't be a very fun movie if they died quickly, don't you think?"

The lights of the theater dim, then flicker, before growing bright again.

Hope ignites like wildfire in my chest. The Family.

There's a second's pause when Frederick's eyes become wide and he doesn't seem to understand what's happening, and in that second the doors of the theater burst open and a woman enters.

"So kind of you to freeze everyone for me," she says.

I don't know what I expected. Maybe that a member of the centuries-old organization ruling over thousands of witches and warlocks would be older than twenty. Maybe that she'd be wearing a cloak instead of an oversized button-up shirt over a tight little cami, painted-on jeans, and a pair of motorcycle boots. And oh, I don't know, maybe that she wouldn't be a freaking supermodel!

The woman strides down the center aisle with a hip-swaying gait that only the stunningly beautiful can truly pull off without looking stupid. And she totally pulls it off.

Amazingly, when I look at the screen again, the tiger is gone.

"Wouldn't be smart of you to get too close," Frederick says. "We've got the Bible."

She must know he can't open it, though, because she struts past him toward the stage without a pause, her glossy auburn hair—pushed back from her face with a rolled-up bandanna—trailing nearly to her waist. She gives Frederick her back while she inspects Mom and Bishop on-screen with all the calmness of a doctor examining a patient suffering from a common ailment.

"You've angered a lot of people, Frederick." The woman doesn't turn to speak to him, just continues examining Bishop. "We were willing to live in peace, end the war, let bygones be bygones, but you couldn't do that, could you?" She turns now, tipping her head so her hair falls across her high cheekbones, and walks to Frederick with her hands clasped behind her back. "But I have a theory. I think you just can't *bear* knowing that you're"—she pokes him in the chest—"weaker than us."

Frederick looks down at where she touched him. "Weaker?" He wheezes as if this thought is just so funny he can hardly breathe. "You won't be saying that when your neck is in a noose."

"And just why isn't it in a noose right now?" she asks

calmly. Frederick's laughter falters, and a smile spreads across the woman's face. "That's right. Because of a witch's spell. A spell too strong for you to break."

"It's just a matter of time." Frederick's lips form a hard line. "We'll get it open, and you'll be the first one I hunt down when we do."

"I look forward to it." She glances around the theater.

"It's not here," Frederick says. "We're not that stupid, Jezebel."

Jezebel pauses a moment, as if to decide whether Frederick is lying about the Bible, then shrugs. "Even so, I think I'll take Bishop with me."

Frederick laughs. "That little brat—"

"Yes, that one. Release him now."

I speak for the first time in the whole exchange. "What about my mom?"

Jezebel looks at me with eyes a shade of green usually reserved for cats. "What *about* your mom?"

I exhale a small breath. It's hard to decide who I'd rather throw to the tiger for a late-night snack: Frederick or her. "So she's good enough to protect your Bible for years, and now you just toss her aside like, like—"

"Save the comparisons for someone who cares." Jezebel turns back to Frederick. "Release Bishop or die. It's your choice."

"You couldn't kill me," Frederick says.

Jezebel doesn't move, doesn't even blink. There's a

whoosh of air, then a flash of movement, and suddenly a seven-inch dagger is suspended in the air, a hair's width from Frederick's temple. His wide eyes dart to the side, and I have to say, I like the fear I see there. I might be impressed with Jezebel's skills if she hadn't looked at me like a beetle scuttling across the floor just moments before—a beetle she was considering crunching under her boot.

"Now," Jezebel says. "If you'd kindly release my boyfriend, I'll consider not burying this knife in your brain."

20

Hold on, what did she just say?

"Do it now, Frederick," Jezebel says. "My patience is not what it used to be."

Metal clangs in the background. Jezebel doesn't look away from Frederick, just holds up a hand, and the huge black pipe careening through the air toward her head clatters to the ground like a No. 2 pencil.

"Nice try," Jezebel says. "Another move like that and this blade gets better acquainted with your brain." The knife vibrates, like it's struggling to stay back and might speed forward into the sweaty skin at Frederick's temple at any moment. "You have three seconds."

Frederick's nostrils flare. "Fine." He whirls his fingers at the screen, and the rope around Bishop slackens and falls to the ground. Then Frederick tips his fingers forward, and Bishop is sucked through the screen with a loud *pop*.

Bishop stumbles off the stage. He checks out the red marks the ropes left across his arms, then shrugs.

"Now get rid of this." Frederick gives a minute nod toward the knife, because any larger a gesture would mean contact with the blade. "A deal's a deal."

"What deal?" Jezebel's eyebrows knit. "I don't recall making a deal."

"Very funny." Frederick's Adam's apple moves up and down as he swallows.

Jezebel laughs and looks at Bishop, who hikes up his pants as he nears.

"I was just about to save us," he says, "but thanks anyway." Bishop winks at Jezebel. Then, finally, he looks at me. "Hey, Ind. Glad to see you in one piece."

Jezebel glares at Bishop. "Well, it's just a regular old lovefest in here, isn't it?"

"The knife?" Frederick's voice shakes with barely controlled anger and more than a bit of fear.

"Will you not shut up?" Jezebel rolls her eyes, and for a minute she reminds me of another beautiful, bitchy girl I know. "Last I checked, the person with the knife gets to make the rules." She looks at Bishop. "Ready, Bish?"

Bish? really?

She doesn't wait for his answer before walking down the center aisle, doing that hippy sway that I've just decided *does* look stupid on her.

"You get back here!" Frederick calls to Jezebel, like a parent admonishing his child.

"My mom!" I frantically look between the knife still trembling at Frederick's temple, Jezebel's retreating back, and Mom on-screen writhing against the ropes holding her to the chair.

"I thought we covered this topic," Jezebel answers without turning.

I take a two-second break from hating Bishop to plead with him with my eyes. He calls, "I'm not leaving without her."

"Then stay," Jezebel says, without breaking stride.

"Fine," Bishop snaps back.

I decide I hate him a bit less. Which would be great, if I weren't scared shitless, because now the knife at Frederick's temple has disappeared, and Frederick gives me a wicked smile.

"Well, isn't this *interesting*." He adjusts the lapels of his suit.

"It is." Bishop nods emphatically. "I've never seen a sorcerer so close to tears before. Hey, are you okay, man? I can grab you a glass of water from the concession stand if you'd like. Maybe a moist towelette to clean off your face."

Frederick's jaw hardens, and he self-consciously touches his sweat-soaked brow.

The double doors of the theater close with an air of finality. Jezebel's done it. She's left us to die at Frederick's hands.

I shoot my gaze to Bishop and give him a look I hope says "What the hell? Now what? Huh? Huh?" And he sends me one back that says "Relax, I've got this covered."

Frederick wags his index finger at Bishop. "That's very funny. A sense of humor is a great attribute. In fact, you might not know this about me, but comedies are my favorite kind of movie." Frederick grins at me, pale blue eyes sparkling, and my stomach knots up all over again.

"And do you know what I find particularly funny?" He pauses a moment, as if to let us answer. "Irony."

Frederick gestures toward the screen. I slap my hand over my mouth at the sight I find there. The same knife that moments ago was pointed at Frederick's head now trembles at Mom's temple. Mom's wide gray eyes dart to the blade, which gleams in the spotlight. She closes her eyes tight, her body racked by the force of her sobs.

"Bishop, do something!"

The double doors burst open again. An irritated Jezebel stands in the doorway, one hand balled on her hip. Bishop smiles at me, and the look he sends me now distinctly says "I told you so."

"Frederick, release the woman," Jezebel commands.

"Nah." Frederick drops into one of the red seats facing the screen. "I think I'll watch this one through to the end."

Jezebel starts down the aisle with heavy-footed steps, until a large dog—a huge, slobbering rottweiler—appears just feet in front of her, blocking her path. I instinctively hide behind Bishop, but Jezebel doesn't even flinch. Not when the dog growls, a low rumble from deep in its chest. Not when it pushes back its pointed ears and leans back onto meaty haunches, as if about to attack. Not when it leaps into the air with a startlingly loud bark. Nope, Jezebel continues walking, as if putting one foot in front of the other is such an inconvenience, and holds up a hand. The dog hits an invisible barrier inches from her face, then goes flying to the side, landing against the mural-covered wall with a whimper before dropping to the ground.

I'm torn between awe at her power and disgust because it's a dog! Sure, it was going to kill her, but couldn't she have placed it in a magic cage or something else less brutal?

The dog licks its wounds, not even attempting to make a second attack, while Jezebel continues down the aisle. She doesn't make it two more steps when hundreds of arrows shoot from out of nowhere, whistling as they dart through the air, poised to land in her chest. She flicks them away with a wave of her hand, and the arrows fly up toward the ceiling, stabbing into the starburst mural and shattering lightbulbs in the chandelier. A rainstorm of glass falls to the carpet. I look at Frederick, wondering just what he'll throw at Jezebel next.

The red-and-gold carpet rumples up, and Jezebel nearly loses her footing, but then she lifts into the air as if suspended by wire. "Seriously?" she says. "*That's* the best you've got?"

Frederick laughs. "Those were just the previews. I think you'll particularly enjoy the main feature."

I hear their caws before I see them. Birds. Hundreds of black, beady-eyed vultures, owning the air around Jezebel. I thought it wasn't possible, but there's fear—terror, actually—seared into the delicate lines of her face.

"Oh no," Bishop mutters.

"What? What?" I tug at his arm, but he ignores me and watches Jezebel.

She recoils left, then right, whipping her head around as the birds circle her, their wings flapping so hard and fast, it's the only sound in the auditorium. One bird tries to peck at her with its hooked beak, and she swats it away. The bird smacks against the wall just like our dog friend, but I can see that it was an effort, that Frederick has found her weakness.

"Something the matter?" Frederick looks over the seat back and smiles, then twists around to drape his legs over the row of seats, fingers laced over his stomach.

Bishop scoops me up around the middle and lifts into the air.

"What are you doing?" I cling to him, not because I worry

he might drop me, but because I really, really don't like my sudden proximity to the birds. One flies so close to my face that its feathers brush my cheek. I let out a squeal, burying my face in Bishop's chest.

I make a promise to myself that if I somehow, miraculously, make it out of this mess alive, if I somehow *am* a witch, I'm going to get good at magic. Because aside from my mother's life being in danger, I can't think of anything I hate more than this helpless, useless feeling.

Bishop grunts and mumbles under his breath, swatting at the air with big sweeping gestures, until the birds are pushed back and there's a space around Jezebel.

"Snap out of it!" Bishop yells.

Jezebel peeks out from around her arms, held up in front of her face, and her shoulders relax a fraction.

"Do it," Bishop urges. "I can't hold them off for much longer." And he isn't lying. The birds flap angrily at the circle holding them back, inching forward bit by bit.

Jezebel takes a deep, shaky breath, and with one flick of her hand, the vultures smack against the wall, landing in a black heap forming a perimeter around the theater. The sound, like hundreds of football players running into defensive dummies one after another, sends a shudder down my spine. But no guilt, I note, unlike when the dog got hurt, because somehow it's different when I felt my own life in danger. In fact, what I feel is a thrill—we're winning. We're getting out of here alive!

But when I look at the screen again, a choked sob catches in my throat, and my heart sinks down to my stomach like it's weighted with lead.

Mom is slumped forward, pale and lifeless, and a steady flow of thick blood drips around the hilt of the blade buried deep in her temple.

21

"No!" I stretch a hand toward the screen, tears streaming down my face. "No, no, no, no, no!"

Bishop tenses beside me, and we drop to the floor. My feet haven't even touched the carpet when Bishop releases me from his grip and disappears. I sink to my knees, drained of the will to even stand without support.

Bishop materializes behind Frederick's seat. Frederick tries to run, but Bishop snags him around the neck, and they both jerk violently left to right as Frederick struggles against his captor. Jezebel struts up to them, holding a coil of thick rope in one hand and swinging the noose in the other.

"Saw you were a fan of rope," she says, a sneer spreading across her face.

I look away just as garbled choking sounds fill the theater. My stomach lurches. Something surges up my throat, and I puke. I puke and puke and puke until there's nothing left to bring up, not even bile, and my throat stings and I'm heaving for air, and I don't even bother to wipe away the mess dripping down my chin.

I don't know how long I spend like this, sobbing as I stare at the oily spots floating in my puke, until a shadow falls over me and breath rushes against my ear.

"It's over." Bishop scoops me up like he doesn't mind that I'm covered in vomit, and all the while I want to tell him, "Of course it's over—Mom's dead. Her life is over. My life is over," but I can't form words, because that'd involve moving my lips and jaw and that's too much to think about, too much to bear. So I just stare into his dark eyes, and he stares back, and I feel nothing, nothing, nothing. He bends down and kisses me on the forehead. It registers that his lips are soft and that I didn't think they would be, and that Jezebel is his girlfriend and he just kissed me, but that's it.

"We hanged him." There's pride in Jezebel's voice, like I should clap her on the shoulder or jump up and down to celebrate.

I look to where she indicated and instantly wish I hadn't. Frederick hangs from a rope tied to the rafters, his arms dangling lifelessly. His head is bent unnaturally to the side, and his skin is so purple it might be called black. And his eyes—they bulge out of his head, staring at me unblinking and making a whole-body kind of fear rise through me. Even dead he has control over me.

"We used rope," she says. "Get it? Just like he used on Bishop and your mom."

I glare at her.

"What?" Jezebel says. Her confused expression clears. "Oh! You want to give it a go?" She holds out her hand, and a knife appears in her palm. I recoil from it into Bishop.

"Jezebel, for Christ's sake." Bishop gestures to the screen.

She rolls her eyes, and the knife disappears. "What? It's only fair."

Fair. That's a funny word. Is it fair that I get to live, and Mom doesn't? That she was the one to die when she wasn't even a witch, when being a witch is all she ever wanted? The injustice of it fills me with so much rage it tears open a ragged hole in my chest, consuming me, eating me from the inside out. And yet, when I open my mouth to scream or cry or *anything*, no sound comes out.

I watch Jezebel as Bishop carries me down the aisle, and I realize that I do actually feel something stronger than anger and sorrow and pain: hate. I hate the Priory for what they did, and I hate Jezebel. If she'd just pushed Frederick to let Mom go when she had the knife to his temple, instead of leaving the theater, Mom wouldn't be dead.

We're almost out the door when a thought hits me.

"Wait!" I manage, grabbing on to the doorframe for leverage. "What if it's just a trick? We need to get her out. We need to check if she's okay!" I'm frantic with the sudden idea that it's all been some horrible joke the Priory played on me in an attempt to get their way.

But Bishop just shakes his head.

"B-but you can fix her, right?" I ask, hope laced through the words.

Bishop looks away quickly.

I grasp his shirt. "You can fix her, *right*?"

"Jezebel knows a lot of people," he says. "She'll find someone who can get her out of the screen."

"And then?"

"And then you can bury her. It's the best we can do."

I close my eyes right as the doors swing shut behind us.

I don't know how we find Paige. All I know is that by the time we spot her huddled in an alley a few blocks from the theater, a mess of snot and tears, the sun has crept up over the horizon, and the sky has turned the dusky gray blue of dawn.

"Indie!" She barrels into me so hard it would knock the breath out of me if I had any left.

She searches my face, and all her happiness at finding me washes away. "Your mom, is she . . . ?"

I give a tiny shake of my head; the simple act forces a painful groan out of me. Paige pulls me against her and lets me cry into her shirt. And then the three of us wearily stagger down a newly awakened Hollywood Boulevard without saying a word.

The car's right where we left it in the parking garage. It still works, even after the beating it took. So there's that. I lie in the backseat of the Sunfire, my head resting in Paige's lap. I don't remember the car ride, or falling asleep, or being carried up to my room, but it all must have happened, because when I blink my eyes open next, I'm in bed. The sun spills light through the windows, and Bishop is fast asleep in the wooden chair at my computer desk, his head tucked uncomfortably into his chest. I remember Mom, what happened, and my heart aches so intensely it chokes the breath out of me. I burrow back under the covers until sleep dulls the pain.

22

Bishop is gone. A block of sunlight streams through the window, warming my cheeks and lighting up the dust floating above my bed. Cicadas chirp a morning chorus. Children yell and squeal as they play in their yards, and someone nearby mows their lawn. Today's just another day. My world came crashing down yesterday; my gut and my heart and my head hurt so profoundly I can't imagine a worse pain. Mom is gone and is never coming back, and today's just another day.

I want to scream. I want to scream until this hole inside me goes away.

Knuckles rap softly on my door, and Paige pokes her head

inside. "Oh good, you're up." She steps inside, only to shift awkwardly at the entrance.

"Is she really gone?" I whisper, so quietly I'm surprised she hears me.

She climbs onto the bed and pulls me into a hug. I want to scream, but instead I cry.

We stay in bed all day.

———•———

I wake Wednesday morning to clanging in the kitchen. For a bittersweet moment I think it's Mom, but reality rears its ugly head as I wake fully, and I remember she's dead.

I swing my legs over the side of the bed. My bones creak from underuse, and when I stand, I waver for a minute before finding my balance. A film coats my teeth, and my bladder feels like it's going to explode.

I leave Paige snoring in bed and slog across the hallway to the bathroom. Mom's toothbrush glares at me from the holder next to the sink. I know if I pull open the shower curtain, I'll find her special smelly soaps sitting in the rack under the showerhead. The ache inside me roars to life. Getting out of bed was a bad idea.

But I do want to know who's in my kitchen. I walk downstairs toward the sound of pots banging and find Aunt Penny elbow-deep in pancake mix.

"I'm making pancakes," she helpfully points out.

I try to force a smile, but it's like those muscles don't work anymore.

Aunt Penny angrily whisks the pancakes with a cheerful smile. It's so bizarre to see her smiling right now that I sink into a chair at the kitchen table and just watch her. Paige walks in moments later.

"Hope you're hungry!" Aunt Penny says.

With a flourish she places a heaping platter of crumbly pancakes on the table. Paige bravely forks one onto a plate and cuts a small bite, while Penny eagerly watches.

"Well?" she asks as Paige swallows.

"You probably should stick to acting," Paige finally says.

Aunt Penny's smile breaks away and she dissolves into tears that leave her gasping for breath.

"I was just joking!" Paige cries. "Oh my God, I didn't think you'd get so upset." She looks to me for help.

"I just don't get it," Aunt Penny hiccups, messy tears streaming down her face. "Why Gwen?"

I plug my ears like I'm five. I just don't want to hear this. But of course I do anyway.

"What have the police said?" Paige asks.

"That it was a random crime," Penny answers, shaking her head. "A mugging gone bad."

It's a ridiculous story, but with just one glance I know it's the story Paige and I will run with.

Aunt Penny tears at her hair. "How could she leave me? I don't know how to do this without her. I don't know how to raise a kid!" She takes a deep breath and sobers up, chewing on the corners of her fingernails as she paces the kitchen. "My apartment is too small for three girls, let alone four. I'll have to move in here. I wonder what the mortgage payments are for a place like this. Indie, do you know what the mortgage payments are? Oh God, why did I quit the Bistro? The tips weren't *that* bad. I wonder if they'd take me back if I apologized about the whole plate incident."

And then it hits me. Aunt Penny is my new guardian.

———————•—•———————

It turns out funerals are the hottest social event next to prom. Hundreds of people show up, the whole of Fairfield High crammed into the pews and packed along the walls like sardines in a can. Devon sits a few rows behind me, dressed in the same dark navy suit and salmon tie he wore to his uncle Leonard's funeral last June. A few spots over from him is Bianca. If this had all happened a month ago, it'd be her sitting next to me instead of Paige. The few feet separating us feel like miles. And though I'd never give up Paige's friendship—not in a million years—a small part of me wonders if this tragedy will be what brings Bianca and me back together. If this will be the one thing that makes her realize what a terrible friend she's been, makes me somehow find it in my heart to forgive her. But I shake off that thought almost as quickly as it comes.

The priest drones on in his heavy monotone, and I don't feel bad about tuning him out. Mom wasn't even Catholic and wouldn't have wanted a church funeral—a fact Aunt Penny just couldn't understand and I didn't have the energy to fight. And so I count the panes in the stained-glass mural, wondering who does that for a living—stains glass for churches—so that I don't have to think about what I'm doing. Which is attending Mom's funeral.

At some point, the priest must have said my name, because everyone is looking at me, and Aunt Penny gently nudges me forward. The church grows so silent you can't even hear a single rush of breath as I reach the altar. I pull my carefully folded note out of my pocket, but I can't get past "My mom was," no matter how many times I try. The entire congregation erupts into sobs at the sight of my raw emotion. It's almost like they're here because they care about me. Almost.

I stay just long enough not to be rude, carefully avoiding Bianca and Devon (I don't want to talk to them in a vulnerable state, lest I end up forgiving them both), and then I slip out the back and wait in the car until Aunt Penny and Paige find me.

And then Friday. There are no more official funeral preparations to take care of, and the casseroles have stopped coming, and everyone's left the house—even Paige, because she isn't as lucky as me and doesn't get a whole week of bereavement leave—and Aunt Penny's off taking a business class to learn how to run an occult shop she has no interest in running but has to because how else is she going to raise me? And I sit down at the kitchen table and realize that Mom really died. That she'll never come back. And that I am alone. Cold hands reach out for me, threaten to pull me into a dark place where I might never escape, and I let them.

It's like I'm trapped in a block of ice that nothing can penetrate. Everything around me is just a blur of color, a flash of movement, garbled sounds I can't quite decipher and don't want to. Time passes like sludge.

I burrow under the covers of Mom's bed and breathe in her scent, which still clings to the fabric. And then I take out my cell phone and listen to Mom's voice-mail message— "You've reached Gwen. Leave a message and I'll get back to you as soon as I can"—over and over and over, until sleep finally claims me.

Aunt Penny comes in every now and then to leave food on the dresser and to try to coax me to come downstairs for this reason or that, but I don't get out of bed. I don't care if I starve. I wish I'd died too.

———◆———

I wake at an ungodly hour to the sound of low murmurs outside the bedroom door. I sit up and rub the sleep out my eyes just as the door swings open, and Aunt Penny and Paige are there.

"I've had enough of this," Aunt Penny says. Paige just shrugs apologetically.

I lie back down and roll onto my side, defensively pulling the covers up to my chin. But Aunt Penny marches to the end of the bed and yanks down the covers so that I'm exposed in my pajamas.

"Hey!" I yell, sitting up and reaching for the blanket.

"Look, I'm sorry to have to do this," she says, holding the blanket away from my reaching grasp. "I know what happened was terrible, really terrible, but I care about you, and I can't watch you do this. It isn't healthy. Yes, your mom died, and I'm sorry about that—you don't know how sorry I am. But you have to get out of bed. And for God's sake, woman, you have to shower."

Paige throws open the blinds, and offensively bright light streams in the window. It's almost like she's on Aunt Penny's side or something.

"Breakfast is waiting downstairs," Aunt Penny says. Reading my thoughts, she adds, "It's takeout from Coffee Bean, so you have no excuse."

Paige follows her. The door clicks shut, and I'm left gaping at the empty space. I have the feeling that I should be mad—it's only been a week since my mom was murdered. But I'm not mad.

I amble downstairs toward the scent of coffee and fresh bagels. In the kitchen, Paige and Aunt Penny have their backs to me as they bicker about which station to watch on the little TV. They speak to each other in the way that only longtime friends do, and I have to wonder how long they've been doing this—conspiring to get me well. Something sparks inside me. I hadn't thought it was possible, but a tiny hole has chipped away at the ice block, and a sliver of light streams inside.

23

Bereavement leave is over, and I have to return to school. (Okay, so technically the leave was over a few days ago, but I guess I just needed more time to grieve the death of a parent. I must be weird.)

Following my little experience returning to school after Jarrod's party, I'm used to staring. Staring I'm prepared for. Staring I might be okay with. It's the pity I can't stand. Every person I see in the halls of Fairfield High drops what they're doing when I near so they can show me their best abused-puppy impressions. People I don't even know squeeze my shoulder, pat my back, mumble apologies as I pass through crowds.

And I get it—they're trying to be nice, trying to make me feel welcome—but it makes it so much worse.

I'm unloading my second-period books into my locker when the *clack clack* of heels announces Bianca's arrival. She's wearing a blush-pink, flutter-sleeve top I've never seen before, and her peroxide-blond hair is cut shorter than I'm used to. It tears at a part of me I didn't know still existed. Because none of this would have surprised me if we'd still been friends. I'd have shopped for that top with her; I'd have helped her agonize over the best haircut. I wonder when this is all going to stop hurting so badly, because right now it feels like I'm grieving two deaths.

"How are you?" Bianca asks, placing a hand on my arm.

"Great," I say. "Except for the whole part where my mom died and you slept with my boyfriend."

Bianca's jaw hits the floor.

So maybe now's not the best time to confront her. But maybe I don't care. Did Bianca ask me if it was a good time when she stripped naked and hopped in bed with my boyfriend? (Hint: no, she didn't.) The horribleness of Mom dying is not going to overshadow what she did to me.

"You know, I think I finally figured it out," I say. "I've been thinking about it a lot, and I just couldn't get why my own best friend would treat me so bad. For a while I thought it was because of Devon, but it didn't make sense why you were so mad. You didn't even like him. I mean, it wasn't like I stole him from you. But then it hit me: you wanted us to be popular together. It was okay if I was popular, just not more popular than you."

"That's not true!" she says, too quickly. "I was just drunk, that's all. It was a stupid mistake, nothing more—"

"No, let me finish, I'm on to something here. Devon wanted me, and you just couldn't stand that. You couldn't stand that I had the hottest guy in school. So you cut me down to make sure everyone knew you were better than me."

"That's *so* not true." Bianca crosses her arms and juts her chin up, but I can tell by her flaring nostrils that I've hit on the truth. I don't care if she admits it; I know I'm right about this.

"You know, a real friend would've been happy for me." I can feel the prick of tears beginning, but I don't want to cry anymore, so I change course. "Oh, and in case you were wondering, I'm not going to make it to practice this week. Just not feeling very peppy."

I skirt around her. I should feel triumphant, having finally told her what was on my mind. But I don't.

———·—·———

I'm sitting in math class, pointedly ignoring Bianca and contemplating the impact of what I've done, when a crumpled-up note slides across my desk. I glance behind me and catch Devon retracting his arm, pretending to be focused on the blackboard.

I take the note into my lap and flatten out the edges. *Glad your back*. "Your" instead of "you're," scrawled in the messy script of a boy. I stare at it for long seconds, unsure how to respond.

I reread the note and decide there's no secret motive or hidden meaning. He's just being friendly, though a part of me wonders if he still has feelings for me. It's stupid and hypocritical that I'd care—there isn't a world where I'd take back a cheater—but I can't deny it's nice to feel wanted.

Thx, I add, resisting the middle-grade urge to write, *Do you still like me? Check yes, no, or maybe.*

Mr. Lloyd has the biggest stick up his ass about people not paying attention to his lectures, so I wait until he turns to write on the blackboard before slipping the note onto Devon's desk. When Mr. Lloyd drops his chalk and bends to pick it up, another note bounces across my desk. I catch it just before it falls, cradling it in my lap against Bianca's prying eyes.

You still up for homecoming?

Homecoming? I glance at the date Mr. Lloyd has written in the corner of the blackboard. September twenty-fifth. I recall the homecoming posters—A MIDSUMMER KNIGHT'S DREAM—plastered all over the school. Homecoming is less than two weeks away. A few weeks ago this was the most important thing in my life, and I've completely forgotten about it. Guess evil sorcerers killing your mom has that effect.

I stare at the note for a long minute, trying to decide what to say. It's not fair that I chewed out Bianca, while meanwhile, here I am making small talk with Devon—I won't let him gloss over what he did to me either. Finally, I simply write: *Why?*

I'm fully aware of how immature it is to hash this out via note, grade-school-style, but I didn't want to talk about it before now. And who knows if I might ever want to again? I slip him the note.

Another one tumbles onto my desk a moment later. *Don't mean to be pushy. I asked around, but everyone good already has a date now.*

I roll my eyes.

No, I meant why did you do it, I reply in angry bold writing, then chuck the note at him so hard it almost flies off his desk.

He takes an inordinate amount of time to reply, and I can hear his pen scratching out reply after reply. I wring my hands under my desk and realize that I'm praying he comes up with something so satisfying it makes the whole cheating scandal go away and life return to normal. It'd make everything so much easier.

Finally, another note tumbles across my desk. *I'm sorry. Don't ruin homecoming for us both because of a stupid mistake.*

You'd think he'd at least wait until my second day at school to remind me that he's an ass. I spin around and give him a heavy-lidded stare. After thirty seconds have elapsed and he's sufficiently uncomfortable, I say, "Just in case you didn't get that, the answer is no."

I face the front of the class. Everyone is staring at me, Mr. Lloyd included. He doesn't reprimand me, though. That's the thing about pity: you can get away with a lot.

In all, my first day back at school is a success.

Aunt Penny's still not back from her business course when I get home from school. And since Paige is at her violin lesson, I'm left watching episodes of *Days of Our Lives* that Mom DVR'd, while I listen to her voice-mail message over and over, because it turns out I like to torture myself.

Someone knocks on the door. I guiltily stow my phone away before peering through the keyhole.

Bishop.

"You going to let me in or what?" he says.

I chew my lip.

"Hello? Burning midday sun? You know how I hate being exposed to the elements for long periods of—"

I open the door, and Bishop's face cracks into a smile.

"How'd you know it was me answering the door?" I ask. "Some kind of reverse keyhole magic?" I glare at him. I don't even know why I'm mad, but it seems like the thing to do lately, so I just go with it.

"Actually, I knew it was you because you're the only person who wouldn't answer the door right away. And I heard your footsteps."

I huff. "Look, can you just tell me what you want so I can—"

"What?" He cocks his head. "Go back to listening to that damn voice-mail message on repeat?"

My mouth drops open. "Have you been spying on me again?"

He rolls his eyes. "Please. Paige told me."

"Oh."

"Yeah." He walks around me into the living room and spins around in front of the couch. "Is there anything else you'd like to accuse me of? Ring on the coffee table? Doormat slightly askew?"

I rake my hair back with a shaky hand.

"I'm kidding," he says. "I understand."

I look up and meet his eyes, but for some reason I can't hold his stare, and drop my focus. He shines his ring on his slim black pants.

"So where's your leather, anyway?"

He looks down at the light gray T-shirt he sports, tattoo-covered arms held out in front of him, and shrugs. "Didn't feel like wearing leather today."

"But you wear leather when it's eighty degrees outside."

"Yeah, so?"

"So if it's not practicality, what is it?"

His eyebrows knit, as if trying to decide what's come over me.

"Never mind." I shake my head, turning away.

"Because we're going to try out your magic today, and I wanted to be comfortable." Before I can even think about a reply, he takes two long strides up to me, so he's blocking the sun slanting in through the venetian blinds. "You have to practice to protect yourself. I can't do it forever."

I glance up quickly.

"What? You thought it was just pure luck there haven't been any attacks since that night? Jez and I have been watching the house."

"So you *have* been watching me," I say, my arms tensing at my sides.

"Not inside your house. I'm not a pervert, as much as you and the State of California would like to think I am."

"And what's *she* doing here, anyway? I don't want her near my house."

"Jezebel wants to help you."

"Help me? Why didn't she help me when my mom was still alive? She didn't seem too willing to help then."

"Trust me, this is unusual for her. I've known Jez a long time and she's never done something out of the kindness of her heart. I'm thinking it's guilt, but she'd never admit it."

"So let her feel guilty." I ball my hands into fists, nails digging into my palms. "I don't want that . . . that *tramp's* help."

Bishop waves a hand for me to continue. "Go on, get it all out of your system."

"She didn't care about helping me when Mom was tied to a goddamn chair! When a tiger was ready to eat her for a snack! I don't want *her* help!"

"Done?" he asks.

I let out a hard breath. "God, you're so infuriating. Why did you come here? Just to make me feel worse?"

"I told you, I came here to help you test out your magic. They've fallen off the radar—Leo, the rest of the Priory—we don't know where they are. They've got the Bible, and for whatever reason, they think you're the only one who can break the spell on it. An attack could happen at any moment. You need to be prepared." He grips me by the forearms. "If you don't practice, if we don't fight back, you're just telling the Priory that you give up, and then your mom's death means nothing. But if you do something, make something positive come out of this"—he raises a hand to stay my objection to the word "positive"—"you won't just be telling the Priory that they can't kill at will, that there are consequences to pay, you'll be telling them you'll be prepared if they come for you, so they don't stick a knife in *your* head next time."

I exhale, my heart pounding hard and fast in my chest.

"I'm sorry." Bishop relaxes his grip. "But it's true. That could be you, if you don't do something."

I can feel it coming. I try to push the memory to a corner of my mind, but it's too strong to be brushed aside.

Mom is slumped against the ropes that hold her taut to the chair. Thick crimson blood drips from the hilt of the knife buried in her head, down onto the frayed ropes and over her blue-veined skin.

Something like a scream crossed with a whimper slips out of me. Bishop pulls me against his chest and shushes me, pressing down my curls with his big hand as I cry into his shirt. He feels warm against my cheek and smells like laundry left out to dry in the sun. I stay there against him, breathing in his scent, until I catch my breath again. When I've quieted, he pushes back to look at me.

"Look, I have a deal. I can't give you your mom, but there is something I can do."

"What? What is it?"

"It's unhealthy, and I really think you need to start moving on, and I'd never suggest this if you'd given me any other choice—"

"Say it, Bishop."

He sighs. "You give me a day to practice magic, and I can let you hear her voice again. And not just on voice mail."

A spark starts low in my stomach. "How?"

"Through a complicated scientific theory proposed by Stephen Hawking, called the—"

"Bishop," I warn.

"Magic, obviously. How else?"

I tilt my head to the side, challenging him to crack another joke.

"It doesn't always work," he continues. "And even if it does, she won't speak to you directly, just on playback. Like with the voice-mail message, except with real conversations she had."

Except it won't be the same one line, over and over. The spark in my stomach shoots up into my chest like a firework.

"But I have to warn you: you may hear things you don't like. People say things when no one else is around, things they don't want others to hear. Maybe it's best to leave the memory of your mother alone—"

"I'll do it."

"Are you sure? Because—"

"I said I'll do it."

Bishop nods once. "Okay, but remember the other half of the deal. I do this for you, you give me one day—one full day—of magic."

I pretend to mull it over a minute before saying, "It's a deal."

He doesn't have to know I was already going to agree.

24

Finding a parking spot on Melrose is a nightmare on a good day. It's about a bazillion times worse when a huge chunk of the street just past the shop is closed off for filming of the latest A-list, crash-bang blockbuster.

Hordes of paparazzi and squealing, fainting fans hoping for a glimpse of a muscled-up celebrity clog the sidewalk and the cordoned-off area surrounding a prop ambulance. I'm not sure whether I want to hate them all, or envy them for having nothing more important to do than watch some guy doing his job. And I don't care that it's hypocritical, and that weeks ago I'd have been right there with them, elbowing my way to the front of the crowd.

"Want to check it out?" Bishop asks as we approach the shop and the chaos of the movie shoot looms closer.

I don't even dignify that with a response. Save to glare at him.

My footsteps grind to a halt in front of the shop. I stare up at the big cursive letters on the shop's canvas awning. THE BLACK CAT. I give a wry laugh, recalling the day nine years ago when Mom received a loan approval from the bank, and before doing any of the more practical things, like finding a location, ordering stock, or taking a bookkeeping course, she insisted we pick a name for the place. Something original. Something to entice tourists in off the street. When I suggested the Black Cat—about the least original name for an occult shop—she happily agreed. Agreed because it made me happy. Tears well in my eyes, which makes Bishop shift awkwardly next to me. I'd forgotten how weird he is about that.

"Does it really get better?" I ask, wiping my face. "I mean, everyone says it'll get better with time, but does it really?"

I hold my breath, because everything depends on his answer. How can I do this, go on with life, if every memory knocks the wind out of me, every day steals my breath away.

Bishop stuffs his hands into his back pockets and stares vacantly at nothing. And then he finally speaks. "Not better. Just less"—he shrugs—"intense, I guess. I don't know how to explain it. It still hurts to think about my mom, but now I cope with it better." He looks at me, a twist of dark hair falling in front of his face.

"Less intense," I repeat.

I guess less intense is okay. I'll take any emotion over what I feel now, which is the worst kind of pain. Pain times a million. Pain on acid.

"Was she a witch?" I ask.

Bishop smiles so brightly his eyes crinkle in the corners. "One of the best."

And now I can't look away from his face, because I've latched on to the idea that one day, some time from now, I might be able to think of Mom and smile the way he's smiling: a real smile that reaches all the way to his eyes. "How did she die?" I ask.

His smile melts away.

"Don't answer that," I say, burying my face in my hands. "It was rude of me to ask."

"Cancer." His voice is even, but there's bitterness laced in the word.

It's so unexpected, I look up from behind my fingers. "But—but she was a witch?"

He nods. "A witch who smoked two packs a day."

I shake my head. "But wasn't there some magic spell that could make her healthy again? That's just such an ordinary way for a witch to die. I mean, not ordinary." I pinch the bridge of my nose.

"There are some spells that work for a while, but then the magic fades and the cancer comes back stronger than before." He gives a bitter laugh. "But I wasn't a warlock then. There was nothing I could do anyway."

His voice cracks, almost as if he might cry, but then he cleas his throat and claps his hand on his thighs. "Well, there goes my lifetime supply of sappy minutes. We going in or what?"

I touch his arm to let him know I can see past the veneer of his joke before fishing in my purse for the shop keys. My hands shake like a crack addict's in withdrawal. I don't know why I'm so nervous—the house holds as many, if not more, memories than the shop—but somehow this place is entirely Mom. It was hers, and she loved it so much.

I'm not ready to go inside, but I slip the key in the lock, because I'm desperate to hear her voice. Bishop says the magic he plans to use only works where the energy of the dead is the strongest—something about energy never being destroyed once it's created—and I can't think of any better place to find Mom's energy than here.

The door pushes open with a creak that sends a chill through me.

And I don't even have to walk in to know the magic will work. Mom's presence here is as undeniable as traffic in Los Angeles. It's not just her scent, which is so strong it's like burrowing under ten of her duvets. It's the fading smell of Murphy Oil, the only wood cleaner Mom trusted on her floors. It's the sequined scarf slung over the chair behind the till, the inkwell and pen next to the till's ledger, the unique way she arranged books on the shelf—laying a stack horizontally every now and then, "for variety." It all screams Mom.

I step into the fractured block of sunlight coming through the big picture window, circled by dust motes that dance lazily around me. When I close my eyes, I can almost see Mom at the bookcase, dusting off the spines of the how-to witchcraft books, wild curls spilling down her back. She turns and sees me, and a bright smile lights up her face. Then she makes some crack about gracing her with my presence, because I'm always so busy with school and cheerleading.

A second later, a shadow falls across my face, and I'm pulled into the present again.

I open my eyes and find Bishop leaning against the window. He looks at me—"appraises" would actually be a more fitting word—and his face takes on an unreadable expression.

"What?" I ask.

"It might not work, you know."

"Yeah, you said that. Like six hundred times."

"I just don't want you to be disappointed. It's not really complicated or anything, but it only works if, well, if . . ."

"What?"

He sighs. "If you're really close with the person who died. Not just anyone can summon the voice of the dead." He holds up his hands in defense. "I'm not saying you weren't close, I'm sure you were. I just want you to be aware that there is a chance, that for whatever reason—"

"It'll work." My voice is even, giving him no room to argue, but as soon as the words leave my mouth an ice pick of worry chips away at my confidence. Maybe it won't work. Maybe I *was* too busy with school and cheerleading. Maybe I wasn't as close with Mom as I thought. "So how do we do this?" I ask.

Bishop looks around. "Too bright in here," he mumbles.

"I can take care of that." I walk around him and pull down the blinds until we're cloaked in darkness, save for the thin strip of light that creeps around the blinds' edges. "What now?"

"Now we light candles."

I snort.

"What's so funny?" Bishop asks. "Candles give our magic extra power. Like an energy drink for witches."

"Candles? Really?" I remember the night of my two hundredth full moon, when Mom and Paige both suggested we light candles and I'd said that it wasn't a séance. They'd been right all along. "Okay, well, there are candles on the shelf over—"

There's a quiet *pop*, and then Bishop's holding a tall taper candle. A golden flame flickers under his chin.

"Oh. Uh, great."

Bishop smiles before striding backward and dropping into a cross-legged position. He places the candle in front of him and pats the floor, indicating for me to sit.

"Should I bust out a Ouija board too?" I sit across from him and mirror his cross-legged pose. "Okay, what now?"

"Now you relax and quit asking so many questions." He gives me a pointed look, then reaches around the flame to take my hands in his. I swallow, looking first at his warm fingers cradling mine, then at his eyes, which are tightly closed, séance-style. Jezebel enters my mind. Beautiful, bitchy Jezebel—his girlfriend.

"Why are you helping me?" I ask.

He doesn't open his eyes. "I thought I said no more questions."

"Last one."

He sighs. "You wouldn't be able to summon without me transferring power to you."

"Oh." A feeling I don't want to think about analyzing squeezes my chest, but I won't let him off that easy. "But why are you here at all?"

He exhales. "I don't know. Can we just focus on this? Close your eyes."

"How do you know they're not already closed?"

He pops one eye open, then closes it again. "Close your eyes, Indie."

I do as I'm told. And I decide that it's true what they say: when you lose one sense, the others become heightened.

How else can I explain the way the hair on the back of my neck stands on end when Bishop brushes his thumb along my index finger? The way I've become acutely aware of the sweat collecting along the lines of my palms. The way the sound of the wood floor creaking as I adjust my position echoes like an old house in a storm.

I don't have time to analyze the phenomenon further, though, because my hands suddenly grow so hot that I know it has to be the magic working. The heat borders on uncomfortable. I try to pull my hands back, but Bishop grips my wrists, not letting go. My fingertips begin to sting, an almost too painful to stand, pinprick burning, like taking the first step into a hot bathtub.

"Bishop." I try to wriggle free, but his grip becomes like iron shackles around my wrists. Panic ignites inside me. I open my eyes, because I'm sure my hands are on fire, that the candle is burning me, but it's not. Bishop's chest rises and falls with slow, even breaths, and his jaw is so relaxed that his lips part slightly.

Doesn't he feel this? Doesn't this hurt him too?

But just when I think I can't stand the heat any longer, it shoots up my arms like a current of electricity, collecting in my chest in a swirling, molten ball of lava, like the sun has been plucked from the sky and shoved into my body. Only now it's not painful. In fact, it's undeniably exhilarating.

"Wow." I exhale, breaths coming hard and fast.

"Think of your mom." Bishop squeezes my hands.

I need only that little reminder for her image to come charging back into my mind. And I'm thankful that, for once, it isn't Mom from the theater, but the smiling, wild-haired Mom I thought of moments ago.

"Will I be okay leaving you two alone?"

I suck in a quick breath.

Mom.

I open my eyes and whip my head around, sure that I'll find her in this room, but she's nowhere to be seen. Disappointment weights my shoulders. I stare into my lap, biting down on my bottom lip to stop it from trembling. This is still great, I remind myself. I heard her voice.

I think about what she'd said. *Leaving you two alone.* Who was she talking to?

Bishop sighs. "Close your eyes or it won't work."

I close my eyes, and as soon as I do, another surge of heat shoots up my arms, and Mom's speaking again.

"I'm kidding, but, Indigo, could I speak with you for a moment?"

Indigo? So she was talking to me. But why can't I remember this conversation? I rack my brain for a clue, but all I get for my efforts is a vague déjà vu feeling.

"I don't mind your boyfriend coming over, it's just . . ." She pauses.

I don't remember having this conversation at all—how can I not remember this conversation?—and yet it's as though my responses are just out of reach, sitting on a virtual ledge in my mind, ready to tumble over and out of my mouth with the tiniest puff of wind.

"Just don't let him near the book, okay?" Another pause, long this time, and I worry Mom won't speak again, that the magic is over, but then she says, *"I'm serious, Indigo. If that book gets into the wrong hands—"*

My stomach pitches. The book did get into the wrong hands, and look what happened. Tears spill down my cheeks, and even though it's been quiet for a long time and I feel Bishop watching me, I don't wipe them away.

"I told you that you might regret it."

I open my eyes and lock them with Bishop's. "I don't regret it." How could he think I would regret hearing Mom's voice, even if it has opened up so many new questions? Even if I can't seem to shake the strange déjà vu sensation—the same sensation that's been pricking my senses more and more lately—that the summoning caused.

Bishop shrugs. "Whatever you say. Magic time?"

I take a big breath and tuck my hair behind my ears. "I guess."

He pushes to his feet and reaches a hand out to help me up.

———◆———

Daylight seems cruel after the dark of the shop, and I have to shield my eyes against the bright sun as we venture back outside. Bishop follows me and pulls the door closed.

"Give me the keys so I can lock—"

A bloodcurdling scream pierces the air, interrupting his statement.

Tires screech to a halt. A siren wails, and the red lights of an ambulance flash behind the crowd gathered around the movie set.

"Did the big bad ambulance scare you?" Bishop jokes, hopping down the stairs next to me, but his words float right out of my head. In its place is an image. A memory. Blood. So much blood. A body in the street. Leather.

Someone yells "Cut!" and the ambulance lights flick off.

My heart pounds an erratic beat.

"You okay?" Bishop touches my elbow, his dark eyes narrowed with concern. "I was only joking, you know."

I blink at him.

"Indie, you're starting to worry me, and I don't worry." He steps in front of me and takes me by the shoulders. I stare at the faded leather of his collar.

"Why do I remember you hurt on a sidewalk?" I blurt out.

Bishop's hands fall to his side. "You remember that?"

I don't tell him I have no idea what "that" is, because I'm scared he won't tell me the truth when he finds out how little I really understand. "Yes, I remember. What I want to know is why I forgot at all. You don't tend to forget stuff like that."

"Crazy," he mumbles. "Why wouldn't the wipe hold?"

"Wipe? What are you talking about?"

He pushes hair back from his face with shaky hands. "This is crazy. I've never heard of this happening before. It must have been the summoning. It must have unlocked something in your brain—"

"Yes, it's crazy. Can you just explain what's going on, please? How come you were hurt, and why didn't I remember it until now?"

Bishop sighs, looking around like he's considering how best to tell me what he has to say. Or not say.

"Spit it out. I want the whole truth, Bishop."

He turns to face me, looking me dead in the eye. "The Priory killed me before they stole the book."

"Killed you?" I ask, incredulous.

He nods.

I let out a humorless laugh. "So, what are you, a ghost? Because I don't see how else that can be possible."

Bishop spins the ring on his finger. "Remember when you asked me about this ring? Well, it's much more than a family heirloom. It's the most important thing I have."

I look at the chunky silver ring, the number two etched deep in its center, that occupies Bishop's middle finger. "What's the two mean?"

"It's the number of lives I have left."

Extra lives? I exhale. "So where can I get mine? Because that'd really solve a lot of my problems right now."

He shakes his head. "No can do. Only one way to get a

ring like this: a dying witch has to transfer her powers to you. So unless you know a witch on the outs or keen on killing herself, you're out of luck."

I chew my bottom lip, turning his words over in my mind. "Your mom gave it to you, then? Before she died?"

Bishop drops his gaze to the sidewalk, still twirling the ring.

"Okay, why did the Priory want to kill you?"

He shrugs. "It's like they knew about the Bible, somehow, though I'm not sure how. They've been tracking any witch or warlock sent on a Family mission, but they've never killed anyone until now. I don't know how they knew. But the point is it didn't work. Pain in the ass busting out of the ambulance strapped to that gurney, though." He shakes his head. "Come on. Let's go." He starts toward the car.

"And I saw you?"

He spins around and walks backward while talking to me. "Yep. You wore this horribly cute miniskirt with suede boots. Not that I was looking or anything. And let me just say this: it's a good thing I had an extra life, because I sure wasn't getting any help from you."

I want to say something, *anything,* but I can't, because I have no idea what he's talking about. I jog to catch up to him.

"So why don't I remember any of this?" I get the impression he's trying to change topics. And judging by the way he's practically running away from me, I think I'm right to suspect he's still hiding something. "Be honest. You're not telling me everything."

He stops walking and rubs his forehead like he can erase the crease in his brow.

My stomach knots up so tight I'm not actually sure I want to hear what he has to say. But it's too late.

"They erased your memory."

My stomach does a nauseating flip. "Wh-who?"

"Frederick and Leo. They erased your memory. Not everything, obviously"—he scratches his nose with his thumb—"just, you know, stuff about the accident and about them. . . . They did it to everyone who saw me die. That's why you can't remember that conversation with your mom. It was right after you saw me land on the street."

My skin prickles as the distinct sensation of being violated creeps over my body. I'm about to ask when this happened when I remember the day I awoke in Mrs. Malone's office, only to forget why I was there in the first place. I'd thought I was going crazy.

I give my head a tiny shake. "But how?"

"They're powerful sorcerers, Ind. Use your imagination."

"Well, what's stopping them from doing it again?" I ask, ignoring his badly timed jab.

"A sorcerer can't erase a witch's memory. You're only at risk before you come into your powers. Same with mind reading. So cross your fingers you're a witch."

"Yeah. I'll get right on that."

The vague, nonsensical comment Frederick made that night in my bedroom about plucking what he needed out of my head suddenly makes sense.

"You're lucky, if you think about it. Those guys could have killed you like they did me and made the whole thing disappear. I think the only thing that saved you was that you had information on the Bible."

I snort. "Oh yeah, I'm really lucky. Luckiest girl on the planet." I recall the drive to the Chinese Theatre the night Mom died, when I'd questioned Bishop about recognizing him from somewhere, and he hadn't bothered to tell me about the time I saw him die. I glare at him through eyes narrowed to slits. "Why would you hide this from me?"

"Whoa, there," Bishop says. "What's with the suspicious tone?"

"What's with all the secrecy? In fact, I don't think I want to go anywhere with you until you can give me a good answer. Why didn't you tell me before now?"

"You want to know why?" Bishop stalks over, so that his shadow falls across me. "For one, those guys could have wiped out your whole memory. The fact that they didn't meant they might be back. Two, I wanted to protect you. What they did to you, it doesn't feel good, does it? Feels like you've been violated? Yeah, that's what I thought. I didn't want to tell you because I care about you, and I didn't think seeing me die and then coming face to face with evil sorcerers were memories you wanted to cherish for the rest of your life. I thought, 'Hey, I would be happy to forget those memories,' but then maybe I'm just weird. Maybe I need therapy. There. You know the truth now. Are you happy? Do you want more information? Like where I get my hair cut? Franky's on Sunset. And I got this T-shirt at the thrift store on West Pico. And Quilted Northern is my preferred toilet paper brand." He storms off toward the car.

I should be angry—I think I'm pretty within my rights to have been suspicious—but everything he said after "I care about you" flew right out the window. Despite just finding out some pretty horrifying news, despite losing Mom, my best friend, and my boyfriend all in the span of a week, a tiny bit of hope flutters its wings inside my heart. Because it turns out I still have a lot to be thankful for. I just didn't know where to look.

25

I slide the car into drive and merge with traffic. When Bishop turns up the radio, I don't slap his hand away or complain we only listen to his music. In fact, I'm incredibly grateful to the aggressive punk-rock lyrics for sucking up the silence that I'm sure would radiate with awkwardness in the wake of his outburst.

"So, where to?" I ask.

"Mount Washington," Bishop answers, buckling his seat belt.

"We're trying flying first? Don't think you're going to lob me off the side of a mountain and hope I learn fast, because I'm not in the mood."

Bishop shakes his head. "Nope. We start with the basics. Moving small objects: paper clips, pencils, et cetera."

I roll my eyes. "Sounds like fun. What do mountains have to do with this?"

"They don't. We're going to my place."

I glance over at him, expecting to see humor in his face, but he bobs his head to a song on the radio.

He can't be serious. Mount Washington is one of the city's most exclusive neighborhoods. Plunked among rolling green hills in the northeast of Los Angeles, the neighborhood features views of downtown L.A., the San Gabriel Mountains, and, oh, roughly one zillion canyons and valleys. And of course, homes so huge they can only be referred to as mansions.

"*You* live in Mount Washington?"

Bishop laughs. "What? Where did you think I lived?"

Actually, now that I think about it, I've never really put much thought into where Bishop lives. He's always just been there. Though I guess he does have to go somewhere at night, hang up his leather jacket, lay his head down to sleep. But Mount Washington? Really?

I navigate the Sunfire through rush-hour traffic so insane there is no chance for thoughts of anything but avoiding an accident, until the lush green hilltops announce we've arrived in his neighborhood.

"This one here, on the left." Bishop indicates what is, hands down, the nicest mansion on the block.

The Spanish-style home rises three stories high and

stretches out for what seems like an entire city block. Towering palm trees and lavish gardens spring up from every corner of the property, lattices of ivy climbing the white stucco walls all the way to the terra-cotta roof. I start counting the arched windows, framed in ornate cast-iron grilles, but lose count around eighteen and give up. And I always thought white houses were boring.

I pick my jaw up out of my lap long enough to ask a question. "You live here?"

"I'm starting to get offended," Bishop says.

Shaking my head, I pull the car around the giant fountain in the middle of the horseshoe driveway. "It's just a lot fancier than I expected from a guy who wears leather constantly."

I glance at the fountain as we pass and realize that it's a mermaid, and that the water is shooting from her nipples. "Ugh."

He laughs.

I park the car, and we step out into the fading evening sun.

Bishop leads the way to the entrance and pushes the big wooden doors open without having to unlock them first.

"Bit laissez-faire on the security, don't you think?" I say, following him inside.

He digs into his back pocket and tosses his wallet onto a glass table in the foyer. "I'm a warlock, remember?"

"And they're sorcerers." I spin around, admiring every detail of his home, from the exposed wooden ceiling beams to the smooth archways leading down various corridors to the spiral staircase rising to the second floor.

"Exactly. You think a locked door will give a sorcerer pause if he wants to get inside my house?"

"Guess not," I answer. "But what about other people? Your run-of-the-mill burglars?"

He shrugs. "Then I'd just drum up some more stuff, I guess."

The pieces of the puzzle begin coming together. "So that's how you afford all this?" I gesture around the house. "You created it with magic?"

"Created the money, anyway. Too much energy to conjure objects for long periods of time."

Before I can ask another one of the boatload of questions on my mind, my ears perk up at the sound of metal rattling upstairs. I dart a glance at Bishop, but it's as if he hasn't noticed. The rattling intensifies, and a dog barks—a jarring sound that is all too recognizable.

"Bishop . . ." My voice warbles with uncertainty.

There's a crashing sound, and then thundering steps overhead. My heart goes into overdrive, but when I look at Bishop again, there's a smile spreading slowly across his face. The thudding becomes louder and louder until my fears are confirmed, and a rottweiler barrels to the top of the spiral staircase, a frantic mass of meaty limbs tripping over each other in their desperation to reach us. The dog regains its footing and charges down the stairs two at a time.

Every one of my instincts tells me to run, but something about Bishop's smile roots me in place. Still, I recoil as the large dog approaches and Bishop still doesn't use his magic against it. And when the dog is just one leap away, I can't help the scream that escapes me.

The rottweiler jumps up against Bishop's chest, and delivers sloppy kisses all over his face.

What the . . . ?

Bishop kisses the dog back, murmuring, "Good puppy," and "That's my baby," into its fur. I relax my shoulders a tiny bit, but my heart still races as Bishop finally straightens and pats the dog on its head. "All right, Lumpkins, that's enough."

When he faces me, my mouth is hanging open.

"What?" He adjusts his shirt, which twisted up during the lovefest.

"Is that . . . ?" I gesture hesitantly at the dog.

"The dog from the theater? Yes."

"And his name is?"

"Lovey Lumpkins."

"But . . ."

Bishop scratches the dog behind the ears, and Lumpkins's eyes loll back in his head. "But he needed a home, and I just happened to have one."

"But he's evil."

Bishop draws back like I've just insulted his mother. "Indigo Blackwood."

"He tried to kill Jezebel!" I cry, though now that I think it over, that is one of his most endearing qualities.

"That was before," Bishop says, and bends low to hug the dog around his thick neck. "And plus, Frederick made him do it. He's learned his lesson. He knows not to mess with Daddy. Isn't that right, Lumpkins?"

"Daddy?" I laugh, because this is just too ridiculous.

"You hungry, or should we just get started?"

I shake my head to snap out of the spell this sight has put me under. "No, I'm not hungry."

Bishop straightens and hikes up his pants. "All right. Follow me."

He leads me upstairs, and down a wide, light-filled corridor, Lumpkins following disconcertingly close on my heels.

When Bishop opens the door to what has to be an office, Lumpkins runs inside and hops up on a leather couch, curling into a slightly less intimidating ball. I decide he's okay for now, and enter.

Pale sunlight streams in through ceiling-high arched windows, lighting the room in soft white. The walls—or rather, the tiny cracks visible around the collage of random framed pictures of every shape and size that clog the walls—are such a rich shade of gray that they almost appear black. The leather couch Lumpkins rests on is pressed against one wall; opposite it is a long black desk, flanked on one side by a potted ficus tree and on the other by a tall, skinny bookcase with an odd assortment of items like a broken globe, a battered copy of *Catch-22,* and what appears to be a bowling trophy. A fluffy bearskin rug covers the dark wood floor, and beanbag chairs in every color cushion the corners of the room.

It's so Bishop that if I hadn't seen the naked mermaid fountain outside, this room alone would convince me that this really is his mansion and he isn't playing a trick on me.

I crane my neck to see the framed pictures that reach all the way to the ceiling, trying to assign a common theme to the randomness. There's a giraffe, a woman's naked back, the Ramones in concert, a man holding up a huge fish, Britney Spears circa 1999, and a picture of a mountain under the words REACH FOR THE TOP that seems like it would be better suited in a guidance counselor's office.

"Who's this guy with the fish?" I ask, pointing to the picture of the man.

Bishop sidles up behind me and leans over my shoulder, so near that his chest brushes along my shoulder blades. A surge of heat runs down into my stomach.

"That's my uncle."

"Really?" I ask, my voice higher than usual. "The one from Texas?"

He nods.

I examine the picture closer now. The man's middle-aged, with short gray hair poking out the sides of his baseball cap and a large belly poking out from under his neon life vest.

He looks nothing like Bishop at first glance, but when I peer closer, there is something similar in his smile, in the lines around his mouth. I wonder why Bishop lives all alone in Los Angeles when he's got family in Texas.

"Is he . . . ?"

"Alive?" Bishop finishes for me. "Yes."

I want him to elaborate without me having to ask, but he doesn't go there. In fact, he doesn't say anything at all. And so then it becomes really strange that he's still pressed up against me. My heart gallops like a prize racehorse. He must realize how weird this is too, because *how could he not?*

I swallow. "Do you see each other often?"

"Not anymore. I lived with him for a year after my mom died, but I haven't talked with him much since he asked me to work for him remotely. Big honor." I can practically hear him rolling his eyes. "Guess a year of living with me *is* a lot for one person to handle." He says it self-deprecatingly, but I get the sense that he's hiding something under the humor.

"What is it you do for him, exactly?" I ask. "I haven't noticed you doing a lot of work since I've met you."

"Odd jobs, really. Nothing interesting."

I narrow my eyes at him over my shoulder. "Well, that's vague. What does your uncle do?"

"He's a councillor for the Family."

I remember Bishop telling me at the Hollywood sign that it was his job to fill me on all things witchy if I turned on my two hundredth moon. "Nothing interesting, hey?"

He smiles, shaking his head so that his hair falls in front of his face. "Not until recently."

I face the picture again, processing this new information and adding it to the Bishop picture that's being painted in my head. Bishop's mom died. Bishop's uncle cast him out (at least in his own mind). Bishop has no friends. And yet he's constantly making a joke out of everything. Either he's the most easygoing person on the planet, or else all the flip comebacks, all the womanizer talk, all the crass jokes, they're just his way to hide the fact that he's lonely, that he's dying to connect with someone. I test my hypothesis. "So, do you really think your uncle sent you away because he was sick of you?"

Bishop lets out a wry laugh. "Well, don't try to spare my feelings or anything."

Heat blooms across my cheeks, but Bishop claps a hand on my shoulder. "I'm kidding. He probably thought it'd be a good idea because of Jezebel. Little did he know she'd follow me here."

I let out a false titter, because it's just so *awkward* when he talks about Jezebel.

"So how has your girlfriend been keeping, anyway?" I blurt out.

"She's not my girlfriend," Bishop says.

"Nice try. She said so herself at the theater, and you didn't deny it."

"Jezebel hasn't been my girlfriend in months."

Hmm. "So why'd she say that, then?"

"Because she's not used to not getting what she wants. We dated, I broke it off, she begged me to take her back, I refused. I guess she thinks she can wear me down."

I know I shouldn't ask more, that it's really none of my business, but I can't help myself. "Why'd you break up with her?"

"Haven't you noticed her little attitude problem?" he asks.

"Oh, I've noticed. I just thought you might be more inclined to forgive something like that in light of the fact that you're a horndog and she's, you know, practically a supermodel." I focus intently on the wall, embarrassed at the edge of jealousy in my voice.

He laughs. "Oh, trust me, I tried. And tried. And tried."

"Ugh, thanks for the mental image."

He squeezes my shoulder. "Look, Jez and I started dating at a bad time. I'd just moved to Texas after my mom died. I was feeling a little down, and she was great for a while. Distracting."

I wait for him to continue, but he doesn't. "And then what?" I ask.

"And then it wasn't great anymore. It wasn't real between us. It was just sex. I realized I was using her to try to forget about my mom, and it wasn't working."

I try to think of something encouraging to say, because he's finally opening up and not hiding behind humor, but all I can think of is that they had sex. And it was great.

"Well, at least that answers the question of why Jezebel's been so eager to help out," I say.

"Let's not talk about Jezebel anymore."

I become hyperaware of his hand on my shoulder. That we're both single, all of a sudden, and alone.

I clear my throat to break my train of thought (and whatever else is going on between us). "So, let's get this over with. The sooner I can defend myself, the sooner I won't need anyone to protect me."

I said it offhandedly, but now I realize that truer words have never been spoken. I made a promise to myself that night—that if I made it out of the theater alive, and if I was truly a witch, I'd master my magic and quit relying on others to protect me. And I intend to keep my promise.

Somehow when I pictured doing magic, it didn't involve crappy office supplies.

I stare at the paper clip on the carpet and will it to move. Sweat beads on my forehead. Thoughts of food consume me, and there's a slow throbbing in my temple from all the mental exertion. But the clip doesn't budge, hasn't budged once in the hours I've spent trying.

I blow out through pursed lips, determined that the magic work this time, and reach around inside me for the heat Bishop says is there, that I only have to grasp onto and move to my fingertips, where it can be manipulated to my will with simple incantations. Which just sounds *so* easy when he says it.

Please, paper clip, I think. *Just move so we can end this cat-and-mouse game.*

After another hour of staring, with Bishop splayed out on the couch, reading *Catch-22* with Lumpkins at his feet, my internal dialogue becomes noticeably more terse. *Move it, goddamn it! I haven't got all day. Move it or I'll snap your twisty metal limbs in half.*

Despite the threats of violence, the clip doesn't budge.

"Ugh!" I chuck the clip across the room. It lands with a *plink* against the desk.

Bishop doesn't even glance up from his book. Maybe because it's the third time I've chucked the paper clip, and the third time I've picked it up and refused his offer to break for a snack. I want to get this right. I have to get this right. Mom wanted nothing more than to be a witch all her life; it would somehow make this whole mess just the tiniest bit better if I got to carry out her dream.

"You need to relax," Bishop says.

I walk over to the couch, blocking the last of the sun from his face. He still doesn't look up. I pluck the book from his hands and drop it on his stomach.

"Hey," he grunts. "I was just getting to the good part."

"How sad. So look, can we not try something a little more exciting? Flying, maybe?"

He rolls his eyes. "How do you expect to fly if you can't even summon your magic? You've got to learn the basics first."

It's my turn to roll my eyes. "Can I get a little more direction here? It's obviously not working."

"You need to find it on your own. But no worries—this is the hardest part. Once you know how to find it, it'll always come easy. It's like riding a bike: you can't unlearn it."

"If it's even there," I mumble. "What about candles? Energy drink for witches and all that."

He snorts, which turns into a cough, and I get the distinct impression he's fighting hard to rein in a huge grin.

"What?" I tilt my head to the side, hands on my hips. "You made that up, didn't you?"

He shrugs and sucks in the corners of his lips.

"You jerk!" I punch him in the shoulder.

"Ow." Bishop cradles his arm, full-on laughing now. "What's with you being so violent?"

"You make me this way."

"Oh, sure. Abuser blames the victim. Classic excuse." He picks up his book and flips through the pages, searching for the spot where he left off. "Channel all your pent-up anger and you could single-handedly wipe out the Priory."

"Hardy har har." I turn to retrieve the paper clip from the desk but Bishop's words, intended as a joke, bounce inside my head. Couldn't hurt to try, I decide.

I think about everything that makes me angry: Bishop,

reading his stupid book while I struggle; Bishop, using his magic like it's the easiest thing in the world, while I burst a blood vessel in my brain from all the concentration and get nothing, *nothing* for my efforts; the fact that I have to do this at all, because there's a group of evil sorcerers that wants me dead, all because I might be a witch, something I never asked to be.

My nostrils flare, and my breath comes hard and fast. I clench my fists and dig my nails into my palms, knuckles turning white. A warm sensation starts low in my stomach, like I've just drank hot chocolate too quickly. Sheer excitement almost knocks the heat right back to where it came from, but I force myself to concentrate, to think of the thing that makes me angriest: that they killed Mom, took her from me forever, and in the most brutal way possible.

The heat moves up into my chest, igniting into the ball of fire I felt earlier when Bishop summoned Mom's voice, pulsing not just in my veins but in every cell of my body, surging from my center out into my arms with every beat of my heart.

"Do you feel it?" Bishop asks, bent low to my ear. I didn't even hear him get up.

I nod.

"Repeat after me: *Sequere me imperio movere.*"

I glance over my shoulder at him, simultaneously shocked to hear this strange language slipping so easily from his mouth and sure that he's screwing with me, because I've never heard him utter a word to make his magic work, but he repeats it again, urging me to copy with a little shove.

"*Sequere me imper . . . imperi-*something or other—" I groan as I feel the heat slipping away.

Bishop squeezes my shoulder. "Concentrate. Focus on the clip. And repeat after me. *Sequere me imperio movere.*"

I sigh, leveling my gaze at the paper clip on the desk. "*Sequere . . . sequere me imperio movere.*"

The left end of the desk pitches up so quickly that loose papers flutter to the carpet. A gasp tumbles out of my mouth, my heart pumping at a dangerous speed. The break in concentration makes the desk thunk back to the floor. But before Bishop can say a word, I lock eyes on the desk again and repeat the words. "*Sequere me imperio movere.*"

"What the . . . ?" Bishop's hand falls from my shoulder. He steps in front of me, eyeing the levitating desk with a mixture of awe and incredulity.

Once it's up, I'm happy to discover it's easy to move the desk where I want it simply by willing it there with my eyes. It takes everything in me not to grin like an idiot as I float the desk over the wood floor, over the bearskin rug, and drop it inches from Bishop's bare feet, so that he has to jump back lest his toes be squashed.

I did it. My heart swells up like I didn't think was possible anymore. "Oh my God," I say. "I'm a freaking witch."

26

All I want is to get through one full day where absolutely nothing bad happens so that I can bask in the glow of my magic and try to forget about Mom's death and the sorcerers trying to kill me. I don't think it's too much to ask, but no sooner does my butt hit the chair in homeroom the next morning, I get called to the school psychologist's office, where I'm accosted with lame pamphlets for a crisis helpline and a journal that I'm to bring to my new weekly sessions. Great.

I mean, it's nice that the school is concerned about me, but I'm getting pretty tired of the kid-glove treatment. It's like they all think I'm going to commit suicide if they don't ask me how I'm coping at least three hundred times a day.

I'm sitting in history when the overhead speaker beeps, alerting the classroom to yet another Mrs. Malone announcement.

"Ms. Indigo Blackwood, please report to Coach Jenkins in the gymnasium. Thank you."

Seriously, universe?

I stuff my books into my bag and trudge down the hall to the gym. When I push open the double doors, I'm surprised to find a half-dozen massive floats in various stages of completion spread out across the shiny gym floor, twinkling under the harsh fluorescent lights.

I recognize the squad's float instantly—an old-school gilded carriage with big wheels and a velvety roof, pulled by two white unicorns. The carriage was Bianca's idea—to haul the homecoming-court nominees around at the parade— but I'd suggested the unicorns in place of horses, and the whole squad loved the idea. I know it's ridiculous, all things considered, but I feel a pang in my gut that I missed out on its creation, on what could have been had life not completely changed for me. Maybe I do need a therapy session after all.

I swallow the lump growing in my throat. "Coach Jenkins?" I call.

"Over here," Carmen answers. I follow her voice to the back of the gym and find her standing on the bed of a float, snipping at the blue and silver tissue paper of a giant football with a pair of craft scissors.

"Indigo, thank you for coming," she says.

Like I had a choice.

"Please, have a seat."

I sit down heavily on the bed of the float and pull my bag onto my lap. And the whole thing is so depressing—the stupid floats, the way Carmen won't look at me, the corny speech I'm sure to endure. I just want to get this whole thing over with, no beating around the bush for half an hour. "So, my mom died," I say.

Carmen snips away at the tissue paper without responding.

I sigh. "So, do you want me to tell you how I'm feeling or fill out a journal or something?"

She continues with her arts and crafts project as though she hasn't heard me.

"Look, I know I missed a few practices, and I'm sorry I haven't helped with the float, but I don't plan on missing anything else, and I'm totally committed to the squad and . . . hello?" I lean across the trailer, trying to catch her eyes. "Coach Jenkins?"

She doesn't answer.

I knock on the wood, but she doesn't look up.

A sinking sensation washes over me. I cautiously look behind me, and am beyond relieved when no one's there. But when I turn around again, the scarred man who held the knife to Mom's throat—Leo—stands behind Coach Jenkins, a maniacal smirk on his face. My body shifts into panic mode, and I scrabble back.

Leo scratches his marred cheek, and Coach Jenkins scratches her own smooth one.

"Kind of fun," he says.

"Kind of fun," Carmen repeats.

I gasp.

Leo scratches both his armpits, *ooh-ooh* and *aah-aah*ing in a lame monkey impersonation, and so does Coach Jenkins.

Leo holds up his fisted right hand, like a magician performing a trick, and then swiftly jams it into his neck, chortling all the while.

"No, Carmen, don't!" I scramble to my feet, but it's too late. Carmen jabs her right hand—the one holding the scissors—into her neck. Blood spurts out of her mouth as she cackles, falling to her knees.

Oh God . . .

I ease Carmen onto her back and frantically search for something to stanch the blood flow, but when Leo steps around her I have to give up any notions of dressing her wounds. Because if I don't get the hell out of there—and fast—it won't just be Carmen fighting for her life.

I leap off the trailer and dash across the gym, weaving between the floats so fast I nearly lose my footing. I'm almost to the double doors when I hear Leo's voice.

"Not this again," he says.

Palms out, I slam into the door. But instead of it flinging open, my body crashes against the metal so hard it makes my ears ring. Locked. Of course.

Dammit, dammit, dammit. I wheel around and flatten myself against the door, my chest heaving as I gasp for breath.

Leo saunters up. "Indigo, it's been far too long." He smiles, but only half of his face moves. The sight is almost as unsettling as his predatory black eyes, the left one blinking far too frequently, flicking up and down my body.

I suddenly wish I hadn't accepted Bishop's offer to break for the night and take up training again after school today. Because as proud as I was of my skills yesterday, I somehow don't think moving paper clips is going to help me in this situation.

"You know, I always thought you were pretty," Leo says. "I came here to give you one last chance to break the spell on the Bible, but who's to say I can't have a little fun first?" He moves around the carriage, loosening his pin-striped tie. "Frederick never let me have any fun. Could waste half a day lecturing some dumb-shit teenager about a movie no one cares about, but the minute I try to have some fun, it's all 'we're taking care of business.'" He gives a derisive snort. "But Frederick's not around anymore, is he? Thanks to you."

"B-Bishop's protecting me," I say. "He'll be here any minute, any second." I scuttle along the wall as he approaches.

Leo snickers. "And just where is he now, huh?"

Good question. I'd like to know the answer to that myself.

Leo unbuttons his shirt, loosened tie draped over his shoulder, revealing a sallow chest covered in sparse dark hair.

The sting of vomit burns my throat. I scan the room for an escape route. I spot the fire door at the rear of the gym. I'm willing to bet he hasn't seen it—perfect. Except that I have to get there, past Leo, and all without him noticing so that he doesn't lock it with his magic. I'm sure it won't matter that I appear to be in better shape than him. Strong calves are probably not going to help against his magic.

Come on, Indie, think! Think, think, think. I do another quick scan of the room and stop at the first large object I spot—the carriage.

I've done it only once before, under the direction of a practiced warlock, but I try not to think about these little details. Instead I focus on the heat, will it to come, and it does without effort, tingling and stinging my fingertips. Like riding a bike.

But then I realize there's a problem with this plan: I can't say the incantation aloud, because this whole plan revolves around Leo not turning around for at least fifteen seconds, not guessing what I'm up to. I've never done a spell without saying the incantation, never even tried. Panic surges inside me.

Leo steps forward. He reaches his cold hand out and

grazes my cheek with his fingers. I let out a little whimper, and he laughs.

"Don't be shy, now," he says. "I promise not to hurt you *too* badly."

Sequere me imperio movere, sequere me imperio movere, sequere me imperio movere.

The front end of the carriage lifts up—oh my God, I did it!—so that it's balanced on the back two wheels, hovering just inches from the floor, and I find myself strangely grateful that Leo's too busy noisily unbuckling his belt to notice the slight groan of the metal. The upended float wobbles over the floor. It dips up and down as my magic wavers, and I have to bite down on my lip from the mental strain. When it's a few feet behind Leo, I decide it's close enough.

"Sorry I can't promise the same thing," I spit out.

I let the carriage crash to the ground. For a split second, it teeters on its back wheels like it can't decide what to do, and I worry it might fall the wrong way. But then the carriage gains momentum and tips forward. I jump out of the way just as it crashes onto Leo's back, flattening him to the ground with a crack that echoes through the room.

It worked!

But I've patted myself on the back too soon, because Leo's already squirming under the carriage, his low growl turning into a thundering roar. I give him a wide berth and make a mad dash for the fire door, but when I pass Carmen lying in a bloodied heap on the football team's float, my breath knocks out of me. I can't leave her here.

"Carmen!" I rush to her side and try to haul her up, but she's all dead weight. When I hear rustling behind me I have to give up. "I'm so sorry, Coach Jenkins."

I lay her down gently, then run. The door is unlocked—thank God!—and I burst onto the fresh-mown lawn of the football field, so thick with fog it feels as though I'm running into a scene from a slasher flick starring me as Lucky Victim #2.

Every second counts, but I can't help glancing behind me. Leo's already at the door, hands braced against the frame. Blood gushes from his nose as he huffs through clenched teeth.

But he doesn't follow.

And I don't get it.

He must be up to something, I decide. Something bad. I tear my eyes from him and dart a glance around. That's when I see them: Bishop and Jezebel, dashing onto the football field.

"You're late," I call out, slowing to a jog now that the situation is looking entirely in my favor. "Had to go ahead and save myself."

27

I'm all geared up Monday morning to spend hours fielding questions about Coach Jenkins. I was, after all, called down to the gym right before they found her body and was therefore the last known person to see her alive. But after I give my statement to police officers at the school ("We just chatted about the homecoming float, that's all!") and they decide it was likely an unfortunate accident, everyone's too upset to pay any attention to me.

Thea breaks down in homeroom. A few people from the squad have to go home, and whoever isn't going into hysterics in the hallway is loudly recounting their personal anecdotes about the beloved cheer coach/home ec teacher. But in true Hollywood fashion, we haven't even made it to lunch before she's become the butt of a million jokes. I even hear someone from the football team say that anyone who could accidentally stab themselves in the neck with a pair of craft scissors deserves to die. Nice.

Though I don't see him, I'm sure Bishop's out there, somewhere close by, watching my every move. In math class I test my hypothesis by getting a hall pass to use the bathroom. I haven't made it past the water fountain when he appears.

"You shouldn't be going places alone," he says, falling into step beside me.

"I have to pee," I explain. He makes to follow me into the girls' bathroom, but I push him out. "Nice try, buddy."

"It's for your own safety," he says, but he's grinning. I let the door swing closed in his face. Despite the jokes, I know he's feeling pretty bad about the close call yesterday. About Coach Jenkins. And that, in turn, makes me feel a tiny bit safer. At least I know he's on his toes now.

I don't see him again the rest of the school day, but when there's a knock at the door not ten minutes after I arrive home, I'm not surprised to find it's him. He, however, looks mighty surprised to find that I'm pushing him back outside.

"Let's go," I tell him.

He raises his thick eyebrows high, but doesn't say more. "Aunt Penny's going to the shop tonight to do inventory," I explain. "And if I don't get out of the house before she's out of the shower, I'm probably going to get roped into help-ing." Buh-bye, practice time. And if yesterday was any indi-cation, I could really use it.

"Actually, that works out, because it's a long drive to where we're going. We need to hit the road now or we won't get back before late."

"And where is it we're going?" I ask.

"Indie?"

Crap.

Aunt Penny edges downstairs, a silky pink bathrobe tied around her waist and her blond curls twisted into a braid over her left shoulder.

I sigh and move aside in the doorway. "Aunt Penny, this is Bishop. You've seen him around, but I don't think you've officially met."

"Nice to meet you," Bishop says, giving Aunt Penny a friendly smile that she returns with a tight one of her own.

"You too. Hey, Ind, can I talk to you for a minute?"

And here it is.

"Be right out," I tell Bishop, then push him outside and close the door, turning to face my aunt.

Penny sits on the stairs "So what's with this guy?" she asks.

"We're friends," I answer simply.

"Friends?" Her sleek eyebrows arch up high.

"Yes, friends. You know, buddies? Pals? Confidants?"

"I don't know that I like you guys hanging out so much," she says, ignoring my sarcasm. "How old is he?"

I laugh. "Are you seriously lecturing me about boys right now? Do I need to remind you about Stan, or Michael, or Aaron, or—"

"Okay, okay, I get it," she interrupts, her hands raised in defense. "I'm irresponsible, and I've made some bad choices, and I'm twenty-eight and have nothing to show for it, but I'm your guardian now and I take that job seriously. I have to nag you, so let me do that, okay?" A deep frown is etched into her brow. Aunt Penny, who might as well be pictured in the dictionary under "party girl."

"Don't worry," I say, my tone softening. "I'll be careful."

She gives me a grateful smile.

When I go outside, Bishop is nowhere to be seen. But then a horn honks from a car parked across the street, and I follow the sound to find him waving at me from inside a cherry-red muscle car with a yellow stripe across the body. I saunter up and place my hands on the roof, bending to look at Bishop through the window.

"You have a car," I say.

"It appears that way," he answers, grinning.

I exhale. "Okay, so then why have I been driving everywhere? Why haven't I seen it till now?"

"Because I just picked it up yesterday after you left. I hate cars. Bad for the environment."

"Oh, so you're an environmentalist now?"

He nods happily.

"Well then, I'm sorry to be the one to inform you that muscle cars are especially bad for the environment."

He shrugs. "So I'm a bad environmentalist. There's also the small issue of a war with the Priory. Wouldn't do to show up late to a battle because the bus wasn't on time. Are you going to get in or what?"

I circle around the vehicle.

"You like it?" he asks as I drop into the faded red bucket seat.

I snort. "No, I hate it. It's horrible and ugly and I won't be seen in it."

Bishop beams. "It's a 1969 Shelby GT500."

I run my finger over the wood-paneled dash. "Authentic."

"It's great, isn't it? I was worried you wouldn't like it."

"Who cares if I like it?" I say. "It's your car."

He guns the engine in response.

Sure, why don't you wave a cigarette and a bottle of Jack Daniel's out the window while you're busy making Aunt Penny hate you?

Bishop maneuvers the car through traffic until we hit the open freeway. The engine rumbles beneath me. Hot wind snaps my hair across my face, and the radio, tuned to some obscure punk-rock station, blasts a song I actually know. Bishop mouths the lyrics, tapping his hands on the steering wheel as sunlight reflects off his aviator sunglasses. Before

I know it, I'm singing along too. Bishop smiles. I smile. There's a whole lot of smiling going on. And I just know that this memory will be forever burned into my brain, because this kind of magic—the kind that can't be conjured with a spell, where everything is just right, and all your problems vanish for three perfect minutes—doesn't happen every day.

But then the song fades away, and guilt stamps down the thrill of the ride. How can I have a great moment when Mom's dead? What kind of person does that?

Bishop turns the radio down. "You all right?"

I nod and force a smile, looking out the window. He leaves the radio turned nearly to mute, so that the hum of the tires on the freeway is the only sound in the car.

"So are you going to tell me where we're going, or what?" I ask, just to fill the silence.

"The Guadalupe sand dunes," he answers.

I glance over at him. "Um, why?"

"Because it's big and open and there are places in the dunes so remote it's highly unlikely we'll come across another human, which is a rare thing in L.A., and I'd prefer not to have to wipe anyone's memory if at all possible."

"That's great, except remember that whole part about the Priory trying to kill me yesterday? Don't you think it's a bad idea to go out, just the two of us, to some remote sand dunes? They could attack us."

"That's exactly why it *is* a good idea. No way would the Priory think we're stupid enough to be alone after yesterday. They'd think it was a trap."

"Yeah, 'cause it's definitely *not* stupid," I mumble.

"Just trust me, okay? I've got something up my sleeve if that happens, which it won't. I'm completely prepared."

As usual, he has an answer for everything, almost as if he'd planned out this conversation or something. "Hey, have you done this before?" I ask.

"What? Drive my 1969 Shelby GT500 to the Guadalupe sand dunes with a hot cheerleader? No, I haven't. Why?"

"No, jerkass," I say, grateful he has to pay attention to the road so he doesn't see my pink cheeks. "I meant teach someone magic. Have you taught other gir—er, other people before?"

Bishop laughs. "Have I taught other girls? Nope. No other boys, either."

I shake my head, looking out the window instead of at him so that I can suppress the smile threatening to spread over my face. Soon his laughter ebbs, and the radio takes over the silence again.

After driving for miles, we exit the freeway, and a short while later we arrive at a huge parking lot with a squat information building and a single car parked close to its entrance.

"This is it?" I ask.

"Not quite." Bishop shifts the car into park and opens

the door. "No vehicles allowed past here. We walk the rest of the way."

"Since when do you care about rules?" I slam my door and follow him toward the edge of the lot, where the sand dunes begin.

"I'm making an effort. Don't want to sully your impressionable young mind." He glances back and grins.

"You're not even two years older than me," I point out. But then a thought strikes me. "Unless you're secretly two hundred years old or something?"

Bishop laughs at the horrified look on my face. "Nope. I'm really eighteen."

"Oh good," I say, relieved. There are already too many ways I feel inferior without being a virtual toddler in the life experience department compared with him.

Bishop smiles, then lets his shades slide back down onto his nose.

We've been walking for only minutes, me doing routine shoulder checks for the Priory, when I become aware of the sweat beading my brow, the hot sun tingling my bare shoulders. I'm at least appropriately dressed for the heat, having donned a pair of cute canvas shorts and a loose ballet top this morning, whereas Bishop sports his usual trim black pants, motorcycle boots, and a V-neck band T-shirt. He left his leather jacket in the car, but I still don't know how he can stand all the superfluous clothing.

I squint at the huge sand dunes rolling across the horizon, set against a sky so blue it looks like it's been Photoshopped.

"This far enough?" I ask.

He shakes his head. "Bit farther. Then we'll fly farther in."

I groan.

It doesn't take long for the hard sand under my shoes to turn doughy as the dunes begin to rise in small undulations. Soon, my legs sink ankle-deep into the sand, and I have to lift them higher and higher to travel across the soft soil. It's so much work that I almost forget to be worried about the Priory attacking. As if reading my mind, Bishop stops abruptly and scans the area around us.

"Ready?" he asks, taking off his shades and slipping them into the neck of his T-shirt.

I exhale. "So ready."

And then there's this awkward pause that never existed between us before.

"Should I . . . ?" I hold my arms out to the side.

Bishop jerks into action. "Yeah, sure, good idea." He places one arm under my knees and another around my back, cradling me like a baby. His face is just inches, maybe centimeters from mine, but I don't dare look at him. Not when he swallows, and it's so loud it would be comical if I were in the mood to make fun of him. Not when he asks if I'm ready, and the way his breath—minty and woody, like he's been chewing on a toothpick—rushes against my ear and makes goose bumps rise over my arms. Not when his fingers touch the bare skin on my back, and that touch makes my heart pound against my rib cage so violently I'm sure he must feel it. And so when he lifts up off the ground, I pretend to be riveted by the sand dunes rippling twenty feet beneath us, like giant waves in an angry sea, the sand twinkling in the bright sun.

Something's got to be wrong with me, I decide. Mom's death must be taking my emotions on a wild roller-coaster ride—amplifying everything, not just the hurt. This makes me feel a bit better about myself.

After a few minutes of flying, Bishop lowers us to the ground. When he places me on my feet, I teeter a bit, like I've just had a few drinks.

"Little tip," I say. "Might want to pick another remote location next time. Mount Lukens, maybe? It's boiling out here." I fan out the shirt that clings to my sweaty skin.

Bishop gives a pointed look down at my chest. "No, I think I made the right choice."

I could kick myself for nearly smiling. "If you don't cut it out I'll be forced to rate your performance as Very Poor on the Magic One-oh-one feedback questionnaire."

Bishop gasps. "Scoring poorly on a test! You wouldn't threaten me with something so vile."

"Very funny. Can we get started, please? It's getting late."

"Sure thing, boss." Bishop holds out a hand, and a broomstick materializes in it. Not a common kitchen broom or even a janitor's push broom. Nope, this is a broomstick that TV and movie witches would be proud to ride: a bundle of yellow straw tied to a long brown handle.

I look from the broom to Bishop. "You can't be serious."

"More serious than I'll ever be." He pushes the broom into the space between us.

I push it back. "*You* don't use a broomstick to fly."

He pushes it back toward me. "And *I* also don't say my incantations aloud, but then I've been a warlock for two years and you're only just learning. Take the broom."

I sigh and snatch it from him.

"Great," he says. "Now that you've learned to harness your magic, flying should be easy."

I roll my eyes, because he had said harnessing my magic would be easy, but he ignores me and continues.

"Harnessing your magic was about learning to manipulate the energy in your body, which you used to move the desk yesterday. Flying applies the same principle, but to manipulate energy outside your body. Instead of pulling all your heat into your core and out through your fingertips, you push the heat down and out of your body to manipulate the air currents instead of objects, and voilà—that's flying."

"Sounds simple."

"I'm glad you agree." Bishop points at the broomstick, which I'm holding away from me like a used tissue. "Straddle it."

I glare at him.

He raises his hands. "What else do you call it?"

I reluctantly do as he says. "You better not be screwing with me about this broom or I'll be pissed."

"I'm not screwing with you. It's much harder to focus on invisible air currents than it is a tangible broomstick."

"So it could be anything, then? Not just a broomstick?"

"Just focus, Indie."

Sighing, I close my eyes, and the heat flares to life in my stomach. But pushing it down rather than pulling it up is another beast entirely. I push and shove and slam the heat down, but it's as if I'm trying to jump through a springy new mattress; I can get a few inches of movement, but mostly it's impossible. Yep, just as I anticipated, flying isn't as easy as Bishop makes it out to be, even with the stupid learner's broomstick.

Time ticks by. The sun moves across the sky, reminding me just how long we've been out here alone, and without any witnesses—we might as well be wearing freaking neon targets on our backs for all the opportunity we're giving the Priory to attack. I've already drained the water Bishop packed for the trip, and I can pretty much bet on a wicked sunburn come morning. I don't want to quit—wouldn't normally dream of quitting—but there hasn't been even a glimmer of progress and we still have the long drive home ahead of us.

"Okay, I'm done." I toss the broomstick into the sand

and stalk away from Bishop with my hands laced behind my head. To suck at flying after doing well with moving objects is more than a little disappointing.

"Don't give up." Bishop, for once, jogs to catch up to me. "You were getting so close."

"Close?" I laugh. "No I wasn't. I'm hot and sweaty and tired, but close? Not even slightly."

Thank God he doesn't argue the point, because I'm feeling violent. He chews the inside of his cheek a moment before speaking. "There is something more I can do to help, but you won't like it."

"There's something more, and you haven't told me?" Yep, definitely feeling violent.

"You won't like it."

"Tell me, already. I want to fly. What is it about the hours of practicing in the heat that hasn't given you that impression? I'm willing to—"

"I drop you from a height," he interrupts.

I close my mouth and give him a glare.

"Adrenaline can help you harness your magic in the right direction."

"Yeah, right. Sort of like candles are energy drinks for witches?"

"Fine, don't believe me."

"Great, I won't. You know, you might gain a little more credibility if you stop bullshitting me for fun all the time."

"You don't want to do it, just like I thought—I get it. But you should know I wouldn't let you get hurt. I'd catch you before you hit the ground, if it came to that."

I shake my head and huff and roll my eyes a bunch, but all the while his words are sinking into my brain. "You won't let me hit the ground?" I ask.

He shakes his head.

"Say it out loud. Promise."

Bishop places his hand over his heart. "I, Bishop, hereby promise not to let one Indigo Blackwood hit the ground."

I bite my lip, contemplating. "What the hell. Fine. Let's do—"

Bishop snags his arm around my middle and lifts into the air so suddenly and quickly that I jerk in half like a foldaway bed. My hair sucks around my face and my stomach does a flip, the landscape below becoming smaller and smaller until I'm sure NASA is probably picking up our movement on their satellites. And then the hands around my middle are gone. There's a split second where I reach out to anchor myself on something solid, before I realize there's nothing to grab.

I plummet. A whole-body fear clutches at me, a tremendous rush of chemicals passing up my body like the worst roller-coaster ride times a million. And then all I can hear, all I can feel is the wind. It pushes against my body and warbles my cheeks, instantly drying my damp top as I pinwheel my arms, belly flopping toward earth.

"Push it down. Push the heat down." It's Bishop, plummeting next to me like he's my parachuting buddy or something. The same wind sucks his hair back and flattens his T-shirt tight against his frame, but, unlike me, he couldn't look calmer. Until he appeared, all I could think about was how it was going to feel when I splatted to the ground, but now I remember that I'm supposed to harness my magic, push it down and blah blah blah. But I can't. How can I concentrate with the ground zooming nearer by the second? This was a mistake. I wordlessly reach out for Bishop.

"Sorry!" he yells over the wind, shaking his head solemnly.

"What? Help me!" I say, choking on a mouthful of air.

The sand nears, closer and closer by the wasted second. Forty feet. Thirty. Twenty-five.

"Push it down!" he yells.

I reach out to claw onto the shirt flapping around his midsection, but he pulls away, just an inch out of reach, grinning that infuriating grin. "Push it down!"

My anger makes it easy to find the heat, and for a second I think that maybe it's working this time—going down instead of up—but then the heat sucks back in at the sight of the sand, so very close.

Seconds before I splat to the ground, Bishop swoops under me and plucks me up in a smooth reverse swan dive, rising high into the sky again, holding me tight against him so that we're nearly nose to nose. The crazy noise of the wind falls away, and it becomes deathly quiet.

I want to scream at him. Tell him he's a jerk for waiting so long to catch me, but then I become hyperaware that we're face to face, that the length of our bodies are pressed together, and I don't say any of those things. His chest rises and falls against mine, and I imagine I can feel the drum of his heart between the two thin layers of clothing separating our skin. I risk a glance at his eyes. This close I notice that, though dark as earth wet with rain, they're flecked with gold, like a fire burns behind them. Like he's *hungry*. The thought makes my breath turn so hard and ragged it can't be healthy. His eyes fall to my lips, and he swallows.

He inclines his head so that the tip of his nose nearly grazes mine, so that our lips would touch if a strong wind should arise. I've never wanted to be kissed so badly, so of course this would be the time Mom pops into my head— the Mom from the theater with the knife in her temple. The guilt from the car ride comes crashing over me like a tidal wave. How can I be doing this?

I draw away from Bishop, as much as I can with him still holding my arms in his iron grip. "Oh God, please put me down, I don't want to do this." I'm hyperventilating now, but for a different reason entirely.

Bishop senses the moment's over and floats us to the ground. His expression is blank and unreadable, and that somehow makes everything worse.

"I'm sorry," I say, digging my fingers into my scalp. I turn around and start walking.

I make it only a few steps before Bishop catches my wrist and whirls me around. "You can be happy, you know. It's okay for you to be happy again."

Tears well in my eyes.

He sighs and slackens his grip. "I'm sorry, I didn't mean to yell at you."

I don't say anything, but it's not because I'm mad at him. I just don't know how to tell him how grateful I am that he understood me, that he knew how I was feeling—torn up that I could feel anything but anguish when the memory of Mom dying is still a heavy weight on my heart—all without me having to say a single word. So I show him the only way I know how. I snake my arms around his neck and crush my lips against his. They're soft, much softer than I expected, and for a moment, they're motionless against mine. And then he moans into my mouth. His hands sink into my hair and he kisses me back, hard and fast and passionate, like it's both the first and last kiss of his life. His lips find my jaw, my throat, the spot behind my earlobe, sending a thrilling ache into my belly. I claw at his clothing, tugging his shirt up, and pull him to the sand. He falls on top of me, pressing his full weight onto me. His greedy hands move up my body, and I yank at the sides of his pants, my heart racing in my desperation to get rid of those two layers between us, because I need this, because I need the way it feels to not think of anything else but what I'm doing. Bishop slides his warm hand up my shirt, and my back arches in response.

And then his lips stop moving. He lets out a frustrated groan and becomes as motionless as a statue on top of me.

"What?" I ask, breathless.

He groans again, like he's in actual physical pain, before rolling off me into the sand, white-knuckled fists braced over his stomach.

"What? What is it? Why'd you stop?" I push up on my elbows, catching my breath and watching Bishop splayed in the sand, squinting into the fading sun.

"I don't want it to be like this," he says.

I shake my head. "What do you mean?"

"When you're sad. It was stupid of me. I don't want to take advantage of you."

"Stupid of you?" I exhale and push to sitting. "I kissed you, remember? What happened to all the 'it's okay to be happy' bullcrap?"

"I'm sorry, okay? It's my fault."

Fault. Like he did something wrong. Tears sting my eyes. I can't believe what's happening. Nowhere along the line did I think he'd humiliate me, that he'd make me feel like a sexual predator. I stand up so suddenly pockets of sand go flying onto Bishop. "Forget it, let's go back."

He groans once more, loudly, without getting up, then chases after me. "Come on, Ind. Don't be mad. Can't you understand? It's not that I don't want to."

Oh great, what's next: it's not you, it's me?

"Ind." He catches my wrist so that I'm forced to face

him. I speak before he can delve into any more embarrassing apologies. "Listen. It was stupid—you're right. I shouldn't have done that." My voice cracks a bit when I say it, so I lace some extra anger into my last words. "I shouldn't have done it, I'm sorry I did, and it'll *never* happen again." I shake free of his grip and walk away. "Now take me home. I'm tired."

28

---❖---

I liked Bishop's kitchen just fine the other day. In fact, it was my second-favorite room in his zillion-room mansion. It features the same wooden beams across the roof, smooth archways around the doors, and windows covered in cast-iron grilles as the rest of the house, making it look like the feature spread in *Architectural Digest*. But there are also stone walls, an ornate tile backsplash, fancy tile floors, dark-colored wood cabinets, and a low-hanging candle chandelier suspended over an island full of planters. Together, the look is just so *warm* that I couldn't help loving the room.

But that was the past. Because today, as I perch on the counter, Jezebel pushing back her cuticles as she leans against the massive stainless steel fridge, Bishop drumming his hands on the island with Lumpkins curled in a ball at his feet, I suddenly don't like it at all. I'd rather be anywhere but here, in this stupid kitchen, with the worst company I can think of, except for maybe Leo and the Priory.

Which is why we're here having this little meeting. I finger the edges of the blackened newspaper, the headline STRANGE MEN SEEN LURKING AROUND HIGH SCHOOL CHEER-LEADING PRACTICE stamped in heavy Gothic script across the third page of the local newspaper.

"I propose a permanent twenty-four-hour guard," Bishop says.

I bark a laugh. I know he's waiting for me to look at him, but I won't. I haven't looked him in the eyes since last night when he rebuffed me in the sand dunes. And that's saying something, considering the long drive home.

"That's ridiculous," Jezebel says.

"Why?" Bishop spins around to face her.

Jezebel heaves a sigh and glances up from her nails. "Because that's a lot of manpower, there's a war going on, and the rest of the Family would never go for it, to name just a few of the reasons it's a terrible idea."

"I'll do it myself, then," Bishop says.

My stomach knots up, and I toss the *Los Angeles Times* aside in a flurry of paper. I want to yell at him to quit this I'm-so-concerned act, point out that he didn't seem too worried about me when he ripped my still-beating heart from my chest. But Jezebel's here, and plus, that would mean admitting I'd felt something for him when I should have been feeling nothing but the loss of my mom.

Jezebel's face remains as impassive—and flawless and beautiful—as ever. "And what about when you sleep? You need to sleep sometime. There are big holes in your plan, my friend." She returns to her impromptu nail-care session.

"I won't sleep, then. I just won't sleep," Bishop says.

Jezebel's jaw hardens almost imperceptibly. "Oh yeah?" She marches over to where Bishop sits, perfect red hair falling in front of her face, and narrows her cat-green eyes at him. "And do you think the Family will approve of this little plan of yours? You're already in enough trouble as it is, having lost the Bible, without them discovering you're in a relationship with a student. A student you've been assigned to—"

"Jezebel . . ." Bishop rises an inch from his stool.

Jezebel ignores Bishop's warning and finishes her statement, eyes flicking to mine as she does. "As punishment."

All the air is knocked out of my chest, and my heart squeezes so hard it's as if someone were using it as a stress ball.

"Oh, I'm sorry." Jezebel cocks her head to the side and sticks out her bottom lip. "You didn't know that, did you?"

I don't want to cry. Crying would make everything so much worse. But nothing goes my way.

"Aw, look!" Jezebel says.

Bishop's expression is a blend of horror and remorse, his fingers knotted up into his tangle of hair.

Jezebel faces me again. "Our friend Bishop here was assigned to train you after his little screwup with the Bible. Training newbies like you is so undesirable it's used as punishment where we come from. Yep, that's why he came back. Not because he cared about you *sooo* much he just couldn't stand to be away. He had to, or he'd have been tried for insubordination."

"That was why at first," Bishop says quickly. "Not now."

Jezebel tosses her head back and laughs.

I cover my ears. *I should run away, just leave.* But that wouldn't solve any of my problems. I need to ignore Jezebel's tormenting, pretend Bishop's not here, forget about whatever I thought we had. I shake my head hard, as if to physically remove him from my People I Care About list. "I don't want a bodyguard."

Bishop sighs. "Indie—"

"It's Indigo," I snap.

He winces as if I've slapped him. "Just listen to me—"

"No," I interrupt. "I think I'm tired of listening to both of you, and of the two of you talking about me like I'm not right here. It's my turn to speak." I slide off the counter. "I don't want a bodyguard. I'm not going to live my life like this, waiting for another attack to happen. If we're going to get the Bible back, kill Leo, and wipe out the Priory for good, we're going to have to get creative." I pause, waiting for the laughter to start.

"Go ahead." Jezebel crosses her arms. "Elaborate, O Wise and Experienced One. What do you propose?"

I jut my chin up. "We use me as bait."

"Now we're getting somewhere," Jezebel says, nodding emphatically.

Bishop stands up so quickly he knocks his stool over. "What are you talking about, Indie?"

"I'm talking about using what the Priory thinks they know about us against them. They think that witches and the Family regard secrecy very highly—"

"Which is true," Jezebel interrupts, pointing a long nail at me.

"Yes, I know. So what I'm talking about is luring the Priory out into a public place, where they think no witch or warlock would ever attack, and then hitting them with force. They'd never see it coming, so long as you two stay far back until the right moment."

"No. Absolutely not. Never happening." Bishop crosses his arms and shakes his head, as if I've just proposed the most inane idea possible. Meanwhile, Jezebel chews the inside of her cheek like she's actually considering my plan.

"It could work," she says.

"No, we're not doing it!" Bishop slams his palm down on the island, rattling a potted plant. "You're talking about putting yourself in deliberate danger. You could be killed."

"I'm talking about saving the Bible," I say, not looking at him. "Saving the lives of every witch and warlock on the planet."

"Yes, do try and think of others for once," Jezebel says, glancing over at Bishop. "You know, Indigo, we don't need him on board with this plan. We can do it without him. I've got influence with the Family, more influence than Bishop and his stupid uncle—"

"Don't listen to her," Bishop says. "Of course she'd love for you to die. Less competition for me."

"Now, that is just unkind," Jezebel says, but she's smiling.

Bishop pushes around Jezebel and grabs me by the forearms. I bristle at his touch.

"Look at me." His voice is pleading, and my heart nearly rips from my chest because I want to so badly. But I don't. I focus on the backsplash, counting the individual tiles so that I can breathe, so that I don't think about his wood-and-mint taste and how it felt when I kissed him. "Indie, I'm so sorry about what happened. I didn't mean to embarrass you and I—"

"Just don't!" I yell, a rapid pulse beating in my forehead. The last thing I want right now is to relive the memory in front of an audience.

"Oooh, *this* sounds interesting." Jezebel's boot heels echo as she paces behind us. "Just *what* happened, Bishop?"

Bishop ignores her. "You're trying to punish me, and it's stupid. You'll just kill yourself."

"No." I shake free of his grip. "That is *not* what I'm doing. This is the best plan we have and you know it. Guarding me twenty-four-seven on zero sleep and waiting for an attack that could happen anytime, anywhere, with any number of sorcerers is just plain stupid."

"The girl is right, Bish."

Ugh.

"We do it at homecoming," I say. "Hundreds of people attend, so the Priory wouldn't suspect the Family would attack, and they wouldn't wonder why I'm there, because"—I shrug—"well, because it's homecoming. And it's almost a week away, so that leaves just enough time to talk to the Family and get their support, plus do a bit more training."

"Oh, fun!" Jezebel says, possibly the nearest thing to a genuine smile she's capable of brightening her face. "Kill them in style."

Bishop blows out a slow breath. "Okay, so let's pretend I'm taking this plan seriously. Don't you think it'll look suspicious when you go to homecoming alone? You don't think they'll know something's up?"

I finally look at him so he can see my big, innocent doe eyes. "Oh, I'm not going alone."

He gives me a suspicious glare.

"I'll be going with Devon. You remember Devon, right?"

He laughs, but behind the indifference is an unmistakable flash of jealousy. "The same Devon that screwed your best friend? You can't be serious."

"Make fun of me all you like, Bishop. I'm going, and we're doing this plan, whether you like it or not."

"Amen!" Jezebel holds a hand up and, even though I hate her nearly as much as I hate Bishop, I high-five it over Bishop's shoulder as I give him a hard stare. Lumpkins sits up and barks, and I'm inclined to believe he likes the plan too.

29

Fairfield High Renegades entertain what I like to think is a pretty decent-sized audience most game nights, considering it's L.A. and school spirit isn't really a thing here. So it's no surprise that on the afternoon of homecoming, the bleachers are so jam-packed full they're at risk of collapse.

I scan the crowd as I perform the moves to Bianca's pre-game warm-up routine, but realize that I won't find who I'm looking for. Mom won't be coming to any more of my games. I blink back tears, because now's *so* not the time to get emotional.

Aunt Penny is here, though, front row center, with Bishop. So there's that. The plan was to have Bishop watch the game from afar, so as to give the Priory the impression that I was alone, without protection. But the second I realized Aunt Penny couldn't be talked out of coming to the game—she was homecoming queen her senior year, after all—I had to ditch that plan. At least I don't have to worry about Paige, who agreed to stay home following only minor threats of violence against her if she didn't listen.

Mrs. Hornby blows her obnoxious whistle as she jogs over from the sidelines. Hornby's hard-core into female athletics and female empowerment in general and can pretty much one hundred percent of the time be found wearing a full tracksuit with big pitters. She's been both the girls' volley-ball and girls' soccer coach since forever, and has now taken on the role of cheerleading coach in the wake of Carmen's death. And she's . . . unpleasant. Mrs. Horny, as we've very maturely dubbed her, has made no secret of the fact that she thinks cheerleading is demeaning to women.

"All right, girls," she says. "As you all know, it's an important game today. And there is no way the football team can manage to win without you girls out there, shaking your booties and yelling out nice things to the boys. So do your school proud!"

A collective eye roll passes over the squad.

"Isn't it against some sort of rule to be sarcastic to students?" I ask, eliciting a hum of support.

But Mrs. Malone's voice comes over the speaker, announcing our squad, before Horny has a chance to respond.

"Come on, girls," Bianca says, trotting toward the field. She turns around and runs backward. "We wouldn't want to disappoint our *favorite* new coach," she adds. And if I'm not mistaken, I'd say Bianca winked at me before spinning around again. Weird.

We take formation on the field. The music starts, and we launch into our choreographed dance.

And I must say, even with me slipping frantic searches for the Priory into the routine, we rock the faces off everyone in the stands. I like to think it's why the Renegades are ahead 16–7 by the time the whistle blows for halftime.

On cue, the homecoming-court nominees head over to the carriage—which I guess sustained only minimal damages in the altercation with Leo—at the head of the processional of floats surrounding the field for the parade.

Bianca and I arrive at the carriage doors at the same time, and there's an awkward thirty seconds where we both go to climb up at the same time, step back, then try again with equal success. Finally she steps back.

"Go ahead," she says.

"No, you go ahead," I respond.

"No, seriously," she says. "I'm sorry I jumped in your way. It was wrong." She gives a weak smile. It's a bit much for the situation, and I get the distinct impression she's apologizing for more than cutting me off. An actual apology would be more impressive, but it's a start.

I climb up the steps into the carriage. Devon is already there, with two seniors from the football team who were also nominated for homecoming king, along with Mandy Allard, the strikingly gorgeous, black-haired sometimes-model and the only senior girl on the ticket for homecoming queen. She doesn't bother to glare at us, and really, why should she? Juniors are never elected king and queen, even when we're nominated.

Devon has the decency to look embarrassed when he sees Bianca and me enter the carriage together.

"Ladies," he says, dipping his head at us before he launches into a conversation with one of the senior guys. We take our places for optimal viewing around the carriage as the marching band warms up, their horns and trumpets tooting and honking above the roar of the crowd.

I glance over at Aunt Penny and Bishop again. They're making small talk, and Aunt Penny doesn't look like she wants to jab his eyes out. Which is annoying. She waits until I hate the guy to decide he's all right? Bishop glances over and catches my eye, giving me a little wave. I give him my back.

The driver guns the engine and the float jolts into action. The crowd goes nuts, waving their pennants and madly blowing into their noisemakers as we tour the track around the football field, led by the marching band. It's easy to get lost in the energy of it all, and I find myself legitimately smiling as I wave at the audience. Weird, considering I could be attacked at any time. The thought puts me back on my game, and I spin around like a freaking contestant on *Dancing with the Stars* to make sure I'm not caught off guard. But the parade comes to an end, and the Priory doesn't attack. In fact, the football game ends—Renegades win, 30–11, woo—and still no murderous sorcerers descend on the stadium.

Devon jogs up to me at the end of the game. "Hey, you have a second to talk?"

I glance over my shoulder and confirm my suspicion that Bishop is watching this whole interaction much more intently than any other portion of the game. I nod at Devon.

"Good," he says. "So look . . ." He laces his fingers together and cracks his knuckles. After a few false starts he gets going again.

"I know you said you don't want to hear any excuses about what I did with Bianca—"

My face glows red at the mention of the incident. "Stop right there," I say. "I don't want to get into it again. Just because I agreed to go to the dance with you tonight doesn't mean we're getting back together. It's like you said—no use ruining homecoming for both of us."

"That didn't come out right," he says, and it's his turn for his cheeks to turn pink. "Look, I know we're not getting back together, but . . . can we at least be friends?"

My instinct is to kick him in the nads, but that'd probably make for some awkward homecoming dance moments. And so I mumble a "fine" instead. A huge smile instantly lights up his face, and he envelops me in a bear hug.

"Thanks, Ind. I really mean it." He plants a kiss on top of my head before taking off for the parking lot.

"Friends don't kiss!" I call to his back, but he's lost in the crowd. I shake my head.

"You did so great!" Aunt Penny squeals, bounding up behind me with Bishop in tow. She takes me by the shoulders. "You're a rock star."

"Made up with Quarterback Jack, I see," Bishop says oh so casually, as if he were just reporting on the weather. Which is exactly why I know he's jealous.

I give him an insincere smile.

"Sorry, Bishop," Aunt Penny says, linking arms with me, "but I have to get this girl home. If we don't get started on her hair now, she'll never be ready in time."

I try not to take that as an insult.

Aunt Penny stands behind me, critically assessing my reflection in the bathroom mirror.

"Something's missing," she mumbles, chewing the side of her fingernail.

I can't imagine what that could possibly be. After three hours under her "professional guidance" (she once worked as a makeup artist on her friend's indie movie), I've had so much gunk caked on my face I was sure that when I finally looked in the mirror I'd be ready to entertain at a children's birthday party. I've had my hair straightened, curled, pulled into elaborate updos, and coated with toxic levels of hair spray, only to be pulled down and washed so many times I've lost count. All this only to end up with a simple low bun at the nape of my nape with a few curly tendrils framing my face, paired with light, shimmery eye shadow and bold pink lip gloss. Strangely, it's my favorite look yet.

"Wait here."

Aunt Penny leaves the bathroom, returning moments later with a handful of tiny white flowers.

"You just happened to have baby's breath on hand?" I ask as she scatters the flowers throughout my curls.

"An artist is always prepared," she says.

She steps back after poking at least eighty more bobby pins into my hair. And this time, she smiles.

"Done?" I ask her reflection.

"Done," she responds. Her smile fades suddenly and she bites her lips.

"Aunt Penny?"

She tries to smile again but fails. "She loved you so much," she croaks.

My eyes fill with tears at the mention of Mom. "And I loved her too," I manage, my voice thick with emotion.

Aunt Penny puts her arms around my waist and rests her cheek against my shoulder. Our gazes meet in the mirror.

"You know, you're doing a good job," I say.

She lets out a little sob. We're still for a moment, the memory of Mom so strong between us it's practically a tangible thing. And then she straightens up and shakes off like a dog come in from the rain. "Okay, enough of this, you're going to ruin your makeup, and then what'll we do? Turn around, check yourself out."

I spin to take in all the angles of my hair and makeup.

"You're *good,*" I say, to which Aunt Penny responds by squealing and clapping.

"I told you to trust me. Devon is going to shit when he sees how hot you look."

I roll my eyes. "I told you, I don't care what Devon thinks. We're just friends. Not even, really. I'm just going with him because everyone else already has a date."

She cocks her head, a hand on her hip. "So you're telling me not the tiniest part of you wants him to regret cheating on you?"

"Of course she wants that," Paige says, poking her head around the open bathroom door. "What girl doesn't want their cheating boyfriend to grovel and beg for forgiveness on hands and knees?"

"If even just to have better access to kick him in the teeth," Aunt Penny adds, and they both nod.

"No, actually, I really and truly don't care," I say. "I mean, of course I want him to regret it, but no, I don't care about him. . . . Ugh!" My cheeks flame. What I really regret is telling Aunt Penny that Devon cheated in the first place. And not just because I had to convince her that the whole ex-UFC-fighter thing was totally unnecessary.

Aunt Penny pats my shoulder, as if to say, "See, I know you better than you know yourself."

"All right," Paige says. "Let's get you into your dress."

A better plan has not been hatched.

It takes Paige under three minutes from the time we enter my bedroom to get me into the dress Mom helped me pick out months ago—a strapless, corset-back gown that fits tight around my bust, then billows out in a puff of navy-blue, crystal-embellished taffeta that reaches just past my knees (optimal dress length for running, thankfully)—buckle the clasps on my strappy heels (Paige insisted I wear flats, but I argued I can run just as well in heels), and hook my sequined clutch onto my arm. All just in time for the doorbell to ring.

My heart races, and I take a measured breath so that I don't hyperventilate.

It's really happening. After days of slapdash training, of Bishop begging his uncle to use whatever influence he has to turn down our plan, of Jezebel pleading with the Family until they miraculously agreed to our plan, of Bishop caving once he realized we really were going to do it with or without him, homecoming night is finally here.

"I'll get it," Aunt Penny says, a blur in the hallway.

"Devon's right on time," I say. "Now, there's a shocker." Especially considering Bianca is hosting a pre-homecoming party the whole universe except me is invited to. Not that I'd go even if I were invited. But Paige doesn't laugh at my joke, just twists her hands together.

"Wish me luck," I say, my traitorous voice cracking.

"I still don't see why I can't help," Paige blurts out. Behind her glasses tears well up, which she doesn't even try to wipe away.

I sigh and swallow my own tears, because one of us has to be the strong one.

"I know, I know," Paige says. "You never thought you'd see the day when I was begging you to go to homecoming. But I just can't stand sitting on the sidelines while you're in danger."

"Potentially in danger," I correct her. "They might not even show up. It's not like they didn't have plenty of opportunities at the game today."

"I know," she says. "It's just . . ." She shakes her head, mumbling something under her breath. Not for the first time, I worry that she's just pretending she's going over to Jessie's for an anti-homecoming *Jeopardy!* party. That she's going to follow me the minute I leave the house. I take her by the forearms and shake her until she looks up at me.

"Seriously, Paige. If the Priory knows anything about me, they'll know you're my closest friend. They could take you hostage. It's hugely unsafe for you to be there."

"I don't care about that," she says, pushing her chin up.

"But I do," I tell her. "Yeah, my magic has improved, but I'm nothing compared with the Priory. The last thing

I need is to have to look after you on top of myself. I won't even have a chance then. Promise me you're not going to follow me."

She's quiet a moment, her lips pressed into a line as a rogue tear slips down her cheek. Finally, she lets out a slow breath. "Fine. I don't like it, but fine."

She twines her fingers with mine and squeezes so hard it hurts, giving me a weak smile that I translate to "Good luck, stay safe, and in case you die, I love you." It's a complicated smile.

And then I walk downstairs.

Devon stands in the doorway, sporting the black tuxedo with a powder-blue vest and navy bow tie that we picked out because it both matches my gown and makes his eyes look impossibly blue. I could stand less gel in his hair, but that's just me being picky—he looks great. And I feel nothing. Despite all my reassurances to Paige and Penny that I didn't care about Devon, I will admit now that I did worry our date would somehow rekindle my desire for him, and then I'd end up being one of those lame-o girls who takes back her cheating boyfriend. I couldn't be happier to find that the Devon-fire is safely dead.

Devon's eyes go from my hair, linger around my on-display bust, and then move down to my legs.

"You look amazing," he says. And even though I'm his date because there's no one else left to ask, he actually looks sincere when he says it. "I have this." He holds up a little plastic box with a corsage made of white orchids.

"Oh!" I turn to retrieve the box with Devon's matching boutonniere from the coffee table, but Paige is already on it.

Aunt Penny snaps pictures while Devon slips the corsage around my wrist and I fumble to pin the boutonniere to his lapel. It feels silly to be doing all these things with him, and not just because the point of the evening is to lure the Priory out and *not* to make lasting high school memories. Though, if everything goes to plan, I'm sure that'll happen too.

After hundreds of horribly posed pictures at various locales around the living room, Devon and I head for the door.

"Wait!" Aunt Penny calls to my back.

I spin around. Aunt Penny chews the inside of her cheek, her index finger pressed to her lips.

"What is it?" I ask.

Her eyes flit to Paige and then to Devon before settling on me again. "Just be careful, okay?"

Ew. It's one thing for Aunt Penny to help out with my hair and makeup but another thing entirely when she gives me sex advice. Cool aunt or no.

"Careful. Yeah, sure." I snag Devon's arm to get out of here fast.

"Wait!"

Ugh. I spin around in the doorway. "Yes?"

Aunt Penny opens and closes her mouth as if trying to

find the right words. I'm about to blurt out that she needn't worry, because I'm not having sex tonight, when she finally speaks. "If . . . if you find yourself in a tough position"—she bites her bottom lip—"you can always call on Alica Frangere."

Alica Frangere? I've never heard of the woman. I exchange confused glances with Paige. "Who's that?" I ask.

Aunt Penny presses a hand to her temple, a pained look crossing her face.

"Are you okay?" I ask.

She waves me away. "Just a headache. Forget about it. You'll be fine, and have a great time tonight." When I don't move, she shoos me to the door. "Seriously, go, have fun." She smiles so widely I'm forced to believe she's okay.

Devon links arms with me and leads me outside. I crane my neck to look back inside the house until Aunt Penny closes the front door. He leads me down the three steps as though I'm a fragile doll that might break just because I'm wearing a dress. It's ridiculous, but then I remember that Bishop and Jezebel are watching somewhere in the falling twilight, and I cling to Devon's arm like the leading lady in some black-and-white movie all the way down the drive to Devon's car.

Take that, jerkwad.

All I can say about the drive to Elysian Park, where we're meeting up for photos with the group who went to Bianca's party, is thank God for Jay-Z. I don't know how I ever thought Devon and I were a good match, but in the many instances of awkward silence and stilted conversation that occur in the short drive, it has become very clear that we're not. We're *so* not.

Devon circles the parking lot and finds a spot at the rear. He opens my door for me, and that's where the chivalry ends. He spots his friends climbing out of Jarrod's car a few rows over and practically sprints over to join.

Right away I see one of the Amy/Ashley twins and Julia with their respective football-player dates, but it's only as I get closer that I spot Bianca. It's kind of hard *not* to spot her, with her white-blond hair, tanned skin, and hot-pink, painted-on dress that scoops low at the neck to show off her ta-tas.

Something like anxiety grips me. I don't know how I'm supposed to act around her after her sort-of apology. It was much easier when my feelings weren't so unclear (read: when I hated her guts).

Bianca smiles as I approach, a proprietary arm linked around a disinterested-looking college-age guy with an acne problem who I instantly recognize as Sebastian. He gives me a not-so-subtle up-and-down appraisal that Bianca catches the tail end of, and I can practically see the friendliness drain out of her, like it's my fault her date is a douche.

She passes a critical eye over my dress. "Nice, did Sears have a sale?" Amy/Ashley laughs, and I shoot her a hard look that shuts her up.

So it's like that now? Bianca knows my family has a hard time with money, knows *just* what buttons to press.

"That's funny, Bianca. And I assume you found your dress in the children's section at Barneys?" I say, bringing to light her little secret. "Because there's no way that thing"—I circle a finger around her tiny dress—"was made for anyone over ten."

"Oh, come on, girls," Jarrod says. He produces a twenty-sixer of Jack Daniel's from the backseat. "It's homecoming. Have a shot."

I cross my arms and look away.

"I'll have one." The swish of liquid tells me Bianca's snagged the bottle from Jarrod. "I'm not a *loser,* after all."

Must remember priorities. Must not punch her in the ovaries.

"Hey, that must be the photographer," Julia says.

"'Bout friggin' time," Bianca says. "We're not paying her just to stand around the parking lot. If we're late to our dinner because of this I am so going to lose it. *Lose it.*"

I roll my eyes. At this rate I'd be pleased for the Priory to come swooping in, just so that I can throw Bianca in their warpath.

I've almost convinced myself this is true, but when my cell phone buzzes in my handbag, I feel like I might have leaped out of my skin if my corset weren't so tight. I glance at the caller ID, and my heart picks up its pace. Paige. I casually wander a few steps away from the group to answer.

"Hello?" I whisper.

"Any sign of the Priory yet?" Paige asks.

"No, and don't say the P word. Jessie could hear you."

"I'm in the bathroom, and I'm just really nervous, okay? Call me as soon as you know what's going on."

"You'll be the first to know." I stow the phone in my purse and rejoin the group for photos.

And then it's another wonderfully awful forty-minute drive to the Athenaeum in Pasadena, the venue for this year's homecoming dinner and dance.

A ripple of fear runs through me as Devon leads me to the entrance of the massive white stucco building. Because here's where I leave my protection behind. It was easy to be sort of confident about this whole thing with a practiced warlock and witch out there watching my every move, but when I go inside, Bishop and Jezebel—and the Family, but they won't arrive until we *really* need help, so as not to tip off the Priory—won't follow.

I take a slow breath and remind myself that they'll be watching closely, that Bishop wouldn't let the Priory get too close without charging inside to help

I don't even have to enter the Athenaeum to know that Fairfield High has pulled out all the stops to make this year's theme come to life.

The stone path leading to the entrance has been trans-formed into a drawbridge, complete with fully costumed, sword-and-shield-carrying guards standing sentinel at the entrance. As we enter, a herald blows a trumpet draped with a flag, then announces to the room that Lady Indigo Blackwood and Sir Devon Mills have arrived. Next to him, a woman in a crinoline gown plays the harp. It doesn't stop there.

Inside, the Athenaeum looks like I've just stepped into King Arthur's court. Swaths of deep red fabric hang from the ceiling, gathered in the center by an ornate gold chandelier. Navy pennant banners are slung between each of the turret-peaked white columns that act as a perimeter around the long dining room tables—each of which is draped in alternating red and gold tablecloths and is decked, buffet-style, with everything from whole cooked turkeys to dessert trays, flower garlands laced between the acres of food. But by far the most noticeable of the themed decor is the giant papier-mâché dragon whose spiky green tail snakes around the columns, its fire-breathing head looking out toward the dance floor. I wouldn't be surprised if they passed around samples of the bubonic plague at dinner, for authenticity's sake.

We mill around inside, admiring the decor, until, at the urging of the herald, we take our seats in the dining room.

I'm not hungry, but I pick at my dinner anyway—strength for battle and whatnot. By the time the butlers (seriously) have cleared the table, there's still been no sign of the Priory. I do get another call from Paige, though, which I let go to voice mail. The girl can be annoying, God love her.

The soft dinner music cuts out to a DJ, who blasts Top 40 music through giant speakers set up in all corners of the room. The lights dim, and we're ushered onto a dance floor teeming with artificial smoke and strobe lights. Just like in King Arthur's court.

Still no Priory.

I must say, it's hard to find a rhythm when you're worried about a sorcerer killing you at any moment, but I try, because the whole point is that I appear to be casual, that I don't look like I'm trying to lure the Priory out so we can reclaim the Bible and kill them.

Minutes turn into hours. The bottle of JD makes the rounds, and soon the dance floor is a writhing mass of teenagers bumping and grinding against each other in a formalwear orgy.

The end of the night nears, and it becomes obvious the Priory isn't coming, that they must have been on to our plans, when the music abruptly cuts out. My pulse drums harder than the beat of the club music still echoing in my ears.

But it's not the Priory—just Mrs. Malone, dressed in an embarrassingly tight sequined dress, tapping the microphone onstage. There's a table draped in red velvet behind her, atop which sits a large and a small version of the same jewel-encrusted gold crown.

"I trust you're all having fun?" Mrs. Malone asks, nodding as if she knows the answer already.

The crowd erupts into cheers.

Mrs. Malone smiles brightly. "All right, you're all probably wondering why I'm interrupting your evening, so I'll cut to the chase." She pauses, and the crowd grows quiet. "It's time to announce this year's Fairfield High homecoming king and queen."

Her last words are muffled by raucous applause.

Mrs. Malone waits a moment before holding up a hand for silence. "First, the homecoming king."

The students roar. Our principal sweeps her gaze over the crowd, clearly loving her part in all the excitement.

"Over one thousand students voted, and it was unanimous: this year's homecoming king is . . . Devon Mills!"

Whoa—an underclassman won homecoming king.

The football players lead a "Devon, Devon!" chant, and the rest of the crowd joins in.

"Come on up here, Devon." Mrs. Malone waves him over.

Devon high-fives his friends before he jogs onstage. He bows low so that Mrs. Malone can place the larger gold crown atop his gelled blond hair, then waves to the audience in his best royalty impression.

Mrs. Malone returns to the microphone. "Doesn't he make a charming king?" She allows the crowd a moment more of applause. "And now, what you've all been waiting for."

The DJ begins a drumroll.

There's a commotion on the dance floor, and Mandy

Allard is pushed to the front of the crowd, rolling her eyes and smiling widely in her sad attempt to be humble.

Mrs. Malone continues. "It was a close call this year, but the votes are in; this year's Fairfield High homecoming queen is . . . Indigo Blackwood!"

The crowd erupts into the same raucous applause that Devon received.

"What?" Mandy and Bianca say together. My jaw is somewhere on the booze-slick dance floor.

I couldn't agree with them more. Me? A junior? Homecoming queen? After everything that happened? After falling out with Bianca and after befriending the girl everyone thinks is the school's biggest loser?

It has to be pity, I decide. People feel bad for me because Mom died.

Hands push me forward, and I stumble onstage, squinting against the bright light and the flash of cameras in the audience. I bend down like Devon did so that Mrs. Malone can place the crown on my head. It's heavier than expected, and I straighten carefully so that it doesn't topple off. And then, finally, I allow myself to look out at the audience.

Bianca and Mandy sulk off toward the bathroom, Julia hot on their heels. But that's it: just those three girls in the entire room of students appear the least bit upset with the decision, and the rest cheer as though they're genuinely happy. And for the first moment, I realize that maybe not everyone loves Bianca. Maybe other people realize what a terrible person she is. It makes me feel sort of bad for her, which is shocking after the whole Sears dress debacle.

But then I see Bishop, and all thoughts of Bianca slip away. He's inside, leaning against one of the turret-peaked columns that border the room, his hands plunged deep in the pockets of his suit pants, his wing tips crossed at the ankles. He looks up at me from under the bowler hat that sits cocked slightly forward on his head, under which spills his familiar tangle of black waves. I don't think I've ever seen him in anything but rocker clothing, and though I'm not entirely sure this doesn't qualify as that, it makes me suck in a little breath. That, and the fact that he shouldn't be here. And since he is, I guess it means everyone else has given up on the Priory too.

Bishop tips his hat and sends me a crooked grin, and I find myself smiling back before I remember that I'm supposed to hate him.

An arm wraps around my middle, and I jerk my gaze away from Bishop as the crowd begins chanting, "Kiss, kiss, kiss!"

Before I even get a chance to process what's happening, Devon dips me backward and plants a wet kiss on my lips. For a moment, I'm too shocked to react, but then I realize that Devon's kissing me, kissing me in front of the whole school, in front of Bishop, and that it's not what I want. I put my hands onto his chest to push him away, but it's too late. He's already pulling me back to my feet.

And Bishop is gone.

Panting for air, I scan the columns at the back of the room, desperate to find him. But a strange movement in the room catches my attention. I squint into the darkness, sure that my eyes are playing tricks on me, because what I just saw *cannot* be right. Then the massive, green-spiked tail of the papier-mâché dragon flicks again, and my doubts are cast aside. The dragon is coming to life.

30

When I scan the length of the dragon's body, I find that the rest of it is as lifeless as any arts and crafts project should be. But I know it's only a matter of time before the whole thing roars to life along with its tail, prepared to rip me—and anyone standing in its path to me—to shreds.

Panic sucks all the air out of my lungs, and I forget what I'm supposed to do next. I'm only vaguely aware of what's going on around me. Mrs. Malone speaks into the microphone and people stare at me frozen onstage, but all I can think is that Bishop's abandoned me. He saw me kiss Devon and was so pissed that he took off, leaving me to die at the hands of the Priory. But then the fire alarm sounds, and I remember I was supposed to run at the first sign of the sorcerers, run far and fast so that none of the students get stuck in the battle zone, and when we were clear, Bishop and Jezebel would attack. Bishop must have activated the alarm when he realized I'd panicked and not come through on my end of the plan.

Devon tugs my arm, trying to lead me offstage as Mrs. Malone attempts to reassure the confused crowd.

"Calm down, students. I'm sure this is just an error and that we can resume the evening shortly, but until the fire department arrives and we can ensure your safety, I'll have to ask that you all file into the parking lot."

Students grumble and groan, collecting their purses and jackets from the tables. Some even line up outside the bathroom.

When I dart a glance back at the dragon, it blinks—a heavy-lidded blink—as though waking from a deep sleep.

I snatch the microphone from Mrs. Malone. "Come on, people, get outside! There's a fire in the kitchen! You're all going to die!"

Hysteria races through the crowd. Students cram into the doorways as though sucked there by a vacuum, and our principal flies offstage, running around like a headless chicken, trying to rein in the chaos. So, overall, much more effective than Mrs. Malone's announcement.

"What are you talking about?" Devon asks. He's been with me onstage and knows that I haven't been near the kitchen. "Let's get out of here," he says.

I shake free of his grip. "You go ahead."

His eyebrows draw together, and he glances back anxiously at his friends' retreating backs. "Everyone's probably leaving for the party," he says, actual pain in his voice that he's not part of everyone.

"Go ahead. I'm not feeling well." I give him a not-so-little shove toward the stairs. He stumbles back, with the most affronted look on his face. A low, throaty rumble sounds from behind him. Devon spins around just as the dragon's twenty-foot-long, papier-mâché body morphs into the scaly green skin of a lizard, its massive batlike wings expanding with a whisk of air from either side of its muscular shoulders. High-pitched screams erupt from the clog of people in the doorway.

"Holy shit!" Devon scrambles down the stairs, plastering himself against the wall as he passes the beast without so much as a backward glance at me.

Of course I wanted him to leave so he wasn't killed. But still. What a gentleman!

I root my feet to the stage, fighting the intense urge to flee along with everyone else. I have to remind myself that the point was to lure the Priory out, that Leo won't kill me until I've broken the spell; the dragon is just a scare tactic.

But that's really, really hard to do when china shatters as the dragon climbs to its feet, bones cracking as it extends its long, curved neck to full length. The animal yawns, revealing two rows of serrated, sawlike teeth and a thin red serpentine tongue.

Why, oh why, couldn't this year's homecoming theme be Care Bears?

I stumble backward.

"Indigo, what are you doing?" Mrs. Malone pokes her head in the door. "Come on out here, it's . . . dangerous." She spots the dragon, and her eyes go wide. She lets out a bloodcurdling scream and stumbles from the room.

The dragon sniffs the air, then snaps its head toward me so fast I shriek. Bishop? Jezebel? The Family? Any time now, don't be shy. I know we agreed you'd all stay back until Leo shows his face, but I think a dragon is a good time to intervene too.

The dragon takes a huge breath that puffs up its chest, then exhales, blowing snapping flames across the room, so close to my face that my cheeks sting as though I've just come inside from the cold. I flatten myself against the wall so that I'm not burned. Just when it feels like my face is melting off, the fire finally, mercifully, sucks back into its mouth. But the dragon's not done with me yet.

It takes one step closer to me, rumbling the earth, talons-for-nails clacking against the parquet flooring. Its mouth opens again, and it doesn't take the third-highest GPA at Fairfield High to know what's going to happen next, what's going to happen if I don't get out of here.

A familiar heat burns up my chest, and I slam it down hard and fast. I'm not even sure what's happened until I'm ten feet in the air, looking down at the dragon's fiery breath flaming below me. I'm flying! And from my new vantage point, I spot Bianca, Julia, and Mandy pressed up against the wall outside the bathroom. The fire sucks back into the dragon's yawning mouth. Following my line of sight, it snaps its head in the direction of the girls. And oh, it's so very tempting to let him have a snack and hope he's too full for a main course. The dragon sniffs the air.

I sigh. "Get out of here!" I yell. "Run!"

Bianca stumbles for the door, Julia and Mandy staggering behind her. "I—I knew you were a freak!" Bianca yells.

A hard clapping sounds from deep within the shadows of the room. Leo emerges, smirking. "Brava! You've finally learned to fly. Thought you'd never do it."

I press a hand over my heart; relief oozes through me like warmed caramel at the sight of him, of his marred cheek and half-frozen smile. It means that help is on the way. The break in pressure makes me falter in the air. I fall hard onto the stage, pain slicing up my spine as my crown clatters in front of me.

Leo misinterprets my reaction as fear. "What? You

thought we weren't watching? Oh no"—he shakes his head—"I've been watching everything you do, Indigo. I probably know you better than you know yourself. Favorite cereal? Cocoa Puffs. Favorite shampoo? Pantene Curly Hair Series. Your best friend is Paige Abernathy, your next-door neighbor, though it was Bianca Cavanaugh before that. You hate pumping gas, so you let your car run on empty for days until you fill it up. Let's see, what else?" He taps a finger on his chin.

An involuntary shudder passes through me. "I get it," I say. I stagger to my feet and push my sweat-dampened tendrils away from my face, sweeping my gaze around the room. Where are they?

Leo tips his head to the side. "Looking for your friends?"

"She doesn't have to look far." Bishop sits at a table with his feet up on a chair. He plucks a grape from a tray on the table and pops it into his mouth. And the fact that he isn't panicked at the sight of a huffing dragon not twenty feet away makes my shoulders relax a tiny bit.

"Give us the Bible and we won't kill you." Jezebel enters through the kitchen doors doing her confident, swaying walk.

Leo speaks without even turning to face them. "I think it was you who once said that the one with the knife gets to make the rules. Well, I think the same principle applies here, with the dragon."

"You think we're scared of your crappy dragon?" Jezebel throws her head back and laughs.

Speak for yourself, Jezebel.

Leo nods. "Fair enough. But maybe one of my talented colleagues can summon more impressive magic for you. Shall we see?"

The double doors burst open, and men and women clad in suits almost as severe as their expressions file into the room. Ten. Twenty. Thirty . . .

A chill passes over me, despite the heat and sweat soaking the air inside the Athenaeum.

If Leo can summon a dragon on his own, I don't want to know what dozens of sorcerers can do together. The Family—where is the Family?

Bishop stands.

"Oh, not so confident anymore?" Leo laughs. As if on cue, the dragon stomps closer to me, rattling dishes off the tables. It paws the air between us. I yelp and leap back, its claws narrowly missing my face.

Leo perches on the end of a table on the opposite side of the dance floor from Bishop. "Just quit being so damn stubborn, Indigo, and break the spell."

I look to Bishop for direction. He nods at Jezebel, and not an instant later, they both materialize in front of me. Jezebel holds a hand skyward, and the roof of the Athenaeum blows out in a mass of white stucco shards and red cloth.

"Hold on tight." Bishop grabs me around the middle, and

the three of us dart straight up through the ragged hole in the roof, a storm of debris falling around us. We zip high into the cold air above the clouds, and I don't bother pointing out that I can fly now, not wanting to test my brand-new skills when the Athenaeum is now just a white speck in the darkened cityscape below, and the hundreds of high schoolers milling around outside look as tiny as ants. A homecoming they'll never forget.

Now that we've escaped, the full weight of reality hits me: we failed. My plan failed epically. Not only did we not get the Bible back, or kill Leo, or defeat the Priory, but I exposed witches to the public, ruined homecoming for my peers, and destroyed a city monument. I don't even want to think about the consequences.

"At least we got out!" Bishop yells over the wind, as if sensing my disappointment and shame. He squeezes me tighter.

"Spoke too soon!" Jezebel yells. She nods behind her.

It's so far away that at first I think it's a bird. But it's fast, *really* fast, and it's not long before I can clearly see the veined wings of the dragon snapping up and down against the twilight sky.

"Oh hell!" Bishop shouts.

"Couldn't have said it better myself!" Jezebel yells.

"What are we going to do?" Bishop asks.

No one speaks, the dragon's flapping wings—growing louder and louder—reminding us that every second counts.

"Follow me." Jezebel plunges down suddenly, like a pelican diving for fish. Bishop grips me tighter and follows suit. I'd always thought he didn't hold back any of his power when flying with me in tow, but now I know that he did—a lot. Because the speed at which we descend toward the ground knocks the breath out of me. Yet, by the time we reach the ground, Jezebel is already lifting up a manhole cover. She tosses it aside like it weighs no more than a penny, and a dank, mildewy smell similar to wet clothes left to dry in a washing machine wafts up.

Reading my mind, Jezebel says "Ew" and pinches her nose. Then, without even crouching down, she drops into the dark hole, only a splashing noise to indicate that she's landed.

"Jezebel." My hair hangs around my face as I grip the sides of the hole and peer inside, but it's too dark; I don't see anything.

"Hurry up, it's coming." Bishop pushes my back.

I do a shoulder check and find the dragon fast approaching, cutting across the star-specked sky at an alarming rate. The fear that had gripped me earlier comes surging back like a jolt of electricity. I kick off my heels and take a leap.

The bottom is farther than I anticipated, and needles of pain shoot up my legs as I splash-land into calf-deep water. I buckle to my knees, hands braced against the gritty-yet-slimy bottom of the sewer for support, shuddering as I consider all the things that could be making the water slimy.

"Out of the way!"

Not a second later, there's another splash as Bishop leaps into the hole after me, and then a quiet *pop* as the same taper candle we used for summoning lights up Bishop's face and the faded redbrick walls behind him. "Come on." He snags my arm, and we noisily slosh through the muddy water, the heavy, wet taffeta gown sucking against my legs, tripping up my steps despite its short length.

We make it only feet away from the hole we dropped through when a thundering boom shakes the walls. I scream and clutch Bishop's arm, and he presses my head protectively against his chest. The echoes of the boom still resonate when it is replaced by a squealing roar so high-pitched it makes my ears ring. A taloned paw reaches into the sewer and angrily claws around left and right.

"Quit cuddling and run!" Jezebel yells, waving us toward her from her spot just inside the circle of light cast by the flickering candle.

Bishop pulls me farther into the narrow, snaking bowels of Los Angeles County. The dragon doesn't follow—can't follow—but I'm smart enough about the workings of the Priory to know that doesn't mean we're safe.

Almost as soon as I have this thought, I become aware that the cold, thick water that was licking my ankles not too long ago now reaches to my knees.

"The water's rising!" Hysteria breaks my voice, thoughts of drowning in a sewer constricting my throat.

The others don't respond, as if they noticed already and didn't want to scare me.

Jezebel's boots splash three feet ahead of us, leading the charge. "Just keep running," she says between struggles for air. "We'll get out at the next sewer cover."

But it's kind of hard to run underwater. The cold liquid rises up around the tops of my thighs, an awkward depth too high to run in and yet too shallow to swim in, and I have to lift my legs higher and higher to make any headway. Jezebel's three-foot lead becomes twenty, and I gasp and struggle for air. Even tyrannical hellish cheerleading training under Bianca's tyrannical regime has left me unprepared for this task.

"I don't get it." Jezebel's voice breaks up with obvious exhaustion. She slows to a jog, then stops, doubled over and panting. "Why wouldn't the Family have helped? They promised. It doesn't make sense. The Priory has the Bible. Why wouldn't the Family send everyone they've got? It's their own lives on the line."

It doesn't make any sense to me either, and I can tell by Bishop's silence that he's thinking about it too as he sucks in big gulps of air.

"Come on, we have to keep moving." Jezebel pushes up and breaks into a sloppy jog again.

The water has slicked higher up my body in the time we've spent catching our breath, and though my lungs ache with exhaustion and my overworked heart pounds, I run after her.

Bishop stays at my side even though I know he could have lapped Jezebel twice over. "Take it off." He gestures to my dress. "It'd be much easier."

I give him a hard look. "Nice try, but I'm not reenacting your porno fantasies."

He shrugs. "Suit yourself."

But it's only a few slow, heavy steps later that I realize he's right. In a few minutes' time, the water will be above my waist, and we'll have to swim. "Unlace me."

"Oh God," Jezebel calls from up ahead.

"Hurry up! The water." I spin around to give Bishop access to the corset-back of my gown. He whirls around, looking for someplace to put the candle before sticking it on a small ledge poking out of the brick.

He splashes up behind me, and even above the *whoosh* of water in the intakes and Jezebel's splashing footsteps, I hear him swallow hard, hesitating, fingers fumbling with my laces.

"I didn't come back just because I was ordered!" he yells over the noise.

Familiar tears sting my eyes. Which is stupid, because really—so not the most important thing right now. Water moves up to my hip bones, the skirt of the dress puffing up around me.

"It's true the Family sent me to train you as punishment for losing the Bible," he says. "But they had no idea that I really wanted to do it, that I'd been dying to see you again.

It wasn't a punishment at all." He takes hold of my shoulders, and I draw in a little breath. "The real punishment was being away from you."

My heart swells so much I'm worried it will burst, relief and happiness causing tears to spill down my cheeks.

"And I only stopped that day at the sand dunes because I didn't want you to regret anything. I didn't want you to think back on what you'd done and hate me for it."

Heat floods my face at the mention of that day, and I'm glad my back is to him so he can't see it. But as much as I don't want to forgive him for humiliating me, I know he's right. I would have felt like he'd preyed on my vulnerability if he'd let things go any further.

"Indie." He pleads my name, his fingers brushing tentatively along the cold skin of my arm. His touch sends a current down my body.

"Okay, you're right," I say tersely.

Silence. And then, "What did you just say?"

I huff and spin around to face him, not bothering to wipe my tear-stained face. "I said you're right. You're right and I was wrong. Go ahead and enjoy the moment because it's probably never happening again—"

He takes my face in his hands and kills my words with a kiss. A kiss so intense it would scare me if it didn't thrill me so much. Long and deep and lingering.

"What's taking you guys so . . . long." Jezebel slows to a halt.

I pull back from Bishop, my breathing as erratic as my pulse.

"Oh, well, pardon me," Jezebel says. "I guess I mistakenly thought we were running for our lives." She turns on her heel and keeps running.

I bring my eyes up to Bishop's. "She hates us."

"And I don't care."

I laugh. "Okay, get me out of this thing."

"With pleasure."

I roll my eyes and hold my arms out as Bishop stretches the corset's laces until the bodice hangs loose around my bust. Then I wriggle out of the dress with Bishop's eager help until I'm wearing nothing but my boy-cut underwear and an interestingly shaped bra made specially for open-backed dresses. But Bishop doesn't seem to notice the ugly bra, his dark eyes exploring me.

"Aren't you going to strip down?" I ask.

"Indigo, I have a feeling your boyfriend wouldn't approve of this." He tosses my dress aside—it lands with a slopping sound before sinking from sight—and then shrugs out of his jacket. Much as I'd like to, I don't wait for him to get undressed.

"He's not my boyfriend," I say, leading the way into the darkness where Jezebel disappeared.

"Interesting." Bishop follows on my heels, bringing along the taper. "He looked like your boyfriend when you were snogging earlier. Congrats on the homecoming queen thing, by the way."

"He kissed me. Against my will. And thanks. Now can we concentrate on escaping this sewer before we drown?"

"Sure thing, boss."

It doesn't take long for me to regret our little bonding moment. Not the kiss but the time we wasted; the water now reaches my ribs, and we might as well be trying to run in quicksand for all the progress we're making, near naked or no. We're forced to ditch the candle in favor of a headlamp Bishop conjures, and revert to messy front strokes, craning our heads back every few lengths to look for a sewer cover we can escape through. Panic punches the air out of my chest.

"What if we don't find one?" I struggle to catch my breath between strokes. "What if we can't get out?"

"No worries." Bishop's voice is calm and unconcerned.

"What's the plan? Snorkeling mask? Break through the roof?" I inadvertently swallow a mouthful of slimy water and have to stop, bobbing as I cough and sputter uncontrollably.

"Finally stopped sucking face, huh?"

Bishop pulls up short, shining the light from his headlamp onto Jezebel, who stands just a few feet in front of us. Her hair is sucked flat against her head, the ends fanning out around her like jellyfish tentacles in the water, and her arms are crossed like a petulant child's.

"It's a 'to be continued' sort of thing," Bishop retorts.

Jezebel's nostrils flare, but she changes topics. "Found

one." She gestures up at the barely noticeable outline of a circle in the curved roof.

"Oh, thank God," I say.

"Or thank me. But whatever. Bish, help me with this. Not enough room to fly in here."

Bishop hoists Jezebel up—and I have to remind myself that his arms are around her for a good cause, and that it's petty and stupid to be jealous just because they used to date and she's super hot. Jezebel pushes the sewer cover off with ease. Streetlight falls into the hole as she pokes her head aboveground. "We're good."

Bishop pushes her up the rest of the way, then turns to me. "You're next."

Bishop's more handsy than necessary as he pushes me up, but I don't complain. Jezebel doesn't come over to help, just lets me grapple clumsily at the pavement until I finally make it out. She gives me an up-and-down appraisal as I get to my feet, and I become aware that I'm standing, soaking wet and near naked, on a Pasadena street.

"I so don't get it, but whatever. I guess he's a butt guy."

I cross my arms over my small chest.

"Am not," Bishop says. "I like boobs as much as butts. Little help here?" He extends his arm out of the sewer.

The water is so high now that I can easily reach Bishop. Jezebel and I each take a hand and hoist him out. He lands on the pavement with a loud *slop*.

As soon as he's on his feet, Bishop gives me the same

appraisal Jezebel did. "Hmm, we should get trapped in a sewer more often." He whirls a finger in my direction, and a tank top and shorts—albeit skanky ones—appear on my body, along with a pair of boat shoes.

"You know, this is getting a bit boring."

I gasp. All three of us whirl around at the same time. The dozens of sorcerers from inside the Athenaeum pack the otherwise quiet street, Leo standing at their head.

"I think I might have to kill you and forget about breaking the spell after all," he says, stepping forward.

"He wouldn't kill you," Bishop says. "He'd drain his powers."

"You forget we tried to kill you once already, Bishop," Leo says. He grins, his hooded eye twitching erratically. "Not sure how you're alive right now, after that poor kid lost his powers killing you, but we're not afraid to try again. There are more than a few people here that are very, very dedicated to the cause. Would give up their power in a second to see a witch go down. Isn't that right?" Everyone behind him nods. "And I do have a few other tricks up my sleeve. Tricks I think you'll *particularly* enjoy."

"Don't listen to him, Ind." Bishop moves so he's standing in front of me "If he kills you, he loses his chance at breaking the spell."

"Wrong again, Bishop. Then I target Penny Blackwood. She might be the most useless witch on planet Earth, but I do what needs to be done."

"Aunt Penny?" I croak.

Leo cocks his head. "What? Don't tell me you didn't know your aunt was a witch?"

Bishop's speech at the Hollywood sign slams back into my mind. Based on my grandparents' genes, Mom had a fifty percent chance of being a witch, which means so did Aunt Penny. My heart sinks even lower, right around knee level. Why didn't she tell me? And if she's a witch, why isn't she helping me now? Better yet, why haven't the Priory targeted her? Surely she can't be more useless than a witch with about five seconds of experience. I don't get it.

"You just have to face it." Leo takes two steps closer, rubbing his chin like some sort of gangster. "We're just smarter than you. Like your little bait idea, for example. We were on to you before it was even a thought in your mind."

Something about the word "bait" sticks out, and I latch on to it. The Family didn't help us tonight, like they'd said they would. The Family hasn't helped us, really, since the moment the Bible went missing. It doesn't make any sense. None of it makes sense. But suddenly, everything clicks into place, and a humorless laugh slips from my mouth. "Bait," I mutter.

Bishop shakes my arm. "Indie?"

"You see"—Leo walks closer, the yellow light of a streetlamp magnifying the bright pink craters in his burned skin, making them appear like lakes on a globe of the world—"we've got intelligence in areas you wouldn't even dream. Would never in a million years consider. Not only that . . ."

I tune out his speech, the truth unfolding before my eyes. Bait—I can't believe how obvious it is, how I could have missed it until now. "I'll do it," I blurt out.

"What?" Bishop turns and touches my shoulder. "Indie, you're being stupid—"

"Don't touch me." I shake off his hand. "Never touch me again, do you hear me? I hate you."

Bishop's brows draw together, hurt and confusion muddying his dark eyes.

"Trouble in paradise?" Leo laughs at his own joke, and his minions hurry to follow suit.

I swallow my urge to kiss every part of Bishop's face until the hurt disappears, and face Leo. "I'll do it if you promise to kill him." I cross my arms and jut my chin toward Bishop. "And if you let me and Jezebel go free."

"I like the sound of this," Jezebel pipes up.

"Indie, what are you talking about?" Bishop moves in front of me and bends low, trying to force me to look at him.

"Oh, please. Like you don't know. You are so fake. Fake, fake, *fake*!" I give him a pointed look on the last "fake" and, finally, a glimmer of recognition crosses his eyes.

I move away from Bishop, toward Leo. "Bring me to the Bible."

Leo's eyes narrow, and he doesn't say a word. An icy fear that he's on to me grips my spine.

As if sensing the danger, Bishop grabs my arm and spins me around to face him. "Indie, please. Give me another chance." He leans in to kiss me.

I draw my arm back, then lunge all my body weight into a punch that cracks across his cheek like a bat striking a fast-ball. Bishop stumbles back, hands up around his face.

"What the hell was that?" His voice is high and strained—no acting job there.

"Try it again and I'll cut your balls off, you—you cheating jerk!" I face Leo again. "Take me to the Bible. You know my terms."

Leo looks between the two of us, and for one horrible moment I think he hasn't fallen for it. But then he gives a curt nod. "Take them all to the compound."

Two of Leo's goons surge forward, pulling something black out of their back pockets. He pulls the same item out of his own pocket, and I realize now that it's a bag. "Can't have you telling your little Family members where they can find us," he explains, before snapping the bag over my head.

31

I'm certain of three things. One is that I'm in a car—this much I can tell from the sounds of doors slamming, an engine rumbling beneath me, and the ticking of turn signals. The second is that it takes roughly thirty minutes to get to our destination before the car jerks to a stop.

The stench of Marlboro cigarettes tips me off to the third thing, which is that Leo is in the car with me.

Doors slam, and then I'm pulled out into sticky, warm air and ushered inside a building, my shoes squeaking on tile flooring.

"You better not be lying," Leo says.

I stiffen at the sound of his voice so close to my ear, recalling the day when Leo tried to attack me in the gym. Only this time, my hands are bound so tightly with thick rope that it's impossible to escape. I focus on each breath—inhale through my nose, exhale through my mouth—so that I don't panic.

Leo shoves me inside a room and pulls the bag off my head. My eyes burn from the sudden brightness, but when they adjust I find myself inside a small room tiled partly in seafoam green, with X-rays of bones lining the top half of the walls. A long, stainless steel table takes up the center of the space, glinting from the spotlight at the end of a mechanical arm coming from the ceiling. Steel surgical tools line small trays against one of the walls, and the scent of antiseptic and alcohol permeates the air.

"You like?" Leo asks.

Bile rises up my throat, and I feel the urge to puke. What have I gotten us into? My plan had seemed so clear earlier, but now that I'm here, what couldn't be clearer is that I was wrong.

There are scuffling noises behind me. Two suit-clad men push Jezebel and Bishop into the room.

"Close the door, Armando," Leo says.

The heavyset Latino man who had been pushing Bishop nods and shuts the door.

"Get this damn bag off." Jezebel thrashes against her ropes and the grip of her handler—a tall, thin man with a hooked nose and a widow's peak—but I know she could easily use her magic to escape if she wanted to. She knows we're up to something, and she's playing along. It's just a mystery to me why the Priory hasn't caught on to this fact yet.

"No can do." Leo slaps something onto the table—the Bible—and then hardens his black eyes on me. "Break the spell."

My heart freezes up at the sight of the book. It's been years since I last laid eyes on it—Mom didn't take it out of hiding very often after the last scare—and I'm surprised to find, to remember, actually, that it's plain. Only the title—*The Witch Hunter's Bible*—written in faded gold, Gothic-style script, and the two dull gold latches that secure the covers, distinguishes it from any old book. Yet despite its plain appearance, it feels important. It *is* important—Mom lost her life for this book. I take a shaky breath and focus on Leo. "Untie me first."

So many unthinkable horrors have happened because of this Bible. And if I unlock it now for Leo and my plan doesn't work, everything will only get worse. Pressure builds in my chest.

"No." His tone and the hard lines of his face leave no room for argument. I do it anyway.

"I need my hands to break the spell," I say. It's at least partly true. I don't really know how to break the spell, but my hands were involved in at least half the magic I've learned so far.

"It's true," Bishop says, then grunts when Armando lands an elbow in his stomach.

Leo watches me for a long moment, and I try not to squirm under his stare.

"Fine." He walks behind me. Something cold presses between the rope and my skin, and the ropes come loose. I rub my raw wrists. "Now do it," he says. "No more wasting time."

I take cautious steps up to the table. Pressing my palms against the cold metal, I lean in toward the Bible resting in the spotlight between my hands.

Leo knocks on the table. "Anytime now."

I swallow, focusing my attention on finding the heat in my core and pulling it into my chest. As soon as it's a thought in my mind, the power surges like I lined my insides with accelerant, igniting my chest with a pulsating ball of fire. I move the heat to my fingertips, press them to the Bible, and close my eyes, willing the spell to break. After a minute or so, I open my eyes.

"Did you do it?" Leo leans across the table, practically vibrating with anticipation.

"I think so."

If I was trying to hide my uncertainty, I failed. Leo scurries around the large table and snatches up the book. I hold my breath as he fumbles with the latch.

"You liar." He slams the book down so hard the sound echoes through the room, then pokes a finger into my shoulder, hard. I flinch. Spittle flies out of his mouth as he speaks. "I can't open this. You haven't broken the spell."

A million different emotions—regret, disappointment, fear . . . mostly fear—slam into me all at once. Why did I think this would work? I'm an idiot. Of course I can't break the spell. I'm a beginner; this is way beyond my scope. But I can't let Leo see how I'm feeling.

I shake my head adamantly, my throat tightening as though I'm using a boa constrictor for a scarf. "Let me try again. Please."

Leo's chest heaves, but he allows me to move around him to reach the Bible. This time, my hand is shaky when I press it to the Bible. When the heat stings my fingertips, I focus on the latch, on popping it open. *Sequere me imperio movere, sequere me imperio movere* . . . When the latch doesn't budge, I wipe sweat from my temple and repeat the words aloud. *"Sequere me imperio movere, sequere me imperio movere, sequere me imperio movere."*

Of course it doesn't work.

Leo lets out what can only be called a battle cry and reaches for me.

I stumble back and hold a hand out to stay him. "Just let me try one more time. Th-that's it—once more. What could it hurt?" Tears sting my eyes, and an uncontrollable sob rises from my chest. The full weight of my mistake presses on me. Leo will kill all three of us, and if what he said about Aunt Penny being a witch is true, he'll go after her next. Even after what she's done to me, I don't wish that on her.

I pick up the Bible and clasp it firmly in my hands.

Aunt Penny. Why isn't she helping me?

Tears stream down my cheeks.

Her nervousness, the way she looked at me before I left—she must have known what was going to happen. Why did she let me do it? Why didn't she try to stop me? And then I remember her advice when Devon and I left for the dance. If you need help, call . . . oh, who was it? Some weird name—Alice or something. But I'm sure it's important now, and not just some friend of hers who could give me a ride home if I were too drunk to drive.

"Do it!" Leo hisses in my ear.

"I am." What was the name, oh God, what was it?

Leo paces behind me.

"Alice F-French. Alica French. Alica Francis, uh, Alica Franz."

"Alica Frangere?" Bishop pipes up.

"Shut up!" Leo yells.

That's it! "Alica Frangere."

The room silences, and I open my eyes.

I nod at Leo. "Okay."

He gives me a long look through narrowed eyes, then snatches the Bible up. This time, when he fumbles with the latch, it pops open with ease.

I sigh, folding in half with relief.

Leo hurriedly flips through the pages, and a slow smile stretches across his face. But only moments later, a frown turns down his lips, and he snaps the book closed.

"What is it?" I ask. "Is there something wrong?"

Leo casts a glance around. "Well, I suppose this place is as good as any." He skirts around me, holding the Bible against his chest. "Lock them in separate rooms. Remove everything—I mean everything—from their rooms. I don't want them doing anything stupid before the ceremony."

Armando snags Bishop's arm and tugs him forward. He stumbles along lazily, and I know if I could see his expression he'd be wearing that same casual/bored one I saw on him at the theater when he was tied to the chair. Jezebel, on the other hand, predictably kicks and fights against her captor, but doesn't conjure any of the impressive magic that I know she's capable of. I'm very tempted to tell her that she's going to get us caught if she doesn't amp up the acting job a few notches.

Other Priory minions shuffle in to remove the table, surgical tools, and trays, until it's just me and the X-rays in the room. A very small part of me is relieved to see the sharp tools go, though a larger part knows it's probably not because they plan to be really kind to us.

Leo pokes his head back inside. "Try to escape and I send a unit over to see your auntie."

I stumble forward. "How long? When are you coming back?"

A wicked grin pulls up his marred cheek. "Just until you starve."

The door slams shut with an echo of finality.

32

The first hour passes by quickly. Jezebel screams in the suite next door and Bishop yells for her to shut up from down the hall, which both occupies my thoughts and reassures me that they aren't dead or worse. I wish I could discuss the plan with them, but Leo or one of his goons is probably stationed outside the door.

In the second hour, after their conflict peters out and the immediate fear of the Priory dissolves, the boredom sets in. I count the tiles on the wall until my eyes cross and I give up.

It's not until it's bordering on the twelfth hour that hunger gnaws at my insides, twisting and churning my stomach so that I'm doubled over in pain, wishing I'd eaten more than a few bites at the banquet. The thought that Bishop's probably gnawing on a chicken leg he conjured makes me panic, and I cry until my throat is hot and my voice is harsh and raspy.

I don't know how many hours have passed when I become acutely aware of my parched mouth, of my dry and cracked lips and racing heart. Water is the only thing I think about. I imagine chugging a cold glass filled with clinking ice cubes, and it's so painful in my gut I have to pace the length of the room to distract myself. I know I'm panicking, that people have survived much longer stretches without food or water, but after so long without a word from Leo, I'm worried about just how long he plans to leave us here.

Finally, I give up and lie down on the cold concrete floor.

I think of Mom. I remember her easy smile as I entered the Black Cat after school. I remember her hiccupping laugh, her scent, the feel of her hug after a bad day. I remember her, and it makes the pain worse. In my mind, I ask her to help me. After more hours pass, it becomes painfully clear I'm not getting any beyond-the-grave assistance, and I give up on that too. My thoughts melt away and I stare into nothingness. Exhaustion pulls at my eyelids.

And then the hallucinations begin. They're only tiny spots in my field of vision at first. Then the spots turn into colors—cherry-red, lime-green, ocean-blue—blooming and flashing in front of my eyes like a Technicolor kaleidoscope.

Metal clangs somewhere in the room. And then a voice. "They're ready."

Leo? Was that Leo?

"You sure?" an unfamiliar voice asks.

"Yes, I'm sure. Bring her to the car."

The realization that it's definitely Leo, and he definitely has plans for me, snaps me out of my hallucination and back into reality just as two meaty hands snag my arms and tug me to standing. Blood rushes from my head, and I nearly collapse but for the man who stabilizes me.

"The bag," Leo says.

At the mention of the dreaded bag, I use my last ounce of energy to try to wriggle free, but it's too late. The fabric whips over my eyes, blocking all the light like a blackout curtain.

"Tie her up," Leo says.

I yelp as my arms are painfully twisted behind my back. To my surprise, I don't feel rope against my skin, but barbed-wire needles of pain shoot up my arms at my slightest protest.

"That should keep her still," the man says, laughter in his voice.

Our collective footsteps squeak loudly on the tile flooring. There's a *whoosh*, and the sounds of heavy traffic suddenly surround me. I catch a brief breath of fresh air through the bag, before I'm ducked like a prisoner into a car. I fall sideways against the leather seat, careful to not land on my tied hands. The now-familiar scent of cigarettes burns my nostrils.

"Where are we going?" I ask.

Leo snickers in response.

"Where's Bishop? You promised to kill Bishop." The entire plan hinges on this one part going right, on his ring working like it's supposed to.

"Oh, we'll kill him, all right." Leo spins the tuning dial on the radio until he reaches a station that plays a hearty, almost nationalistic classical song. "Ah, Shostakovich! You know, I should thank you, Indigo, for taking care of Frederick for me. It's great to finally pick the music." He turns the volume up so loud he has to shout to be heard. "Haunting melody. Perfect for the occasion, no?" He breaks into delighted laughter, and I sink into the seat.

I don't know how much time passes, but it's a lot. I try everything to stay awake, but after a while, sheer exhaustion combined with the vibrations of the car lull me to sleep.

I jerk awake when the car stops.

Invisible hands drag me outside into a chill air that smells of earth. Without warning, the bag over my head is pulled away. I stumble, disoriented by the hugeness of my surroundings after so long without sight.

The sun is low on the horizon, the sky awash with thick brushstrokes of red, gold, and orange. Which would be beautiful if not for the bog. It's sunken in a dip in the land and is shadowed by tall skeleton trees, as though the earth were trying to swallow it and the trees cover the evidence. What I can see of the water through the thick moss caking the surface is brown and murky, and sticks and tall grass poke out from the banks. It looks like a place to dump a dead body. Which, I guess, is the point. I shiver.

Another car door slams. I spin around to find Armando pushing Bishop toward us, the hook-nosed man pulling Jezebel from the backseat of the last vehicle in the processional parked along the dirt road.

But what is almost as alarming as the fact that they're herding us into a bog at the side of an isolated dirt road at nightfall is what the Priory members are wearing: hooded black robes with sleeves that flare over their hands and hems that brush along the dirt, making them look startlingly like priests.

Gravel crunches as more vehicles near. They slow to a halt, and dozens more robed men and women spill out onto the road.

When I whirl around to face Leo, I see that he's wearing a robe too. Leo pushes me toward the bog.

"Your promise," I say to him. "I want to see him die." I jut my chin toward Bishop in a defiant gesture, but my voice shakes with uncertainty.

Leo grins. "Promises, promises. That was really more of Frederick's ball of wax."

"Wh-what? What does that mean?"

He laughs. "Victor?"

The man who answers to Victor is average in size, but his severe expression and long, wiry beard give him a distinct "don't mess with me" vibe. Victor yanks my arm and uses it to propel me forward. The movement makes a barb dig into my skin, and I let out a yelp, then bite down on my lip to prevent any further outbursts. I don't need Bishop to know how scared I am, in case he gets any ideas about backing out.

We're led into the chilly water of the bog. My body shrinks against the cold, goose bumps flaring up over my exposed skin—which there is a lot of, thanks to Bishop. Our movements disturb moss on the still water, and it collects on our clothes in thick patches. They lead us out until we're waist-deep, and then Armando pushes Bishop forward, backing away as the other Priory members wordlessly close in, forming rings so dense around him I can barely see him through the cracks between their bodies. But I do see him. His bag has been removed too, and his hands untied, his dark hair sticking up in all directions. Though he feigns a bored expression, I don't miss the fact that his eyes dart around the group like an animal in a cage.

A bird caws somewhere. And then the chanting begins.

It's so low at first, almost a whisper, that I can't hear what they're saying. The sun slips behind the trees on the horizon, and the sky turns a thick, gray-blue color. Flashes of light penetrate from the inner circle, and I realize that some people are holding candles. I lost sight of Leo among all the sorcerers, but he speaks now, and I trace his booming voice to the center of the circle. He holds the Bible open in one hand, reciting verses in a strange language I've never heard before. Bishop twirls his ring—a nervous gesture, and my heart squeezes hard.

The chanting grows louder, and the robed bodies begin to sway forward, more and more violently until it appears they're being propelled toward Bishop by magnetic force, before being rocketed back.

Three people—Armando, Hooknose Man, and a dark-skinned man step forward from the group. Armando and Hooknose grab hold of Bishop's arms, while the third man brings a small dish to Leo. Still chanting, Leo takes a pinch of what looks like salt in his fingers, then throws it onto Bishop. As soon as it hits him, the men holding Bishop pull him back into the water, submerging him like it's some sort of baptism. Leo holds a hand over Bishop and reads from the Bible as Bishop's legs thrash frantically in the water. I clench and unclench my fists. I know that his dying is part of the plan, but seeing it happen is another thing entirely.

The men pull him up. Bishop coughs and sputters as Leo takes another pinch from the dish and throws it at him. And then he is submerged again. Pressure builds in my chest, the urge to scream almost too much to withstand. The men mercifully bring Bishop up for air, but he's allowed only a quick breath before he's dunked again. I can't take it any-more; I cry out and step forward, but Victor yanks me back so hard my arm feels like it's popped out of the socket. Hot liquid oozes down the sores on my raw wrists: blood.

Finally, after the third time, the men leave Bishop above water and back away. He takes huge, sucking breaths, his dark hair plastered to his cheeks.

A woman steps forward, something dark clutched against her chest. She extends her arms suddenly, and swaths of black cloth fall over his head and body, still more material floating on the surface of the water around him. The chanting grows so loud that I can barely hear Leo, and their eyes—the way they roll back in their heads, as if consumed with lust for power, makes me want to cover my face like I'm watching a horror movie.

Another lackey steps forward and hands Leo an athame—a ceremonial dagger just like the ones Mom sold at the Black Cat.

This is it. I cast a quick glance around the crowd for Jezebel and find her staring at Bishop, so still and unmoving I wonder if she's even breathing.

Leo raises the athame high, the jewel-encrusted hilt gleaming in the last speck of daylight. I can't watch anymore, and I bury my face in my shoulder just as the sickening, wet sound of the blade slicing into skin breaks through the air. Bishop doesn't cry out, just makes this grunting noise. When I do work up the courage to look, I find the men letting go of Bishop's arms so that he sinks into the water. Blood pools out around the cloth, turning the already murky water red.

Oh, Bishop, what have I done? Tears streak down my cheeks, and a shuddering sob racks my body.

Someone lets out a battle cry, and soon the whole group is cheering. Leo's voice halts them. "Bring another."

Another. I dart my eyes around at all the faces now focused on me. I try to back away, but the guy pushes me forward. "What about the deal?" I scream. "The deal was to let me go free!"

I didn't think it was possible to feel anything more intense than devastation at this moment, but I do. Fear clutches my spine like a bird of prey, digging its talons into my back and refusing to let go.

The crowd parts as I'm pushed into the center of the circle, where the water is still red and thick from Bishop's blood.

Victor releases me. I whirl around to take in the dozens of eyes that stare at me like I'm the very dregs of humanity. The chanting begins.

Their whispered voices, speaking in that strange language, make the hair on my neck stand on end. But it's the eyes that haunt me, greedy with anticipation. And even though I'm petrified, I can't help feeling a strange pity for them. They're rich in power, and still they aren't satisfied. They still want more.

Before I know it, the whispering has become tribal-like yelling, and the same two men step forward to take my arms. Leo takes a pinch of the white crystals from a dish the black-haired man proffers and throws it onto my chest. I know what comes next, so I take in a big breath just as I'm pulled back into the water. Despite being prepared, my body tenses from the sudden drop in temperature. I don't fight it at first, just lie still and quiet as I listen to the muffled chanting above me, but then the need for air becomes so great it's like a vise is tightening around my lungs, screwing up more and more until they feel as though they're going to pop from the pressure. I kick and thrash against the grip on my arms until I'm finally pulled back up.

I take a few gulping breaths, and then I'm pulled down again. The pressure is unbearable the second time, and I fight with every ounce of energy I have left, but it's useless; the men are stronger than me. By the third time, consciousness begins to slip away, and the pain in my chest disappears. But then I'm hauled back to the surface again, and as air fills my lungs, both mental alertness and pain come crashing back.

The thick black cloth is thrown over my head, stealing all the light out of the world. I know the knife is next. The sound it made as it sliced into Bishop's body fills my mind, consuming my thoughts so that I can't think straight. But even through my haze, one thing is clear: the plan had major holes. It doesn't matter if the Bible was truly fake, if Leo lost his powers when he killed Bishop. Because if they stab me now, I'm going to die. I'm surrounded. Bishop is currently dead, and I don't even know where Jezebel is.

I close my eyes tight, the anticipation nearly as painful as what I imagine the knife will be. *Just get it over with,* I think. *Kill me already.*

A collective gasp rises up all around me, and the chanting cuts short to confused murmurs. I pop my eyes open. I can't see a thing but the black, heavy cloth, but I whirl around anyway, following the sounds of commotion breaking out all around me.

Leo's annoyed voice cuts through the confused murmurs. "What's going on?"

"He's alive," a voice calls out.

"My magic," another voice adds.

"It's not working!"

The murmurs abruptly switch to panicked cries.

The cloth is yanked from my head and the wire around my wrists cut free in one swift motion, so that I'm left stumbling and confused in the chaos that surrounds me. Jezebel's back is retreating before I can even register that she helped me.

I spin around to find Bishop—blood spilled from a gash in his shirt, wrestling the knife from Leo as a mass exodus of sorcerers madly slosh toward shore. Bishop wins the knife and tosses it with a *plunk* into the water. Leo holds his hands up toward Bishop, jaw tense and eyes determined, as if he's trying to summon his magic. But nothing happens. Leo's eyes dart left and right, and he backs up.

Jezebel appears behind him and claps a hand on his shoulder. "Go on"—she nods toward the fleeing sorcerers—"your friends are leaving without you."

Leo pauses a moment, as if to consider whether this is a trick, then bolts. Jezebel laughs, a delighted sound that lights up her face, and holds out a hand. The fleeing sorcerers not already out of the water hit an invisible wall.

"I'm thinking alligators," Jezebel calls, tapping a finger on her chin. "Yes, alligators seem like the way to go."

Ripples form in the water, and the long, scaled bodies of dozens of alligators appear, homing in slowly on the sorcerers backed against the invisible wall. A long snout jumps from the water and digs into Leo's back. I cover my ears as the sound of snapping bones and high-pitched screams break through the night.

"Come on." Bishop turns me away from the scene and pulls me into his arms. I sink into him and let myself be led around the carnage, toward the first car at the roadside, telling myself that they deserve it for what they did to Mom, that I should enjoy their gory deaths instead of being sick over it. "It's over," he says.

"It's over," I repeat, testing out the words.

33

"**O**kay, *now* can someone explain to me what the hell that was all about?" Jezebel paces in front of the booth, wearing a tread in the In-N-Out Burger's checked gray tile.

After everything that happened, I was far too drained, not to mention hungry and thirsty, to jump into a lengthy explanation on the drive back into Los Angeles.

I swallow my bite of cheeseburger in preparation to speak, but Bishop beats me to it, talking around a mouthful of food. "The Bible was a fake."

Jezebel stops pacing to stare at him.

"That's why they lost their powers," I say, wiping my fingers on a napkin and twisting around to face her. "They killed a witch using a fake Bible, only Bishop didn't die because of the ring."

"I have only one life left." Bishop holds up his hand to show her that the ring is now engraved with the Roman numeral one. "That was fun and all, but I don't really want to do it again, okay?"

Jezebel closes her eyes and shakes her head, as if someone were trying to teach her a complicated mathematical formula. "But how? Why is there a fake?"

"The Family used us as bait," I continue. "They must have planted a fake one at Mom's shop to divert the Priory's focus from the real Bible's location. That's why they never sent anyone to help. They used us." My tone becomes bitter. "They didn't care if we died, just so long as their stupid Bible was safe. I bet there are zillions of fakes around the world."

Jezebel shakes her head adamantly. "It's impossible. Secrecy is paramount to the Family. They'd never risk exposure unless it was for something really important, like the Bible. And besides, the Family wouldn't risk me like that. Maybe the two of you, but not me. There's got to be another explanation. I'm one of the best witches they've got."

"And you're deadly afraid of vultures and everyone knows it," Bishop chimes in, then takes another huge bite of burger. "You're a liability."

Jezebel lets out a little snort of derision.

"I'm sorry," Bishop says.

She tilts her chin up. "Don't be. It's not true."

"Okay, so why don't you explain to me why the Family didn't help us when they had a chance at recovering the Bible?" Bishop wipes ketchup from his chin with his sleeve, a thing only a guy would do.

Jezebel's quiet a moment before she speaks. "B-because they couldn't risk it, knowing they could get killed. Did you see the Priory's numbers back there?"

"So they sent you alone?" Bishop asks, incredulous. "And they sent me alone, in the first place, to bring back our most important relic, when sorcerers were following our every move?"

"They trusted me," Jezebel spits, but her voice cracks with emotion. It's probably the first time I've ever felt remotely bad about anything to do with Jezebel. And it will probably be the last.

"They didn't help," Bishop continues, "because the real Bible was never missing."

Dishes clank in the restaurant's kitchen.

"Forget about this," Jezebel says. "I'm out of here."

"Oh, come on, Jez." Bishop reaches out to grab her arm but misses when she recoils. "Don't feel bad," he calls after her. "It's not just you they don't care about. The Family obviously tipped off the Priory about me getting sent to pick up the Bible. Who else would have known about my mission except them?"

The bell jangles, and the restaurant door swings closed behind her.

Bishop gives himself a whole-body shake and settles back against his seat.

"She helped me back there, you know," I say quietly. It's the closest I'm willing to come to saying anything positive about her after she left my mom to die at the hands of the Priory.

He takes another bite of his burger before standing. "She'll be fine. She just needs to cool off."

I force a little smile and stand. "I don't blame her for being mad, though. I'd be pretty pissed too."

"She'll get over it. Trust me."

I hope it's true.

Bishop links arms with me and leads me outside. The Sunset Strip is its typical just-after-bar-close self, teeming with sidewalk traffic so dense it competes with the cars clogging the street. Palm trees sway in the light cast by the neon signs of the clubs; music and high heels and cell-phone chatter fill the night. But when Bishop looks down at me, it's like we're the only two people around.

He pulls me against his side. "So, I guess life is going to be pretty boring without people trying to kill us every day."

I laugh, putting my arm around Bishop's waist. "I'll take boring."

A panhandler jangles a cup of change, and Bishop tosses a few large bills into his tin without pausing. "Where to?" he asks me.

My first thought is home, but then I remember Aunt Penny. She's a witch. There was a Blackwood spell on the fake Bible, and she knew how to break it. I don't know what it all means, why she lied to me and didn't help me when my life was in danger. I just know that I don't trust her, and I can't go home until I figure it all out.

"Your place, I guess," I say.

Bishop looks down at me, grinning like a madman.

"I don't mean it like that." I punch him in the gut, but I'm laughing now. "I just need a place to stay for a while, until I figure some things out."

"I think I can help you with that."

When I look up at him, I expect to see a smirk, but instead I find that same hunger in his dark eyes. Something in the air changes, and suddenly his warm body presses me up against the stucco side of the nearest building, and his lips crush against mine hard and fast. I kiss him back just as urgently, because I've wanted this for so long and it seems I don't know how to do anything without immediacy, without the threat of death looming over me. And then his fingers curl into my hair and his kiss becomes achingly deep and slow, because we're safe for now, and we have all the time in the world.

"So does this mean you're my girlfriend?" he asks huskily when he pulls away for air and my insides are the consistency of melted butter.

"Hmm." I look up for a moment, as if considering. "Okay. But *only* if Betty gets herself a bikini." I brush my fingers along the naked Betty Boop tattoo on his neck. "No way I'm dating someone with a pair of boobs on his neck."

A smile blooms across his face, crinkling the corners of his eyes and making laugh lines sprout up around his mouth. "Technically, the boobs are on my collarbone, but it's a deal."

I smile too and pull him into another kiss.

It's not like everything is perfect, or ever will be again, but right at this moment, pressed against Bishop's warm body, everything is okay. And I'll take okay.

"Should we call a cab or just conjure one?" he asks after I've released him.

I instantly remember my promise to Paige. "Oh shit, my phone." Somewhere between being chased by a dragon and sloshing through the L.A. sewer system, I lost my purse.

"Not a problem," Bishop says, winking at me. He holds out his hand, and a small silver phone materializes in his palm.

I smirk at my boyfriend before snatching it up and dialing Paige's number. It rings eight times before going to voice mail.

"Weird," I mumble, and dial it again.

Voice mail.

"What's going on?" Bishop asks.

"I don't know. She's not answering."

I remember the missed call from Paige earlier. At the same moment I remember that she left a message, and frantically dial the number to reach my cell phone's voice mail. Soon, answering-machine lady speaks to me in her irritatingly monotone voice.

"You have one new message, left yesterday at nine-forty-five p.m." Static plays through the speaker, and then . . .

"Hello, Indigo."

Leo.

I gasp.

"I'm here with your friend Paige, and you know, even though you and I have had our problems in the past, I can agree with you on this one thing: she is an absolute *doll*." There are muffled moans in the background. Someone grunts, and the sound of china shattering pierces through the phone. When Leo speaks again, his cool confidence is gone, and his voice is cut with an edge of hostility. "I was really hoping you'd come by and join us, but since you're not answering your phone, I think we'll just have to come to you."

Epilogue

Four Hours Ago

I blink my eyes open. At first I see nothing but darkness, but when my eyes adjust I find that I'm in a small room. The muted bass of club music thumps above me, vibrating the wooden beams of the low ceiling. A slow, aching pulse pounds against my skull, and when I swallow, my throat burns as though I've just put away a whole pack of cigarettes. I rub my temple, racking my brain for a clue— something, anything—about where I am or how I got here. *Think, Paige. Think.* With a jolt I recall the man with the scarred face. Remember his threats, his scary obsession with Indie, him pushing me into the backseat of the car.

And then nothing.

My heart races, panic setting up camp in my chest. I need to get out of here.

My eyes lock on a thin strip of pale light I hadn't noticed before, illuminating the edge of a door. Swallowing, I push myself to my feet, my muscles complaining against the movements. My head drains of blood when I stand and I nearly pass out, but I hold out my arms and soon the world stops swaying. I take a hesitant step forward. Then another.

A sound outside the room stops me short. Footsteps. Laughter. Coming closer.

I suck in a breath and scuttle backward, my back slamming into a shelf. Something clatters to the ground, and the laughter stops.

Holding my breath, I close my eyes tight and clench my shaking hands at my sides. *Please don't come in, please don't come in.*

The door creaks open.

"And what do we have here?" a man says. His words send a chill up my spine.

I force my eyes open. Two figures stand in the doorway, backlit by smoky gray light. A thin-faced man with buzzed hair and too-tight pants, and a generic-looking blond bimbo who clings to his arm.

The man shakes off the girl's grip and steps into the room. My heart rate accelerates with each step he takes nearer to me. He reaches up over his head and pulls something, and

I'm suddenly blinking against the dim light of a single over-head bulb. The man stares at me for way too long, his eyes traversing every inch of me so that I want nothing more than to melt into the shelf and become part of the decor.

"And just what do you think you're doing here, *human*?" the man says, contempt lacing his last word.

The girl steps forward and throws her arms around the guy's shoulder, assessing me. "She looks young, Bobby."

Bobby grins. "Old enough."

This is a nightmare, I decide. Just a horrible nightmare. I close my eyes tight and try to wake up, but when I open them again, they're still there, sneering at me.

An unwitting sob escapes me.

"Aw, you've scared the little girl," the bimbo says, laughing.

Bobby joins in. "What's your name, little girl?"

I press my lips together to keep from crying again.

"Come on now, don't be shy," Bobby says.

A shadow falls across the room. At first I'm not sure whether the person in the doorway is a man or a woman. The albino-white hair, which matches equally pale skin, is short and slicked back, reminiscent of James Dean's. The eyes are big, framed by white lashes that are bare of any makeup, and all the other features are so androgynous it could go either way. It's only the voice that gives her away as a woman.

"What's going on here?" the woman says.

"Nothing!" Bobby blurts out, and laughs nervously.

"I thought I'd made it abundantly clear that no one was to come into the basement without permission. Was there a problem with my instructions?" She tilts her head very slightly, locking her unblinking eyes on the guy.

I dart my eyes between them, unsure of what's going on—just that I don't want to be a part of it.

When he doesn't respond, she continues. "I hope you weren't thinking about harming the girl."

"Of course not, Rowan," Bobby says quickly. "But, just so I know . . . why are we not harming her, again? She's just a human, you know. I can tell." His laughter peters out when she doesn't join in.

"Because," the woman says, stepping into the room, "I have big plans for this girl."

———•◦•———

Acknowledgments

First and foremost, a huge thank-you to my agent Adriann Ranta for helping to make this unlikely dream of mine a reality. I'm so lucky to have her in my corner.

Thank you a thousand times over to my editor, Wendy Loggia, whose sharp eye for detail and expert guidance turned *Hexed* into the absolute best book it could be. Her insight and enthusiasm know no bounds! Also thank you to Heather Hughes, Colleen Fellingham, Susan Wallach and Alison Kolani for their genius editorial skills; Alison Impey for designing the beautiful jacket; and the entire team at Delacorte Press who read or helped shaped this book. Thank you to Janice Weaver and the team at Doubleday Canada for helping *Hexed* reach Canadian readers.

Two people deserve an entire book's worth of thanks. I can't thank my sister Brandy Allard enough for being my biggest fan and for believing in me from day one. And Ruth

Lauren Steven is not just the best critique partner a writer could ever ask for but also my across-the-pond, Internet best friend. (Maybe we can even meet one day?)

An abundance of thank-yous go out to my online friends. Thank you to the people from the Novel, Chapter-by-Chapter group, particularly Amaleen Ison, whose don't-pull-any-punches critiques made the first thirteen chapters better by a lot. A gigantic thank-you to Amy Tintera for being my go-to girl for insider info on L.A., and to the rest of my friends in Gunning for Awesome: Amy Christine Parker, Kimberly Welchons, Natalie C. Parker, Corinne Duyvis, Gemma Cooper, Lori M. Lee, Stephanie Winkelhake, Deborah Hewitt, and Lacey J. Edwards for always being there for moral support when I needed it the most. Thank you to my blog and Twitter followers for making this whole process fun, especially Paulina W. for her unwavering support and enthusiasm.

Thank you to Amy Fontaine for helping me sort out a huge plot hole over night shift at work, and to Shannon Mancuso for taking my jacket photo.

Of course, a massive thank-you goes to my close family and friends. My mom, Phylis Kaukanen, and my sister Crystal Couture, thank you for reading the earliest draft of *Hexed* and claiming it didn't suck. Barb Hemsworth, thank you for *always* asking how the writing is going and for reading this book on your honeymoon (and thank you, Cody, for yelling out "More magic!" during our phone calls). Thanks to Laura Dennis and Rebecca Stokaluk for cheering me on along the way.

Finally, thank you to my son for having such incredible sleeping habits that I had time to write a book—I love you to the moooon! And to my husband, Logan, thank you for not laughing at me when I strolled into the living room and announced I was going to write a book. Thank you for the endless support, for the coffee when I could barely keep my eyes open, and for telling everyone you know your wife is a writer.

And last but not least, thank you to the readers. I can't wait to share what happens next.

About the Author

MICHELLE KRYS lives with her husband and son in Northwestern Ontario, Canada. She works part-time as a NICU nurse and spends her free time writing books for teens. Michelle is probably not a witch, though she did belong to a witchcraft club in the fifth grade and "levitated" people in her bedroom, so that may be up for debate. *Hexed* is her first novel. Visit her at michellekrys.com or follow @MichelleKrys on Twitter.